#UofJ2

GAME CHANGER

#UofJ2

ALLEY CIZ

Also by Alley Ciz

**@UofJ411: Thought you didn't fumble @CasaNova87?
#OffYourGame #LosingMoreThanTDs**

I had the girl—THE girl.
Kay. My Skittles...**MINE.**
The a blitz from the past flattened me like a linebacker.
Time for a new playbook.

Mason Nova is...argh!
I told myself to stay away.
Warned my heart *not* to fall for him.
Did it listen? **NOPE.**
Now it feels like it's crushed under a fallen cheer pyramid.
Sorry to tell you, but *you* are **NOT** a game changer.

GAME CHANGER is book 2 in the U of J Series and cannot be read as a stand-alone. It picks up right from the cliff LOOKING TO SCORE threw you off of. Can our too-charming-for-his-own-good Casanova win back his pint-sized, rainbow-haired sass queen in this second chance sports romance? The banter between these two continues until Mase and Kay's story concludes in PLAYING FOR KEEPS out now.

Game Changer (#UofJ2)

Alley Ciz

Copyright © 2020 by House of Crazy Publishing, LLC

Copyright © 2020 by House of Crazy Publishing, LLC

Paperback ISBN: 978-1-950884-13-1

Ebook ISBN: 978-1-950884-14-8

Cover Designer: Julia Cabrera at Jersey Girl Designs

Cover Photographer: Wander Book Club Photography

Cover Models: Megan Napolitan & Wayne Skivington

Editing: Jessica Snyder Edits, C. Marie

Proofreading: Gem's Precise Proofreads; Dawn Black

❧ Created with Vellum

To Jenny! You are so much more than my PA, you are literally the other half of my brain most days, as well as my best friend.
#YesWeKnowMaseIsYours

Author Note

Dear Reader,

GAME CHANGER IS BOOK 2 in the U of J Series. You must read book 1, LOOKING TO SCORE, prior to this installment to follow the story properly.

 # UofJ Series:

Cut Above The Rest <—Freebie for newsletter subscribers.

1. Looking To Score
2. Game Changer
3. Playing For Keeps

If I'm new to you and you haven't read my BTU Alumni books you're fine.
If you have met my other crazy squad of friends and Covenettes there are a few cameos in here you might enjoy, with a tiny time gap between the two series.

XOXO
Alley

IG Handles

CasaNova87: Mason 'Casanova' Nova (TE)
QB1McQueen7: Travis McQueen (QB)
CantCatchAnderson22: Alex Anderson (RB)
SackMasterSanders91: Kevin Sanders (DE)
LacesOutMitchell5: Noah Mitchell (K)
CheerGodJT: JT (James) Taylor
TheGreatestGrayson37: G (Grant) Grayson
ThirdBaseAdam16: Adam
CheerNinja: Rei
TheBarracksAtNJA: The Barracks
NJA_Admirals: The Admirals
TightestEndParker85: Liam Parker

Nicknames

Mason Nova: Casanova/Mase
Kayla Dennings: Kay/PF/Smalls/Short Stack
E (Eric) Dennings
CK (Chris) Kent
Em (Emma) Logan
Q (Quinn)
JT (James) Taylor <CTG BFF- Cradle-To-Grave Best Friend Forever>
T (Tessa) Taylor
Pops (James) Taylor Sr.
G (Grant) Grayson
D (Dante) Grayson
Mama G- Mrs. Grayson
Papa G- Mr. Grayson
B (Ben) Turner

Playlist

- "Haunted"- Kelly Clarkson
- "Dark Side"- Bishop Briggs
- "Hate (I Really Don't Like You)"- Plain White T's
- "Blurry"- Puddle Of Madd
- "Notice"- Little Mix
- "Malibu Nights"- LANY
- "All Around Me"- Flyleaf
- "Wasabi"- Little Mix
- "Guys Don't Like Me"- It Boys!
- "Haunted"- Taylor Swift
- "Trust Issues"- Olivia O'Brien
- "Up & Down"- Dana Dentata
- "Make You Miss Me"- Sam Hunt
- "Break Up With Your Girlfriend (I'm Bored)- Ariana Grande
- "Just A Man"- SoMo
- "Unsteady"- X Ambassadors
- "The Heart Wants What It Wants"- Selena Gomez
- "Nights Like This"- Kehlani feat Ty Dolla $ign
- "Fuck Apologies"- JoJo feat Wiz Khalifa

- "Call You Mine"- The Chainsmokers feat Bebe Rexha
- "My Kinda Party"- Jason Aldean
- "Human"- Rag'n'Bone Man
- "Frustrated"- R.LUM.R
- "Low"- Greyson Chance
- "Sound Of Your Heart"- Shawn Hook
- "Suffer"- Charlie Puth
- "Brokenhearted"- Karmin
- "Don't Stop"- 5 Seconds of Summer
- "Close To Me"- Ellie Goulding with Diplo
- "Never Really Over"- Katy Perry
- "Dangerously In Love"- Destiny's Child
- "Falling"- Harry Styles
- "Just A Friend"- Biz Markie
- "STFU & Hold Me"- Liz Huett
- "Hallucinate"- Dua Lipa
- "Pom Poms"- Jonas Brothers
- "A-YO"- Lady Gaga
- "I Love Me"- Demi Lovato
- "F.F.F."- Bebe Rexha feat G-Eazy
- "Teenagers"- My Chemical Romance
- "Distraction"- Kehlani
- "Ruin My Life"- Zara Larsson
- "Play With Fire"- Sam Tinnesz feat Yacht Money
- "Castle"- Halsey
- "Thunderstruck"- AC/DC
- "Unstoppable"- The Score
- "BLOW"- Ed Sheeran feat Chris Stapleton
- "How To Start A War"- Simon Curtis

FIND PLAYLIST on Spotify.

#Chapter1

"THIS WAS A MISTAKE."

Replaying the words in my head does nothing to dilute the painful memory of them.

"That's what I'm trying to tell you," I implored. The irony of it all...the campus playboy, Mr. Casanova, accusing *me* of being a cheater.

"No. I mean this."

Tears fall again at how callously he classified us.

"This is the reason I don't do relationships."

More tears, *so* many more.

"Oof. What the?"

Dimly I'm aware of being stepped on...neither the pain nor the sound of a body stumbling to the ground next to me really registering, lost inside my head...

"Are you breaking up with me?"

Even now I cringe at how pathetic I sounded.

"Yes."

One word. One syllable. One finite answer and he was gone.

"Kay?"

Wait...

That was said out loud. I heard that with my ears, right?

"Kay?"

I know that voice.

"Kay?"

Why is JT calling me Kay? He barely ever calls me that, not since he coined my PF nickname.

PF.

Thinking of the name makes me scowl.

"Why don't you tell me, P. F." Mason spits out each letter of my nickname like it offends him.

How could two letters be the catalyst for destroying such a vital part of me?

"Kay, what's wrong?"

Everything.

"Oh my god, Kay." Em crouches down at my side.

"Why is she in the hallway? Is she hurt?" Q drops down on my other side.

I'm still in the hallway?

Hmm…

I wonder how long I've been here. If they're here, it must mean the game is over, so I guess it's been a few hours. Have I really been sitting in this spot the whole time?

It's happening again—the breakdown, the foggy haze, the complete loss of time, the inability to speak, the shutting down. It's like an old habit I can't break.

The breakup, though debilitating in the moment, isn't even the worst of it. *That's* the biggest blow. I thought I'd grown stronger, thought I'd learned ways to cope, ways to never fall victim to the crushing weight of my emotions again.

"Kay, talk to me." Strong hands grip my shoulders but, again, I barely register the touch, like a ghost floating, taking in the scene from above.

"Kayla, what the fuck is going on?"

Fingers pinch my chin and lift until I'm no longer staring at the floor. Instead, as my vision clears, the haze dissipates and a new stream of tears starts to fall down my cheeks as I meet a concerned set of whiskey-colored eyes.

I watch as those same eyes track the drip of tears onto my chest, like a leaky faucet I can't turn off.

"Why are you crying?"

Because…

I don't answer. I can't even think it; how am I supposed to voice it?

"Em, check the Gram," JT instructs, doing his best to piece together what happened without having the puzzle pieces.

"Were you even bullied? Or is that just some lie you used to get me to stop pushing the issue of posting about us on my social media?"

"Nothing since they figured out she's PF Dennings from NJA."

I flinch at the name, my body having a Pavlovian response. I close my eyes to shut out the pain but then force them open again, anchoring myself back in the present by locking them onto my oldest friend.

"This doesn't make sense." JT runs a frustrated hand through his hair. "She wouldn't just be like this. Something happened."

Just my heart being broken.

"Should we call Mason?" Q asks.

I jerk in JT's hold. Why am I fighting the numbness? I should give in, let it take me away again so I can just stop hurting.

"He didn't answer." Q's voice sounds like it's coming from inside a tunnel, but I still manage to be conscious of her relaying the information to JT.

Of course *he* wouldn't answer.

"Try again," JT instructs.

I should tell them not to bother; the result isn't going to change. Mase—*no!* He's not Mase; it's Mason now—won't answer. He's done with me.

"Are you breaking up with me?"

"Yes."

"Kayla, I swear to god, if you don't open your mouth and use your words right now, I'm calling E."

The threat is enough to pop the last of the bubble of gloom surrounding me.

"Can we stop with the Kay / Kayla stuff? It freaks me out."

JT sags like a deflated balloon, his body falling forward, his head pressing into my lower belly as puffs of air ripple the fabric of my sweatpants.

"JT is just a friend. He's as much a brother to me as E."

"Yeah, and in Biz Markie's song, that's exactly what the bitch says when she's actually hooking up with the other guy."

"Fuck, Kay." JT's arms band around my hips and he holds on to me like he's the one in need of the lifeline and not me.

"You're still doing it." I bring a hand up and start to run it through the short dark auburn hair on the back of his head. The action soothes him, but I do it more to reaffirm to myself that he's real. As close as E and I are, JT has always been my anchor.

Our friendship may not be the most conventional, but it is purely platonic. JT is legit my bloodless brother.

Mason isn't the first person to think there's more to my relationship with JT than there is. It's one thing to think it; it's entirely another to believe it. I know there are parts of me, things I still haven't told him, about how bad things got after my dad died and the events that led to the deletion of my Instagram…but, seriously, after all the stories he's heard about JT and me growing up…how? How did he come to such an incorrect conclusion?

"—you didn't want things posted of us because you were worried about your other boyfriend finding out."

I'm not a liar, and I'm certainly not a cheat. For Mason to accuse me of being both those things is what hurts the most. Yes, I've kept parts of my past secret. It was a way to protect myself, to shed the veil of being a victim, to keep my heart safe.

Fat lot of good that did.

"What happened?" JT tries again.

Both Em and Q fidget, unsure what to do. I don't blame them. Being aware of the fact that I fell apart in high school is tough enough, but witnessing it is a whole other level. For as bad as this scene is coming across, it isn't anywhere near me at my worst.

"J." I choke out the single letter, giving away my desperation. It's as rare for me to drop the T in his name as it is for him to call me Kay.

With a muttered curse, I'm lifted from the floor and cradled in JT's lap. My nose brushes along the skin bared by the V of his cheer uniform's collar and sweatshirt, the familiar scent of sweat and eucalyptus keeping me from the brink of total collapse.

"What can I do? What do you need?" he asks in a distressed plea, taking on the anguish bleeding off me.

"Home," I sob.

I can't be here, in the place where I first started to fall for Mason, surrounded by memories that are mundane but still hold weighted significance.

"Okay." With the ease only a person used to tossing girls over his head can exude, JT rises from the ground, still holding me in his arms, and follows Em's directions to my bedroom.

The welcome relief of the soft goose down duvet on my tailbone after hours spent on a hard floor doesn't last long as those memories smack me in the face.

Mase—fuck! Mason—and me studying.

M-A-S-O-N asking me to be his girlfriend.

Our first sleepover.

Our first time.

Fuck! I need to get out of here.

Em and Q both hover in the doorway, their concerned gazes bouncing between me on the bed and JT shuffling around the room, gathering an overnight bag, my purse, and my keys before slipping my classic black and white Chucks onto my feet.

A screechy pained whine escapes when he tries to pull Mason's hoodie over my head. I can see the questions swimming in his eyes, but blessedly he doesn't ask, instead pulling my own U of J sweatshirt from the wardrobe.

Adjusting the hood to hide my face, he tugs on the strings to tighten the fit. Tucking me tight to his side, he drapes both my bags over his shoulder as well as his own, which he dropped by the door before, and leads us out of the apartment.

I vaguely recall him promising to call the girls later, but that's the last thing I'm cognizant of. The walk to the car and the almost-hour-long drive home aren't even a blur, just another void of time in my memories.

A hand squeezing mine brings me back to the present, and my eyes blink until the Taylor home comes into focus. My head lolls to the side on the headrest and I attempt to meet JT's encouraging smile with a grateful one. I couldn't tell you if I'm successful or not, but this is just one of the many things that show how well he knows me. I haven't uttered a word about the demise of my relationship with Mason, but still he sensed I couldn't be at my house a few blocks away.

Pinky idles in the driveway, the heat from the vents ruffling the curls hanging limply around my face as JT waits for me to be ready to move.

I give an almost indistinguishable nod, and he grabs our bags out of the back seat then rounds the Jeep, pulling my door open for me to hop down.

He holds his arms open and I fall into them, sinking into the hug, the back of his blue Kentucky sweatshirt clutched in my hands. God love him, he doesn't even flinch at the fabric getting covered in tears and snot.

The shudders racking my body eventually subside in his hold. Once I'm calm enough, he lets me go with a pat on the back.

The sound of the front door opening brings attention to our arrival, and Pops steps into the foyer a few seconds after us.

"Jimmy, my boy." Pops automatically pulls JT into a hug, but the jovial mood drops along with his smile as he catches sight of me. "Who do I have to kill?"

The automatic protective response brings the first twitch to my lips.

"Dad," JT cautions.

"Come here, baby girl."

Without any hesitation, I go to him, letting him fold me into his fatherly embrace. Growing up as the best friend of my dad, Pops has always been like a second father to me. Their longstanding friendship is how JT and I became CTG BFFs (cradle-to-grave best friends forever).

"You kids want anything to eat?" He starts to lead us to the back of the house where the kitchen is located.

I don't, the knots in my stomach are more than enough to fill me up, but I follow anyway, taking a seat on one of the stools at the counter. I concentrate all my energy on breathing in and out, anything to not succumb to the depression I feel welling up inside me. I still can't believe any of this is real.

"Shit, Kay." Tessa rushes me as soon as she spots me. I really must be in worse shape than I thought if both Taylor children are calling me Kay.

"What am I, chopped liver?" JT asks in response to the *Please, I can't human right now* plea I give him over her shoulder. "Don't I get a hug?"

"You're an idiot," T retorts, but she lets go of me to go to him.

Both Taylor siblings are a good mix of their parents. JT got his whiskey-hued eyes from his mom, where on Tessa they tinted the blue eyes inherited from Pops to a deep midnight blue. The deep auburn of JT's hair comes from a mix of Pops' once rich brown hair that is now gray at the temples with the same bright strawberry locks Tessa has.

"Come on." JT releases T and holds out a hand for me to take.

With the Taylors, I don't have to worry about being seen as rude for not saying anything as I leave to follow JT upstairs.

The path to his bedroom is as familiar as the one to my own, the door still ajar from when I slept over the other night when Pops was on shift at the firehouse. I toe out of my sneakers as I walk to the bed, leaving them scattered in my wake and dropping my hoodie amongst the mess.

I slip under the covers, burying my face in the pillow on my side of the bed. A wall of heat envelops me from behind as JT crawls in next to me and pulls my body in to spoon with his. I couldn't even count the number of times JT and I have shared a bed during our lives. Most parents keep their babies away from others who are sick, but not our moms. The only way one of us would sleep then was if the other was in the crib too.

Like all those years ago, the feeling of someone reaching inside my chest and squeezing my heart in their fist starts to fade, though it doesn't stop the little whimpers from slipping out periodically.

"I need to know what happened, Kay."

Fuck! I hate that he's still calling me Kay.

"Mason—" My voice breaks, the pain from just uttering his name like a physical blow. "Broke up with me."

"The fuck?" There's a faint whistling sound as JT sucks a breath in through his teeth. Guess he wasn't expecting that answer.

"He thinks the reason I wouldn't let him post pictures of us on his Instagram is because I was afraid they would get back to you." The image of Mason's usually sparking green eyes deadened in anger flashes through my memory and cuts through me like a hot knife.

He was so angry. So mean.

"What?" The incredulity in JT's voice soothes the sting a little.

"He thinks we're really a couple and the whole PF and Kay thing was a way to cheat on you both."

Waves of anger pulse off his body the longer I speak. Even though I'm technically a month older than him, JT has *always* treated me as his younger sister, *exactly* the same as E. Honestly, it's this fact that makes Mason's kneejerk reaction hurt so much more.

If only he trusted me and came to me instead of jumping to conclusions.

This…

This is what kills me, how he automatically thought the worst without giving me a chance to explain.

Fucking social media. I *loathe* it. Why does Mason have to be so hung up on it? Will it ever stop being the bane of my existence? Hasn't it done enough damage to my life?

"He said it was a mistake to date me." I sniffle, trying to clear some of the snot building up inside my nose so I can breathe. The cotton of the pillowcase is already wet under my face from the tears that started back up the moment I stepped into the safety of the bedroom. "On the plus side, at least this one isn't using me to get close to E."

"*Sonofabitch*," JT curses under his breath. "I'm going to kill him."

While I can appreciate the instinctive drive to come to my defense, I can't handle thinking about everything any longer. I close my eyes, my body both numb and screaming in pain simultaneously. I will sleep to come, desperate for a reprieve, even if only for a few hours.

Chapter2

PAIN.

Kay's smiling face on JT's Instagram.

All I can feel is pain.

Why does he get to post pictures of her when she fights with me about doing the same? How is that shit fair?

My body hurts from punishing myself in the weight room and later at practice today, but it's my heart that hurts the worst. It misses Kay.

Hell…*I* miss Kay.

PF Dennings. JT Taylor and PF Dennings—@CheerGodJT and @FlyerQueenPF—won multiple Worlds titles.

PF Dennings.

NJA coach PF Dennings.

Needing a way to shut off *anything* related to Kay—she played me, I'm done—I drive straight from her dorm to the nearest liquor store and buy the biggest bottle of Jameson I can find.

It's Chrissy/Tina all over again.

I haven't spoken to anyone about what happened. Instead, my bottle of Irish whiskey and I trudge up the stairs of the frat house and lock ourselves in my room.

PF. P. F. P motherfucking F.

Not needing the temptation of torturing myself by looking at posts about "Kay" and her "friend", I power off my phone and settle in to get drunk, seeking the solace only a good bout of inebriation can bring.

This fucking sucks.

#THE GRAM

#Chapter3

UofJ411: More info #SpillingTheTea #CasanovasMysteryGirl
***REPOSTED—picture from JT's IG of him and Kay in their
Admirals uniforms after winning Worlds—CheerGodJT: Me
and @FlyerQueenPF kicking ass and taking names!! Love
this chick!! #WorldChamps #CheerWorlds #CantTouchUs
#WeSetTheStandard #CTGBFF***
@The_book_queen: Her name isn't PF. I went to high school
with her. Her name is Kayla Dennings. #CasanovasMysteryGirl
@The-mumma-life: Oh yeah. Isn't she related to Eric Dennings
on the Baltimore Crabs? #CasanovasMysteryGirl

UofJ411: It's true. #Siblings #CasanovasMysteryGirl
***old picture of E in a Penn State football uniform with his
arm around Kay wearing her own PSU #87 jersey and smiling
for the camera***
@_The_art_of_reading_ Oh shit! She is. Look at this picture of
them from back when he played for Penn State
#SisterOfTheEnemy #CasanovasMysteryGirl
@UnCheckedOther: Is she really a spy for the Nittany Lions? Is

that why she's dating @CasaNova87 #SecretAgent #CasanovasMysteryGirl

@Work2play: Are we even sure this is the same girl though? #IsItFakeNews? #CasanovasMysteryGirl

@Lala_powergirl: Did she pick @CasaNova87 because he also wears #87? #MagicNumbers #CasanovasMysteryGirl

UofJ411: We found the proof that @FlyerQueenPF and Kayla Dennings—Eric Dennings' little sister—ARE the same person. #HowDoYouLikeThemApples #CasanovasMysteryGirl
old picture of E with Kay in her NJA uniform making silly faces at the camera

@_Bdsmbutch: Def the same girl. #MysterySolved #CasanovasMysteryGirl

Chapter4

THE SCENT of coffee followed by the dip of the bed behind me rouses me from sleep. For a few blissful seconds, the only thing I have to contend with is the annoyance of having to leave dreamland, but as the pale blue walls of my best friend's bedroom come into focus, the events of yesterday come crashing onto me like an anvil in an old cartoon.

The video of JT and me stunting at The Huntington.

People making the connection to me being PF Dennings.

Mas—Mason breaking up with me.

"This was a mistake."

That has me burying my face in the pillow, wishing for sleep to take me again so I can go back to forgetting. My entire body hurts like I spent a whole day doing full-outs.

A gentle hand smooths what I'm sure is a wild mess of curls from my face and tucks them behind my ear. "PF," JT says, exaggerating his usual *Pffff* pronunciation. At least he's back to not calling me Kay. Gotta take that as a good sign.

It's a struggle to open my eyes again. They're hot and painful from crying myself to sleep, probably swollen into something resembling Will Smith in *Hitch*.

JT sighs when a buzzing sound fills the room. I realize it's a phone—his or mine, I'm not sure.

"I know you don't want to, but you need to get up. E has been calling all morning."

Pushing to sit up, I roughly shove the rest of my wayward curls out of my face and gratefully accept the mug of java salvation held out to me. My hands curl around Pops' *I'm a firefighter and a dad—nothing scares me* mug. We aren't just funny t-shirts in this family.

"I take it you told him about what happened with… Mason?" Saying his name is just as painful as it was yesterday.

Fuck! Post-breakup day one sucks as much as the day it happened.

Don't they say time heals all wounds? Well time better hurry its ass up. I know, I know—I'm being unreasonable. Forgive me, though. I'm brokenhearted and undercaffeinated. At least I'm mature enough to not say it's the worst thing to ever happen to me, so there's that.

"No." JT sends another call to voicemail. "In light of everything else that's been happening, I didn't think he needed that *particular* piece of information. I remember what he was like after *him*"—he spits out the word, knowing not to say my ex's name in my presence—"and I didn't want to be the one to send him off the deep end."

E's not the most reasonable person when it comes to me, that's for sure. Logically, I know he can't do anything to Mason, but he didn't let a little thing like logic get in the way when he tried to get *his* scholarship pulled.

I'm petty enough to be disappointed by the NCAA's strict regulations that led to E's failure four years ago.

I jolt, the rest of what JT said registering. Cautiously, I lift my gaze, and the way he looks like he sucked on a lemon is almost enough for me to chicken out on asking, "What do you mean 'everything else that's been happening'?"

He glances down at the darkened screen of his phone then back to me. "You've been outed."

The way he chooses to phrase it has the first hint of a chuckle breaking free. It also gives me hope. Yesterday was a bad, *bad* day for me, but at least now I know I have grown—even if only marginally—from the girl I was in high school, because if I hadn't, I would still be an incoherent mess hiding under JT's covers.

"Are you trying to tell me you *didn't* keep the Kayla Dennings who is related to Eric Dennings hidden in a cabinet under the stairs?"

"You're such a Potterhead." I rub at the sleep coating my eyes, wincing at the sting of pain when I do.

"So are you. I don't drive all the way to Espresso Patronum by myself, sis. *You* are always riding shotgun."

Oh, how I love Lyle's coffee shop. It's such a happy place. Except thinking about it—or anything else I had in common with Mason—only makes me think of him, *again*.

"Come on." JT holds a hand out for me to take. "Get up. Drink that and let's do what we can to prevent E from coming up here and throwing you over his shoulder to take back to Maryland with him."

E has done many things since Dad died in an effort to "take care of me", but calling in Jordan Donovan might take the cake. Talk about an overreaction.

Opening the door of the Taylor home to see the hockey-royalty PR dynamo, you can tell by the height of her spike-heeled stilettos, the sharp cut of her black and white checked cigarette pants, her white silk shirt, and black moto leather jacket she is a force you don't want to reckon with.

To say I feel underdressed in a pair of black leggings, socks, and one of JT's NJA hoodies is an understatement.

I haven't had many interactions with Jordan throughout the years she's handled E's publicity, but the smile she gives me as she steps inside is filled with matronly affection, despite her not even being thirty years old.

Knowing there's no way to avoid the conversation—no matter how much I wish I could—I lead us into the kitchen.

JT leans against the counter, thumbs flying across the screen of his phone. He's most likely texting E, saving me from having to fake my way through my own conversation with my brother.

He looks up when we enter, fingers pausing as he gives a quick glance to confirm I'm alright before he resumes typing. JT may have pushed me to be the one to handle this meeting with Jordan, but he's hanging around in case I need him.

"Listen." Jordan pulls out one of the wooden chairs, draping her jacket over the back and settling in while flipping open the cover on an iPad I didn't even see her take out of her bag. "I'm going to tell you right off the bat that your brother has *a lot* of…" She pauses as if to think of the best way to put what I'm sure were demands from E. "*Opinions* on how we should handle your recent uptick in social media presence."

"I'm sure he does." I shake my head as I take the seat perpendicular to her. "And that is one PC way to talk about trolls on the internet."

"I am a professional." She smirks and gives me a wink. Again, her calm, self-assured demeanor keeps me at ease instead of feeling like crawling out of my skin at the mere mention of social media.

It feels juvenile to worry about what people post about me on the internet, but I know firsthand the damage it can inflict on a person. Mason might have tried to trivialize what I went through…

"Were you even bullied? Or is that just some lie you used to get me to stop pushing the issue of posting about us on my social media?"

But no amount of doubting me and throwing being bullied back in my face will negate it.

Do I think E is overreacting by calling in Jordan? Yes, I already said so. But in the same breath, if I wasn't worried about others knowing I'm his sister, I wouldn't have kept parts of my life a secret.

A comforting hand curls around my wrist. "I know Eric didn't hire me until after you were in the thick of things, but I remember the news articles and *stories*"—the contempt put behind that word tells me all I need to know about her opinion on gossip rags—"we helped bury to the back pages of the search results. Even if you want us for nothing else, my people will make sure that doesn't change."

Headlines flash through my brain like a movie montage of newspaper clippings and magazine articles. The drama surrounding the details of Dad's death and the ensuing trial combined with the Liam cheating drama and subsequent bullying all added up to one hell of a bad made-for-TV movie. Thank god Lifetime never picked it up. I shudder at the thought.

"That's good." It is. The last thing I want is for people to be reminded of how badly I lost it and the extent of my breakdown. If only dredging up embellished, and sometimes fabricated, news stories was the only thing I had to contend with.

"But my biggest concern is how the internet trolls are going to affect my life. I deleted *all* my social media years ago, yet…here we are."

This whole scenario is in direct response to people posting about me, dragging up old pictures and the like, trying to make them relevant again. It already cost me the man I fell in love with; what else will it take from me?

"There are a few schools of thought on how best to handle it, and I can sit here and give you facts and statistics until I'm blue in the face." There's this gleam, almost one of mischief, that enters her hazel eyes as she leans back in her chair. "Eric has been *very* vocal about what he thinks you should do, but…ultimately the decision is going to be up to you."

I bet that's a very mild description of how my brother has been. The number of phone calls he has made today while having practice is staggering. Thank god for JT serving as my buffer, because I can only imagine how much E was able to cram into each of his conversations.

I hate that I feel like I'm being forced into a decision that should be inconsequential and is total first-world problems.

My stomach cramps, and the bagel I managed to choke down with my second cup of coffee threatens to make a reappearance as flashbacks from high school hit me.

Cornered in the girls' bathroom.

The taunting: "If I dick you good enough, do you think your brother can put in a good word for me *with the college scouts?"*

The whispers: "It's cute you think you were good enough to lock down someone like Liam Parker."

Phones constantly pointed in my direction, waiting for the next GIF- or meme-worthy moment.

Underneath the thick blue camouflage cotton of my sweatshirt, my skin breaks out in goose bumps and beads of nervous sweat roll down my spine.

I used to be the girl who could make friends with anyone. Put me in any social situation and I flourished.

With the exception of the woman sitting next to me, you'd be hard-pressed to find a sister prouder of their brother or quicker to boast about his accomplishments.

Then Dad died.

E and I still champion each other, but it's only done privately.

I'm not the first daughter to suffer the loss of her father, and sadly, I won't be the last. It's just his death was the initial spark in setting my private life aflame.

Liam didn't just betray me romantically by cheating on me. No, he betrayed me on a basic human decency level.

Who was the number one source for the press and stalkerazzi looking for dirt on or photo ops with one of the NFL's top draft picks? Liam Parker. If only we could have proved it.

What started as a human interest story about how an up-and-coming NFL star eloped with his college girlfriend in an effort to maintain guardianship of his minor sibling was twisted into ludicrous and sensationalized stories of how the great Eric Dennings took on the responsibility of caring for his suicidal sister.

I was extremely depressed, especially during that first week after we learned about Dad being killed. Even now, it's a complete void in my memory. Though I wasn't suicidal during that time, the media cared more about selling head-lines and advertising space than they did about the truth of our family's pain.

Stinging radiates from my hands, and I hiss. JT lifts his gaze to me, his eyes dropping to my hands as I unfurl my fingers. Drops of blood mar the skin of my palms from where my nails dug in hard enough to pierce, and a towel appears in my field of vision.

We don't like to talk about—or even think about—the soap-opera-worthy details surrounding the circumstances of Dad's death. The press using them as fodder to sell newspa-pers was one thing. We were able to come to terms with them…sort of.

But having my most private moments of pain turned into memes for my schoolmates' entertainment is why I ran away from social media and never looked back.

"Eric explained to me—at *great* length—how you've sepa-rated your identities to minimize recognition." Jordan starts to scroll through open tabs on the iPad, and when I catch a glimpse of Instagram, I glance away, physically incapable of looking at it. "I wish I could tell you I think it's possible for you to continue on this way." Her eyes flit from the screen back to me, and her throat works with a swallow.

If she's nervous to say her part when it's something she is

paid to do, how the hell am I supposed to feel? I'm not sure I can handle another bomb. After yesterday, I'm barely keeping it together. The tape holding all my broken pieces together is of the Scotch variety, not the duct.

"But with you dating such a notable player from your school's football team, the interest in you"—she clicks on the CasanovasMysteryGirl hashtag and scrolls through the posts —"is only going to increase *because* of the original secrecy."

Of course it is.

We live in a day and age where people feel they are entitled to know things about their peers. And if that peer happens to be a celebrity—not that Mason is a celebrity outside of campus, but we all know he will be one day—they feel it is their *right* to have all the information.

The invention of the internet has made that information both easier to come by and more readily available. The problem with the interwebs is it also gives those who should have kept their opinions on said information to themselves a platform to spew them without consequence—at least without consequence to themselves.

"I know E probably asked you to come up with about a dozen different contingency plans because we *all* knew this was an eventuality." I suck in a breath, knowing the next words out of my mouth are going to cut me like razorblades. "But how different would your strategies be if I *wasn't* dating Mason?"

"Are you breaking up with me?"

"Yes."

God, I hate being reminded of my new single status.

"What do you mean?"

In the distance, I hear the front door open and close, so T must be home from school.

"In your professional opinion...if I were no longer connected to Mason, how fast do you think the interest in *me* would die down?"

"Please tell me you aren't thinking of breaking up with Mason over this, Kay?" Bette's question is tinged with panic. Guess it wasn't T arriving. I want to say I'm surprised she drove up, but I'm not.

She's here to mom the crap out of me. As much as I wish I didn't need her here to do just that, I do. I totally do. The little girl inside me who only ever wanted her mommy growing up weeps at how quickly Bette has come to lend her support. She doesn't even know the half of what happened and still she came without being asked.

"No." I shake my head, rattling the dull throb left over from my cry-fest.

"Good." Bette lets out a sigh of relief. Too bad it's premature.

"He dumped me."

#Chapter5

HIDING out from the guys is harder than I thought it would be. Right now, I'm wandering around aimlessly, walking each floor of The Huntington like I'm a ghost tasked with haunting the hotel.

With the game tomorrow, I can't get blindly drunk like I did last night, but fuck if I'm not looking for a way to shut the voices in my head up. Okay, so it's not voices, it's voice, but my inner coach has been both extremely vocal and suspiciously quiet. It's an oxymoron I have had zero luck in figuring out.

I still haven't had it in me to check Instagram again, but based on the questions I've been getting when I *am* around, two things are glaringly obvious.

1. No one has figured out Kay and I broke up.

2. The fact that Eric Dennings is her brother is now common knowledge.

"Bro, why didn't you tell us Kay is related to Eric Dennings?"

"Holy shit! Was Eric Dennings the family you met in Maryland?"

"This is epic. You gotta hook us up with a meet-and-greet."

The ones from my teammates were easy enough to ignore

—what they were asking wasn't any of their business. The ones from my boys, though, not so much.

"Why isn't Smalls answering when we call?"

"For reals. Doesn't she know it's our night-before-the-game tradition?"

"She's messing with our superstitions."

Questions like those just kept coming, and I didn't answer a single one. I didn't know how.

#Chapter6

UofJ411: Umm…am I the only one seeing this? #OffYourGame #CasanovaWatch
boomerang of Mason fumbling
@68blackburnc: Since when does @CasaNova87 fumble? #ButterFingers
@Acolon1729: Is this from his first or second one today? #LostCount #CasanovaWatch

UofJ411: Where's Waldo? #GetTheMilkCartonReady #CasanovasGirl
picture of the empty seat where Kay and the boys usually sit
@Annielaurel: Could this be why @CasaNova87 played like shit? #WheresTheGF #CasanovasGirl
@Ash_lovesbooks: Anyone have connections at Penn State? Is she at their game instead? #PlayingBothSides #CasanovasGirl

Chapter 7

"WE NEED TO TALK," Trav says—well, more like *demands* as we step inside the AK house.

Bypassing the pledges setting up for tonight's party, I follow my best friend up the staircase to his bedroom. I quirk a brow when I hear the lock click.

"I'm not risking anyone interrupting us before we have it out." He leans against the edge of his desk, crossing his feet at the ankles and his arms over his chest.

I mirror his stance against the wall opposite him and blow out a breath. I knew I wasn't doing a good job of keeping anything from him. We've been best friends for too long for him not to pick up on the most minute changes in my demeanor, and though I'm loath to admit it, this breakup has affected me in a major way.

Silence stretches and swells between us, both waiting for the other to speak first. I don't know what Trav wants me to say, but I'm not in the mood to have a Dr. Phil session with him.

"Is it Kay?" Her name slams into me like the tackle I took in the third quarter.

My head thunks against the drywall, no longer able to maintain eye contact. "Is what about Kay?"

"I hate when you try to be all aloof and play dumb." He chuckles, but there's no humor in it. "How quickly you forget I was there when you were losing your shit in the shower."

The slap of my palm against the wet wall echoes like a gong.

My shampoo bottle gets chucked out of the shower stall, skidding across the floor from the force.

"I would have thought you'd go to Kay's to talk shit out…" Trav runs his gaze up and down my body, assessing me. "But since you've been a miserable motherfucker the last two days, I'm starting to suspect you didn't and you're just letting things fester."

Two days—that's it? It's only been about forty-eight hours since I broke up with Kay.

"Nah, bruh. You're overthinking things." I try to brush it off again. I really, *really* don't want to talk about this.

"Nova, you're so full of shit your eyes have turned brown." He shoves off from the desk and starts to pace. I'm not sure how helpful it is, the space inside the room so minimal he only manages two steps before he has to turn around in the other direction. "Fuck!" Trav slaps his hands against his thighs. "This is *me* you're talking to. Why are you lying?"

After about a dozen laps, he resumes his position and levels me with a heated glare. I don't defend myself against the accusation I see in his eyes because, honestly, I can't. Things are only going to get worse once he finds out the details.

"I'm an idiot." I lift my hat off my head and toss it onto the bed, running my own hands through my hair.

Trav, being the asshole he is, laughs. "That isn't new information. What I really want to know is why did the guy who hasn't had a single collegiate fumble have *two*"—he waves two fingers in front of my face—"in today's game?"

And there it is, the real kick in the jockstrap. The Hawks lost our first game of the season—a conference game, no less.

I played like shit. Honestly, I'm shocked Coach Knight didn't bench me. For the first time *ever*, my heart wasn't in the game. Instead, it was somewhere on the floor where it landed after it was ripped out. And, yes, before you get on my ass like my inner coach, I am well aware that the wound was self-inflicted.

"I feel like this is a dumb question because you're fine at away games, but was it because Kay wasn't at the game?"

I told you girls were nothing but drama, but NOOO, you didn't want to listen to me. I bet Brantley has been blowing up your phone. What would your future agent have to say about how shitty you played? *taps chin* No wonder you're too much of a chickenshit to turn it on.

"I thought she never planned on coming today anyway? Didn't she have cheerleading shit to do with her friend who's in town?"

My hands clench into fists and a growl rolls through the back of my throat at the mention of her "friend".

Don't you think it's time to find your balls and tell him what you did? My inner coach is a dick.

"I broke up with Kay."

"WHAT?!" Trav jumps to his feet. "Why the hell would you do a dumbass thing like that?"

"So what I really want to know, Kayla—if that's even your real name…"

"Because she's just like Chrissy!" I shout, taking my frustration out on him because he's here.

"The fuck she is." He may have cursed, but his tone is calm and even.

"Look at all the signs." My fist punching a hole through the drywall echoes through the room. Trav, to his credit, doesn't even flinch at my loss of control.

"You really had me fooled."

Secret Instagram profile.

Secrets in general.

Different name in an official capacity.

Claimed by someone who isn't me on Instagram.

I tick each of these off, the expression on Trav's face only darkening with each one.

"You know what?" Trav shakes his head, his disappointment dripping off of him. "You're right." See? It isn't just me. "I should have seen this coming. I'm sorry I didn't."

"Not your fault, man. At least this one didn't try to ruin our friendship."

I'm barely managing to function as it is. If I had to worry about the strength of our bromance right now, I don't know what would happen.

Also…

For as bad as the Chrissy / Tina thing was, I didn't love her. Sure, my dick and my immature teenage heart thought I did, but that's because I didn't know how to differentiate lust from love like I do now.

That's what makes all this that much worse. My love—present tense, not past—for Kay is so strong, it might have ended up being the *one* thing capable of destroying my life-long friendship with Trav.

What the fuck does that say about me?

"I'm not talking about Kay. I'm talking about how I should have seen how *you*"—his finger presses aggressively into my pectoral—"would lump *her*"—another poke, his finger bending back with the force—"in the same boat as Tina."

What the what?

"It's been four years, Mase. Stop letting the bitch fuck with your life. Tina is not worth it."

"But Kay—"

"Is *not* fucking Christina Hale. She's not pretending to be Kay with you and PF with her friend."

He resumes his earlier pacing, this time with a lot more agitation. He's muttering under his breath, yanking at his hair, and a few times comes close to punching the wall himself. For as·fucked up as I was—am—over the whole Chrissy/Tina thing, it hit Trav twice as hard.

"Did you even stop to think that maybe the reason her gym has her listed as PF is *because of* her brother? You would think people wouldn't care, but the Gram is *insane* with posts about her right now."

My gut churns, acid pushing its way up my esophagus. "What do you mean?"

"Hashtag Casanova's Mystery Girl has far surpassed Casanova Watch."

"They already know who she is—why would they still be using that hashtag?"

Worry prickles along the base of my skull as I recall E talking about bringing in his publicist if needed. Kay laughed it off, like her brother was merely overreacting, but...

Could it have actually been more?

Dammit, Kay! Why did you never go into detail about your bullying?

You were the one who threw the bullying back in her face.

FUCK YOU very much, inner coach.

"I mean, don't get me wrong..." Trav's voice breaks me out of my internal argument. "They still wanna know *every-thing* about our girl down to the type of toothpaste she uses, but now all the conspiracy nuts are out."

A part of me I didn't know still existed sparks to life at my best friend calling my girl *ours*. Fuck me for jumping to conclusions. I had Trav with me when I was spiraling and yet I held everything in and jumped off the deep end.

"What conspiracies could people be coming up with?" My eyes roll. Everything about all this drama is ludicrous.

"How she was only dating you to break up with you and give Penn State the edge over us, stupid fucking bullshit like that."

A grinding sound fills my head as my molars rub together.

"What?" Trav asks at my *Oh, shit!* expression. That particular theory is about to get worse.

Now I'm starting to see why E could be worried about the press. No one really cares about an athlete's family unless they themselves are famous, but something like this? Juicy tidbits that can fan the flames of rivalry? Fuck, I've lost count of the number of times Brantley has harped on using anything at your disposal to sell tickets and magazines.

"Back in high school, Kay dated Liam Parker."

Trav's blue eyes widen enough that I can see a full ring of white around them. Guess he wasn't expecting *that* to come out of my mouth.

"Well...this just got all Kardashians up in here." He's such a smartass, but I'll take the injection of levity into the situation. "Okay, bro." He pulls out his desk chair, sitting down and taking both a notebook and a pen from the drawer. "Sit your ass down and start from the beginning." He points at his bed, the covers roughly tossed up to make it look made. "I'm going to need *all* the details of your dumping to help you fix it."

"Should I start calling you Cupid1 instead of QB1?" I taunt while doing as he asked, retrieving my hat in the process.

"Hmm..." He scratches at his chin like he's deep in thought. "Fuck yeah, I like it. Now give me the deets."

I do. I tell him every accusation I made.

"You told me you don't like having your full face show in pictures."

"Outside of you wearing my hoodie and when we're sitting next to each other in class or at lunch, you keep as much space between us as you do between you and our friends."

Every insult I tossed out, all the ways I belittled Kay about her hang-ups with social media and what she went through in the past.

"I gave you an easy solution to shut the haters up. You wouldn't have to do a thing except smile for the camera, and yet you refused."

"Were you even bullied? Or is that just some lie you used to get me to stop pushing the issue of posting about us on my social media?"

I purge my guts to one of the few people in this world who won't judge me.

"At one point, I slow-clapped her. I *fucking* slow-clapped." I'm not just an idiot; I'm an asshole and a douche.

There may not be judgment, but there are eye rolls, a reaction I'm sure Trav picked up from Kay herself.

"You really are a fucking idiot, Mase."

"I know." I lift my hat off and replace it on my head, working the brim between my hands before releasing it to grip the back of my neck.

"Lucky for you, helping you serves a more selfish purpose for me, so yes, I accept the job as your Cupid1."

I know better than to ask what those selfish reasons could be, but I do anyway.

"Because...as your best friend, I probably fall under the persona non grata category. The way Short Stack cooks and always feeds me is not something I want to give up."

The absurdity of Trav's statement manages to get the first genuine laugh out of me in days. This guy is forever thinking with his stomach.

"Real bro code mentality right there," I quip.

"Whatever." He pops a shoulder. "Not a risk I'm willing to take."

I nod. No use arguing. Besides, we have more important things to discuss.

Time to come up with a plan to get my girl back before it's too late.

Chapter 8

"PF, WHERE YOU AT?" JT's voice echoes down the hall of my family home, and Herkie jumps down from the couch to greet my bestie instead of waiting.

I don't bother answering. He'll find us in less than a minute.

"Oh, good. Bette did your hair," JT says when he spots me curled up in the corner of the sectional, recently straightened hair hanging around my shoulders.

I didn't have it in me to stop Bette from fussing over me earlier and letting her style my hair was a painless thing to allow. Plus, having someone else wash your hair for you is one of the best things ever.

I may feel like crap on a stick, but yes, my hair is on point. The real question is why JT cares.

"If this is your subtle attempt at getting Bette to do your own hair, you know you don't have to bother."

"Ooo, good plan." JT makes double bouncing finger guns at Bette. "You can hook this up"—he points to his head—"while this one"—he thrusts his arm out to me—"goes to get ready."

"Ready?" I shake my head, my hair fanning out at the aggressiveness of it. "I'm not going anywhere."

"Oh, but you are." He takes my hand and pulls me from the divot I've worn into the couch with my ass. "We're going to King's, and you don't get to have an opinion on the matter."

That explains the dark jeans, stylishly ripped white tee, and Vans.

"I'm not really in the mood to go to a Royal Ball." All my effort goes into pushing back against the hands curled around my shoulders, trying to prevent them from guiding me up the stairs.

"Too bad, so sad for you, PF." I don't need to look back to know he's sporting a shit-eating grin. "Now go get changed, and keep in mind it's a race night." He doesn't stop until we come to my bedroom door. "And make sure you do something"—he spins me around and circles a finger an inch from my face—"about this mess."

Guess the coddling portion of the breakup period is over. JT is a tough love specialist if the situation warrants it. Besides, I can't really fault him. The skin around my eyes is looking rough. I had to wear more than one ice mask to get the swelling down enough not to scare people at The Barracks this morning, and eye drops are a necessity to control the redness around my irises.

"*Really* feeling the love right now, bro."

"Calm your sarcasm, sis." He spins me again and pats my ass like a ballplayer, directing me into my room. "You have half an hour then I'm dragging you out, ready or not."

Thirty minutes later, dressed appropriately in my own pair of black skinny jeans, black and white Chucks, white V-neck, and leather jacket, I sit in the passenger seat of Pinky while JT drives us to King's.

My hot pink Jeep sticks out like a sore thumb amongst the

sea of matte black sports cars parked around the huge empty lot surrounding the buildings that serve as home base for Carter King and the Royalty Crew.

The bonfire that is a staple of these Royal Balls is going strong. T and Savvy are already here, standing with the other high schoolers staying far enough away so the smoke won't give Savvy an asthma attack.

JT tucks me under his arm and leads us to where Carter and his aptly named second, Wesley Prince, hold court. He takes one of the open seats around the fire and pulls me to sit in his lap.

JT falls into easy conversation with the guys while I give a handful of chin jerks hello. I managed to hold it together during our stunting clinics last night and practice with both the Marshals and Admirals today—the latter significantly harder because of the Roberts Twins—but I'm all tapped out on social interaction.

I may not be a regular at these things like JT is when he's home—until T and Savvy started attending, I used to hang with them instead—but nobody seems to be bothered by my silence. The lack of judgment and pettiness is actually one of my favorite things about the Royals.

With a two-year age gap between us and King, we didn't mingle with him and his crew much past our mutual connection of T and Savvy's friendship. But when shit started going down and the bullying got out of control at Blackwell Public, JT took matters into his own hands and sought out a more active friendship with the king—no pun intended—of Blackwell.

Being a member of one of the town's founding families, Carter has connections all the way from the mayor's office down to the gossiping elders. He has way more pull, and dare I say power, than one would think is typical for a person who is barely old enough to legally drink.

Outside of the obviously illegal street races—he inherited the operation then grew it into the biggest circuit in the tri-state area in a handful of years—no one really questions all the things the Royals are actively involved in.

I suspect the reason JT dragged me out tonight was to remind me that though Carter may be more his friend than mine—hence why he isn't the CK in my life—he's a friend nonetheless. There wasn't anything they could do digitally, but King and his Royals were the ones to shut down the bullying that happened inside the halls of Blackwell Public.

Even after Carter graduated, Wes continued to uphold the Royal protection decree. So, being dragged to a Royal Ball instead of letting me wallow in a pint of Ben & Jerry's? This is JT's way of making sure I remember there are people who will have my back when he has to return to Kentucky tomorrow night.

When "Wasabi" by Little Mix comes on, I know T and Savvy have taken control of the sound system, and if I wasn't so depressed, I would find them for an impromptu dance party. Instead, those nerve endings that would be tapping my feet and swiveling my hips are deadened, and my legs remain hanging limply over the side of the chair.

Like a box of Rice Krispies, the fire snaps, crackles, and pops. My attention is drawn to the dancing orange and red flames, watching the way the oxygen moves from the heat at the peak of the high teepee of stacked wood.

I'm free to zone out, but I can't tell if it's a blessing or a curse. It's nice not having to fake being alright when I'm the farthest thing from it, except the flip side is any time I have too much time to think, my thoughts turn to Mas—*fuck!* —Mason.

I'm angry.

I'm hurt.

If you told me my heart had grown tear ducts, I would

believe you since it literally feels like it's weeping out the pain of missing him.

Guess I better get used to my new reality.

#Chapter9

BY THE TIME Trav and I emerge from his room with a plan to get Kay back, the Alpha party is in full swing downstairs. I come to a halt at the threshold, Trav bumping into me at my abrupt stop.

"Oh, shit," Trav whispers at the sight of Grant Grayson glaring at us as he pauses in unlocking his own bedroom door.

Having been lost in my own head these last few days, I didn't even think about the lack of communication from him. He warned me not to hurt his best friend, and that's exactly what I did. His response—or more accurately, his lack of one—is a clear sign of whose side he's taking in all this.

Guess he went with 'sisters before misters' instead of 'bros before hoes', huh?

We stand in a silent stare-off until the sound of running footsteps precedes Em's appearance at the top of the stairs. "Oh, good." She flicks a glance in my direction but dismisses me instantly, giving her full attention to Grayson. "You're back."

From over Em's head, Grant's dark gaze meets mine again, but he also ignores me and only speaks to her. "You're still here?"

"I was waiting for you. JT knew you'd be mad enough he didn't tell you what was going on sooner, so I'm your ride." Em puts her hands on Grayson's back to move him along the second he has his door open. "Now hurry up and change."

"Have you talked to her?" I hear Grayson ask as they disappear inside the room.

"No. JT said she put her phone in a drawer at his house and hasn't touched it since Thursday."

Desperate for any information I can get about Kay, I hustle across the hall and shove my foot inside the jamb before the door can fully shut.

"What do you want, Mason?" Contempt drips from Em's question as she folds her arms over her chest.

"You're going to see Kay?" I ask, not intimidated by her ire in the least.

"Of course I am. Friends"—she steps close, poking with me each word—"rally around each other in their time of need."

Fuck me.

Oh, buddy. You've committed one hell of a personal foul.

"Do you think we should compare notes on your stupidity?" Trav whispers into my ear, though his voice isn't low enough not to be overheard if the slight curl to Em's lips is any indication.

"I fucked up," I admit, not for the first time tonight, and if I can convince Em to tell me where they are going, I doubt it will be the last.

"You got that right." Em snorts before the brief flash of amusement is wiped clear.

Grayson, unperturbed by the audience, starts undressing. "Is it wrong I'm annoyed she didn't tell me?" he asks Em as he pulls on a pair of dark jeans.

"She didn't want to ruin your weekend with your family." He grunts his displeasure at that reasoning. "If it makes you feel any better, JT said she hasn't even spoken to E. He's been the one fielding all the calls."

"I can't believe she agreed to tonight." Grayson slips a fresh t-shirt over his head.

"I don't think JT gave her a choice." Em gives us her back, continuing their conversation as if Trav and I don't exist. "He's working the *bigger picture* angle."

"How bad is it going be when he goes back to Kentucky?"

"Don't know." Em shrugs. "But from what I've been told…"

The taste of copper fills my mouth as I bite my tongue hard enough to draw blood in an effort not to demand she finish her sentence. I hate that I'm missing not just pages, but whole chapters from Kay's story.

Grayson finishes zipping up a black hoodie and moves to stand next to Em. His six-eight frame is practically vibrating with barely restrained anger as he eyes me. The two adopt similar poses of crossed arms and death glares, and again, I'm reminded that he might be my brother in the fraternity, but he also considers himself one of Kay's brothers.

"I'll deal with you another time." Grant goes to step around me. A frantic need overwhelms my body and I take a chance, reaching out to stop him with a hand to his arm.

"Where is she?"

"You lost the right to ask that," Em snaps. This harsh, mama bear side of her is a new development.

"Emma." I let every ounce of anguish I've been feeling show on my face. "I know I don't deserve it"—I inhale deeply and send up a silent prayer—"but I'm not going to be able to fix this on my own."

Fuck! Even with help, there's a chance the damage I inflicted is too great.

"I…" I bring my hands to my chest, laying my palms flat over my heart. "I *need* to be able to fix this. *Please.*" I swallow thickly. "Please help me."

Who knew silence could be so deafening? It's heavy and stretches on and on until I think I can't take it anymore.

Finally, Em shares a look I can't quite read with Grayson before refocusing on me with an arched brow and a smirk. I should probably heed the warning, but my drive to get to Kay is too strong.

"It's your funeral."

#Chapter10

EXCITED MURMURING SPREADS throughout the lot as a buzz of anticipation permeates the atmosphere. It's enough to break me out of my own antisocial haze.

From my seat, I can't make out what's going on, but the way the crowd is swarming suggests it's a new arrival who's stirring things up. I'm not the only one who has taken note of the change. They aren't being overly obvious about it, only shifting to lean forward in their seats, elbows braced on their knees, hands hanging limply between them, but all the Royals around the bonfire are on high alert.

"You invited people from BA?" I speak for the first time in the hours since we arrived, directing my question to Carter since he runs the show.

BA, Blackwell Academy, is the most expensive and exclusive private school in the state. It also happens to be on the opposite side of town from Blackwell Public, where we all graduated from. The rivalry between the schools and their students runs as deep as any generations-old family grudge.

Luckily for them, their money is green, and Carter allows them in the races. Whoever arrived must have a car nice enough to rival King's based on the reaction.

"No." His jaw is hard, part of it popping out from how he

has it clenched. Carter King embodies every bad boy persona mothers warn their daughters about. He's got a Cam Gigandet vibe to him with his short buzzed blond hair hidden underneath his black beanie, snug black t-shirt, ripped jeans, classic Jordans G would kill for, and leather jacket. "With you being here, I didn't want to risk having that many unknowns around. I'll take those rich douches' money next weekend."

This time it's shock that renders me speechless.

Carter chuckles at my slack-jawed expression. "I get that we aren't BFFs, Dennings, but"—he cranes his neck to look past me to where I can hear Savvy laughing with T—"you have *always* been good to my sister, and you know how I feel about my family."

Unexpected emotion chokes me. The King siblings may not be orphans like myself, but with a dad who died when Savvy was young and a mom who isn't winning any mother of the year awards, it was Carter who took over the majority of responsibility for the younger King. Having grown up in an unconventional family dynamic myself, it never even crossed my mind to be anything less than accepting of Savvy into our own.

"Tonight is about reminding you there are people who have your back and preventing you from forgetting that fact like you did for a time in high school." Carter levels me with a *You'll do best to listen to me* brow raise, and I'm nodding before I even realize I'm doing so. It's not something we talk about openly, but I appreciate how he used his pull for me.

Still…

If it's not BA-ers, what is going on?

Then I see Em, Q, CK, and G push through the sea of people, but it's not them causing the commotion. No, that honor goes to the backward-hat-wearing Adonis striding up behind them.

What the fuck?

My battered heart jumps at the sight of Mason looking too damn good. A pair of dark jeans hangs from his trim hips, the waffle weave of his green Henley clings to the rippling muscles of his washboard stomach, and his distressed denim jacket and white fitted ball cap complete the look.

Though his presence is enough to have me going into a tailspin, it's his car that set the gearheads here off.

"Em," I hiss, grabbing her hand in a death grip and pulling her down to my level.

Beneath me, JT grunts, and I think I may have elbowed him in the junk from my jerky movements.

"*What* is *he* doing here?" I peer around her and find those seafoam green eyes still locked on me like he can see through the body bent between us. All the longing and softness in them evaporates the instant he notices I'm sitting in JT's lap, but I'm too busy reeling from him being here to process the shift.

"Apparently"—Em chances a glance over her shoulder—"Casanova has a death wish." I don't miss how she's fallen back into calling him by his old moniker.

"I'll say," Tessa says from somewhere behind me.

"I know you're a King, Cart, but maybe you should channel a queen and be all *Off with his head*," Savvy suggests to her brother as she too makes her way over.

"Not now, Sav," Carter warns.

There's a snort and my gaze snaps to the left to see Trav flanking Mason. His presence is another punch to the gut, reminding me a boyfriend isn't the only thing I lost this weekend.

There's more bickering, but I tune it out, too focused on Mason. The agony in my heart makes it painful to look at him.

"This is a closed party," Carter declares.

"It's okay, King." I reach out, placing a hand on his knee to keep him from getting up. Mason's eyes blaze as they lock on the touch and his nostrils flare. He can be jealous all he wants, but he lost the right to be possessive over me when he broke up with me. Besides, me controlling Carter is more for his benefit. All it would take is one tilt of his chin to set his Royals in motion.

"Why are you here, Mason?" I ask.

"I came here for you."

Again…

What the fuck?

#Chapter11

AFTER INSTRUCTING both Trav and me to change, neither Em nor Grayson speak to us except to say to follow them. When we drive past the *Welcome to Blackwell* sign an hour later, I'm not surprised to see this is where Kay is. What does come as a shock is that we don't go to her house.

Probably a good thing. I know he has a game tomorrow, but what if E came up for the weekend? *takes ball cap off and scratches head* I don't think he would be as inclined to let you off as Grayson did—at least for now.

Real helpful, Coach, I snark back, my hand gripping the gearshift with a little more force than needed to drop into third for the turnoff.

We pull into a massive lot that's home to two large buildings—one that looks like a garage and the other a warehouse—and dozens of sports and muscle cars, most of them in matte black paint. In the midst is a familiar candy-colored Jeep.

I follow Em's Lexus RX to an open section to the left and park. Given how Kay reacted when she saw my 1967 Ford Mustang Shelby GT500 the night of our first date, the way people swarm my car should have been expected. Same goes for the chilly reception I receive from Kay herself.

Here's what I didn't expect.

The simultaneous punch to my gut, balls, and heart at the sight of her. Instead of curls, her long hair hangs around her shoulders straight, the colors hidden in the strands that peeking out in the flipped ends curling around the swells of her cleavage, which is displayed by the dip in her tight t-shirt. She has a badass biker chick vibe going on in her leather jacket.

Then there's the extra whammy of her sitting in JT's lap.

As if I'm not reeling enough, there's also the way Mr. Poster Bad Boy sitting in the next chair tries to act like he can make me leave.

Followed quickly by how *wrong* it is to see Kay's tiny hand on him when she tries to prevent him from getting up.

"I came here for you."

At my declaration, Kay's beautiful stormy eyes bounce around the area surrounding the bonfire burning my back. "You shouldn't have," she says, no longer looking at me.

"Can we talk?" My words come out like the plea they are.

"Are you serious?" Her eyes snap to mine, a hurricane swarming in the gray depths.

"Yes."

I shove my hands in my pockets to keep from snatching her away.

"*Now?* Now you want to talk?" Her arms fold defensively across her chest.

"Yes." The word is sure even though everything inside me is fueled by uncertainty.

Kay stares at me like I'm out of my mind—and maybe I am—and the vacant, almost-looking-through-me gaze kills me. What I wouldn't give for an eye roll from her right now.

I will her to give in and speak, but when she does, it's not what I want to hear.

"No."

Who knew one word could hurt so badly?

"Please," I implore.

"Seriously?" Her voice screeches at the end.

"Come on, Skit. Ple—"

"DON'T." The word comes out as a whisper and a yell. "Go home, Mason. I'm not getting into this here."

I hate that she's calling me Mason. It's like we're back to when we first met, when she did her best to keep me from getting close, like dropping the shorthand of my name is just one more way to keep me at arm's length.

I didn't put up with it then, and I'm sure as shit not going to now. I widen my stance and cross my own arms. I'm not going *anywhere*.

"Dennings." Bad Boy—I think she called him King earlier —holds up a small black card, similar to a hotel keycard, pinching it between his fingers. When Kay glances his way, he jerks a chin at the warehouse-looking building.

I don't think my heart beats at all while Kay stares at the tiny piece of plastic.

"Thanks, King." Her entire body sags under the weight of the sigh she expels, but she accepts the offering, not even waiting to see if I'll comply before pushing herself up and striding toward the structure.

Every eye in the vicinity is on me, each of them asking, *Well? You going to go after her or what?*

Inhaling a deep breath and a nod of encouragement from Trav, I jog to follow, my hand catching the door a second before it latches.

I pause at the threshold, taking in another deep breath, praying I can find the right words to fix my epic mistake.

"Kay?" My voice echoes in the vast space, the scent of leather and motor oil hitting my nose as I take in the handful of sick sport bikes and the matte black Camaro she's perched on the trunk of.

My steps falter at how broken she looks with her feet

propped on the bumper, elbows braced on her spread knees, face buried in her hands.

Seeing her like this makes every muscle inside me feel like it's been pummeled and in need of an ice bath.

She doesn't move when I call her name. In fact, she doesn't react at all until I lean a hip against the car and reach out a hand to touch her back.

"Don't." It's a strangled plea.

"Please, Kay."

Her head whips around and she shoots daggers at me with her eyes. "What, Mason? What could you want from me?"

There's my full name again. I swallow it down and ask, "Can we talk? *Please?*"

Her eyes widen in shock. "Talk? *Talk?* Are you kidding me with that?"

It feels like I'm buzzing underneath my skin. I've admitted to myself and to others that I fucked up, but I don't think I understood the extent of it until now. I've never seen her seem this…distraught before.

"Please?"

"What's different about today?" She drops her gaze, running her thumb back and forth over the skinny purple metallic paint outline of the glossy black racing stripes. "I wanted to talk to you the other day and you shut me down. It didn't matter what I had to say, or that I could explain. It didn't matter that that particular post was taken out of context. *No.* All that mattered was what was posted on social media. So please, *please* tell me why I should talk to you when you wouldn't give me the same courtesy."

Her words and the pain evident in them tear my already beaten heart to shreds.

"Look." I grip the back of my neck to keep from reaching for her again. "I'm sorry, okay."

"You're *sorry*?" she squeaks, each sign of her pain stabbing me like a hot poker.

"Yes, Kay." I put every bit of sincerity I have into my words. "I fucked up, I know."

"Yeah you did."

I hate that she still won't look at me.

"You know what I don't get?" she says, finally lifting her head so I can see her face, the rims around her eyes red. "You"—she points to me—"pursued me"—points to herself. "*You* were the one who actively sought *me* out." She repeats her pointing. "*You* barreled your way into *my* life."

She's right. From the moment I saw her—even when I thought she belonged to another—I felt drawn to her. If she thinks I'm going to give up after having her, loving her, knowing what it feels like to be loved *by* her, she has another thing coming.

Two days ago, the ghosts of my past had me throwing in the towel. Not anymore. Time to leave the past where it belongs—in the past. I'm recovering my fumble and running it in for the most important touchdown of my life—my future.

"Lord knows I haven't been perfect in our relationship." She buries her hands in her hair, fingers tangling in the straightened locks with a tug. "I was scared and kept things a secret because of my fears, but I never *lied* to you."

"So what I really want to know, Kayla—if that's even your real name—"

I shake off the memory. "I kno—"

She throws up a hand, cutting me off. "Yet that's exactly what you accused me of doing."

"Were you even bullied? Or is that just some lie you used to get me to stop pushing the issue of posting about us on my social media?"

My mouth opens to speak, but nothing comes out. I

genuinely don't know what to say. I decide to go with the truth. "You weren't the only one who kept secrets."

"What secrets could you have that would lead to you coming over to my dorm only to accuse me of cheating on you by thrusting a picture of JT and me in my face? A five-year-old picture was your great proof, proof that PF was some alternate identity I used to…what? Have an affair with you?" She rambles on in an attempt to figure out my reasoning. "But when you think about it, that doesn't make sense since you were around for some of my video chats with JT. Is social media really that important to you that you would only believe in my love for you if it was posted for strangers to see and dissect?"

"I gave you an easy solution to shut the haters up. You wouldn't have to do a thing except smile for the camera, and yet you refused."

"In high school I dated this girl who also wasn't big on social media." My explanation cuts off the tumble of her words. "Unlike you, she did have accounts and did let me post pics of the two of us on mine."

"You told me you don't like having your full face show in pictures."

"I didn't think anything of it at the time, but they were only ones like her kissing my cheek or with one of my hats blocking most of her face."

The urge to punch something hits me with force. Now I'm the one who can't look at Kay. The parallel between our relationship and the one I had with Chrissy is not something I wanted to admit to myself most days—forget about explaining them to Kay.

"What I didn't know at the time was she did that because I wasn't the only person she was dating." I swallow and force myself to search out her comforting grays. "She was also dating Trav."

"How?" Kay sputters at my confession, jaw going slack, eyes blinking in confusion. "How is that even possible?"

Because you were a stupid-as-fuck seventeen-year-old who let himself get led around by his dick. My inner coach is so nice to me. Not.

"Her name was Christina Hale, and she went to school a few towns over from ours."

"For how involved Trav was in our relationship, I find it hard to believe you two didn't talk about the girls you were dating."

"Oh we did." I let out a humorless chuckle. "I told him all about Chrissy, and he did the same about his girl—Tina."

#Chapter12

WOW.

I'm not sure I have any words right now.

Of all the ways Mason could have explained his kneejerk reaction that led to our breakup, this was not one I could have predicted.

I wish that were our only issue.

"Please, Kay. Let me fix this."

I jump off the back of the Camaro when Mason goes to reach for me again. I can't have him touch me. If he does, I'll crumble, and I *can't* let that happen here.

Not in public.

Not where people can see.

I may be protected here, but it's still too risky.

"I'm sorry, Mason." I am. I really, *really* am. "But you can't."

"Bullshit!" he snaps.

The soles of my Chucks squeak against the painted concrete as I start to pace the width of the garage. I make the mistake of looking over at Mason when he curses, and damn him. Why does he have to look so good leaning against a car? This would be much easier if I wasn't so damn attracted to him.

Or, you know, if you weren't in love with him. My inner cheer-leader rolls her eyes, so hard if she were a cartoon and not a manifestation of my conscience they would have popped out onto the floor.

"Mason—"

"STOP calling me Mason."

The splintered pieces of my heart shatter into dust. He wants me to call him Mase. I can't do it. I *have* to think of him as Mason. I *need* the distance it creates between the campus playboy he used to be versus the man who owns my heart.

As much as I wish it weren't true, he does still own it, and if the last two days had never happened, I'd be closing the distance between us and letting him fold me into his strong, muscly arms.

But they did, so I can't.

"You should go."

Please, please, please go before I lose it completely.

"I told you"—he pushes off the car—"I'm not leaving until we fix this."

"If you're looking for forgiveness, I forgive you. I'm not going to lie and say it doesn't hurt—it does—but I under-stand now why you jumped to the conclusion you did." I eye him warily as he starts to move.

"And I'm sorry. *God*, baby, I'm so sorry I hurt you." His steps continue, and for each one he takes toward me, I take two back.

"I believe you, but when you broke up with me…you didn't just break my heart." I choke down a sob before it can escape. "You broke a part of me that was barely even strong enough to be with you in the first place."

"Fuck! Don't say that." He stalks across the remaining space. A whimper that sounds more like a wounded animal than anything that could come from a human leaves my mouth when he cups my head between his large hands, his fingers tangling in the hair at the base of my skull.

Fuck. Losing him was hard. I didn't think I would survive it. But now? After almost three days of dealing with what I consider my worst nightmare since losing Dad, having to push him away because I realize I really am not strong enough to handle being with such a public figure? Gut-wrenching. Skinned alive, dipped in a vat of acid level pain.

"We each have our demons, Mason. The only difference is mine aren't just winning...they won."

I bring my hands up, my fingertips hovering over his chest for a second before I have the strength to actually touch him. Fire spreads through my veins at the contact, and I almost lose my resolve to do what I have to do. The fortifying breath I take almost does more damage than good when it brings the intoxicating scent of his soap with it.

"Maybe if you told me about them, if there were no more secrets, I could help you fight them." He pulls me slightly closer, ignoring the way I'm trying to push him away.

I don't know what's scarier, revealing my secrets or letting him help.

Heat pricks at the backs of my eyes and I lose the battle to the tears I've been fighting.

My knees give out when Mason uses his thumbs to wipe them away.

The color leeches from my fingers as I pull up every ounce of determination I have to stand my ground.

"The reason I fought giving in to your charms so hard is because I didn't think I would be able to handle the risks of being with someone in your position."

The constant attention.

The probing into both my present and also my past.

The judgment and ridicule.

"You can, baby."

I shake my head, finally freeing myself from his hold and jumping away before he can reach for me again.

He's wrong.

He needs someone who can stand by his side during all the good and amazing things coming his way.

One of my biggest regrets is hiding away inside a hotel room instead of attending the NFL Draft with E. I didn't get to hug him or congratulate him when his name was called as the fifth overall pick. He had Bette, but the way he embraced me a little bit tighter, a little bit longer when he made it back to our suite after gave away his disappointment.

Mason deserves to have the person he wants to celebrate with by his side when his moment comes. I am *not* that person.

"I can't. I'm too weak." *Too fucking scared of breaking down from the pressure.* "Eventually you would have figured it out for yourself."

Chapter 13

NO.

No, no, no, no, no.

I don't accept this.

Kay thinks her demons have won? Thinks they can take her away from me?

I may not be all that religious, but I can be her mother-fucking priest and exorcise those bastards.

I fucked up by ending things in the first place, but the main reason it only took a kick in the ass from Trav to set me straight is because deep down I knew the breakup should have never happened.

Now? Nothing, *nothing* is going to keep us apart.

When I move to touch her again, she skirts around me and takes off for the door, literally running away from me this time. I stand rooted on the spot, the slam of the door closing as harsh as a gunshot.

She thinks dating me is a risk? Sure, all relationships are to some extent, but to think she's too weak to handle being with me?

She's out of her damn mind.

There is not one person in this whole world who is more perfect for me than Kayla 'PF' Dennings, and I'll prove it to her. It's time for my inner coach and me to come up with the most important playbook of my life—the one for Kay's heart.

It's game on, and I always play to win.

The chilly night air brushes along my cheeks, but my blood is boiling too hot for me to notice. I scan the area for Kay, but before I can find her, I'm intercepted by JT. He looks nothing like the happy-go-lucky guy I've seen plastered all over social media. No, this person standing in front of me looks pissed as fuck.

He's dressed similarly to most of those here, in jeans and a leather jacket, and not for the first time, I wonder who the hell Kay is hanging out with.

His arms are folded across his chest, staring me down hard, his brows a stern line across his forehead. Though I have a couple inches and a few pounds on him, Trav was right in his assessment about the guy—he is built like a footballer.

"I'm getting real tired of seeing her cry." JT cuts right to the chase.

"Can you stop being such a nice guy?" The strawberry-blonde I recognize as his sister Tessa scolds him as she bounces up to his side.

"Tess," JT chides.

"Don't give me that, Jim," she says, crossing her own arms.

"I think she wants you to act more like my brother," a blonde adds, flanking JT's other side.

"Not a chance, Savvy," JT says as Tessa counters with a, "Screw the Royals. I want him to go full-on E."

I do my best to hide my wince at the thought of what I'm sure E wants to do to me for breaking his sister's heart.

JT rolls his eyes—of course he does; Kay is his best friend, after all. "Wes!" he shouts over his shoulder. "Can you help a brother out and control the mini Royal please?"

Another guy in a leather jacket, his with ribbing and

elbow patches those who race motorcycles would wear, joins us. "I love that you think she listens to me."

JT chuckles in the way any brother with a little sister laughs when they are with a guy who knows that pain. "At the very least you can distract her by taking her to the race."

The guy, Wes something or other, claps JT on the shoulder but shakes his head. "No can do, bro. King's racing tonight. I'm in charge of the book."

The comment has JT shifting his attention away from me and giving it all to Wes. "Carter *never* races in these small ones. Why's he racing tonight?"

"Well, when your girl—"

I growl at Kay being called anyone's girl except mine. Tessa and Savvy giggle, highly amused, and I see a satisfied smirk tilt the edges of JT's mouth as he watches me out of the corner of his eye.

"—started rooting around for the tequila and looking all high school-ly, King thought a little street racing might be just what she needed to stop thinking about this guy for a while." Wes waves at me, but my gut is too busy clenching at the thought of Kay riding shotgun while people play *Fast and Furious*.

"Is Kay safe with this King guy?" Trav asks, stepping up to my left, backing me up should I need it.

"Yeah." JT blows out a breath. "You won't find a better driver in the state than Carter. But fuck me"—he thrusts a hand through his hair—"thank god it's only Bette who's up this weekend."

That catches me off guard. When we were at their place, Bette didn't say anything about visiting while JT was home. Does that mean E did come up?

"Bette's here?" I ask, wondering if I should prepare myself for more than one ass-kicking.

"Hold on." He holds a finger up for me to wait and speaks to Wes. "What do you mean she looked *high school-ly*?"

"You know…" Wes makes a rolling motion with his hand. "How she would retreat into herself when she would go days without speaking"—his fingers form a V and point from his eyes to JT's—"and she could be looking right at you and not see you."

"Were you even bullied?"

My eyes fall closed against how condescending I sound even in my memory. Days? Kay would go *days* without speaking? What happened that would cause that kind of reaction?

"I know she didn't really say…well…*anything* until *he* showed up." Again, Wes points to me. "But this was different."

"Fuck." The mood shifts as JT starts to massage the ridge of his brow.

"What's wrong?" Trav asks before I can, and I feel him shift, ready to fight anything that dares threaten Kay.

JT casts a look around. The crowd has dwindled considerably since apparently a street race is underway, but we aren't alone. "I'm not getting into it here, and the only reason I'm not kicking your ass for the dig you made about her being bullied is because I know she didn't tell you the full extent of what happened."

Fuck me. I *need* to know what went down.

"I'm not going to tell you." *Shit.* "It's not my place." *Double shit.* "What I will tell you is this, and I'm only going to say this once, so you better listen the fuck up."

Instinct has me wanting to question who the fuck *he* thinks he is talking to me like that, but I've given this guy enough reason not to like me; I don't need to be outwardly disrespectful as well.

"Kay—"

"She doesn't like it when you call her Kay," Tessa interrupts.

"Shut it, Tess." She mimes zipping her lips. "Anyway…"

JT gives her side-eye. "Kay is my *family*." He turns away, pacing a handful of steps before turning back. "You may have gotten all growly hearing her be called *my girl*, but make no mistake, she is mine."

The fuck she is. This time I sound practically feral, and Trav's strong throwing arm pressing against my chest is the only thing keeping me from decking the guy.

JT puts up both hands in a stop motion and takes a step back. "Relax, Caveman." His use of Kay's nickname cuts deep. "I don't mean mine in the way she's yours—and she *is* yours. I mean she's mine the same way she's E's. I don't give a *fuck* about actual blood relation. That girl is my sister and *always* will be."

I gotta hand it to him, he earns my respect with each word —okay *maybe* not *each* word, but you know what I mean— that comes out of his mouth. And he's right—the only vibe I've picked up from him is the same I have around E or Grayson.

"JT is just a friend. He's as much a brother to me as E." Kay tried to tell me the same thing, but my asshole response was, *"Yeah, and in Biz Markie's song, that's exactly what the bitch says when she's actually hooking up with the other guy."*

JT and I stare each other down, breathing heavy in a standoff for the same girl, one as a brother and one as the— God willing—boyfriend. I know the moment he sees the shift of understanding in my gaze, and his whole body deflates as his defensive guard lowers.

"Now…as much as she will deny it and is fighting it, Kay loves you."

Skittles may not be the one saying the words, but it still feels good to hear them. The knot that has been a permanent resident in my gut loosens fractionally.

"You have a chance—albeit a small one—to fix this and win her back."

"She—" I clear my throat, emotion getting the best of me. "She said she's too weak to be with me."

"And you believe that?" If looks could kill, I'd be dead where I stand.

"Fuck no."

I get a nod of approval.

"She's not weak. She just...doesn't feel fully healed from the last time."

I'm really going to have to sit Kay down and make her tell me everything that happened after her dad died. I can't come up with a proper playbook if I don't know my opponents.

"It's going to be *a lot* of work, and it will feel like an uphill battle at times. You won't just have this bullshit that's happening now with people trying to dig up dirt on her for the simple reason of her being with you. You'll also be fighting the shit from her past."

"I'll take on the whole goddamn world if I have to. I'm not giving up. Kay is *mine*, and I'm not going to let a single soul keep her from being at my side where she belongs."

#THE GRAM

Chapter 14

UofJ411: More than friends? #MuscialBedMates
#CasanovasGirl
***picture of G leaving Kay's apartment with a duffle bag
hanging from his shoulder***
@AshWonderWoman: @TheGreatestGrayson37, does
@CasaNova87 know you spent the night at his girlfriend's place?
#IKnowWhereYouSleptLastNight #CasanovasGirl

UofJ411: Why so sad? #HeresAKleenex #CasanovasGirl
***picture of an obviously-been-crying Kay at a table in the
library***
@Beccalynn1010: They have to have broken up. Look at this ^^
She was totally crying #DoYouNeedATissue #CasanovasGirl

UofJ411: Someone is missing… #WheresWaldo
#CasanovaWatch #CasanovasGirl
***picture of the crew's lunch table with everyone there
except Kay***

@Behawks87: Why isn't she eating with them anymore?
#DidTheyBreakUp #CasanovaWatch #CasanovasGirl

UofJ411: Is this goodbye? #TroubleInParadise #CasanovaWatch
#CasanovasGirl
boomerang of Kay walking away from Mason
@Ladyjanegray75: I wouldn't walk away from you
@CasaNova87 #CasanovasGirl

#Chapter15

ELVIS DURAN and the Morning Show blares through Pinky's speakers while I hide out in the parking lot, but not even Greg T's antics can cut through the nerves consuming my body. I have fifteen minutes left until I have to be in class, which is fifteen minutes too few before I have to face Mason.

I'm under no illusions that the strategy of coming in late and leaving a few minutes early will work again today like it did the other day. Mason is too damn stubborn to allow that.

He calls—I send it to voicemail.

He texts—I leave them unread.

He shows up at my dorm—I sleep at the Taylors' on nights Pops isn't working.

Why won't he just go away?

Then there's the other *issue*, I think, my gaze sliding to the messenger bag on the passenger seat.

I have no clue what possessed me to bring *it* with me. I don't know, maybe I was afraid if I left it at the Taylors', Pops would somehow find it and take his temper to five-alarm status.

Being the main subject of UofJ411's content on their Instagram feed is bad enough. The speculation, the rumors, the utter glee at the prospect of Mason being back on the market.

It's the turn things have taken since my identity leaked that I never expected. Thanks to the rivalry between the schools, the news of my relationship status with our tight end found its way to the *last* Nittany Lion I would want in the know.

Another glance at the clock on the dash tells me if I'm going to class, I need to leave the sanctuary of my Jeep now.

Gurrrrl, get your ass out of the car, my inner cheerleader scolds.

I adjust the black and white chevron-print infinity scarf around my neck, worrying the thin cotton between my fingers.

I lift and replace the black Yankees hat on my head several times before finally giving in and pushing the door open to exit the vehicle.

Sure enough, waiting outside the lecture hall is Mason Nova. *Damn him.* I hate that I can't deny how flipping hot he looks leaning back against the wall, signature backward cap on, feet kicked out in front of him and crossed at the ankles, hands shoved into the pouch of his U of J football hoodie.

Fight and flight war inside me, but before either one can win, Mason looks up and those beautiful seafoam green eyes lock onto me, sending shivers rushing down my spine.

"Hey, babe." His deep voice rumbles out of his throat and into my chest.

I can't do this. It's too hard.

I turn to flee, but Mason's bear-paw-sized hand wraps around my upper arm, encircling my bicep completely and preventing me from making my retreat.

"I don't think so. Not this time." He gives a *gentle* tug, always conscious of how much smaller I am than him.

Short of literally fighting him off, I have no choice but to follow him into the classroom—except when we step inside, it's not our lecture hall, but rather an empty one.

"As much as I like seeing you in my hoodie, you do work

a leather jacket." He grabs the folded-over lapels, keeping me in front of him.

"Mason." I put my hands on his chest, locking my elbows to keep as much distance between us as possible.

"What do I have to do to get you to call me Mase again?"

Why does such a simple request hurt the heart so much?

"Mason." I try to sidestep, but his hold on my jacket is resolute.

"Skittles."

I squeak at his nickname for me, the familiarity cutting deeper than I thought possible.

The leather of my jacket creaks as his hold on me tightens, the tips of my toes overlapping the tips of his as I'm forced across the last inch between us.

I drop my head, seeking the shelter the brim of my hat affords me, trying to hide from those light eyes that can see right through me.

As if he's read my mind, my hat is gone, falling to the floor with a soft thud, and Mason's warm breath dances across my forehead followed by the softest, gentlest, most heart-wrenching kiss.

No longer able to be stifled, a sob breaks free and tears start to stream. As if I'm not struggling enough, Mason doesn't pull away, only bending to rest his forehead against mine.

"I miss you, baby." His words may be whispered, but it doesn't take away from the steel behind them.

I miss him too. So much. I'm barely sleeping, food's lost all taste, coffee is (barely) sustaining me, and the only time I feel a micron of peace is when I'm at The Barracks, though even that is touch and go because seeing the twins only makes me think of him.

"You need to let me go, Mason."

"No."

Damn stubborn bastard.

"Pl-Please."

I don't know how much more I can endure before I break down completely. Every cell in my body wants to merge with his, every breath I take filled with the intoxicating aroma of his body wash.

It's too much.

He's too much.

"I'm no good for you."

I can't stop seeing those same words penned in harsh black Sharpie.

> *I had to guess so I hope I got the size right. Figured he deserves a heads-up about what a train wreck you are. Unless...the rumors are true, and he's already realized you're no good for him, realized being with someone like YOU can only be career suicide. You ARE your mother's daughter after all.*

It was the last line in the note accompanying the package Liam sent that *really* hurt.

"The *fuck* you aren't," Mason snarls, completely unaware of my inner turmoil.

He pulls away so fast there's a breeze. When I finally chance a glance at him, peering through the loose curls that have fallen in front of my face, the only way I can describe his expression is thunderous.

He stomps toward the door, and I don't know whether to cry out in relief or beg him not to leave. I'm a disaster. I want him to stay but need him to go.

Tears continue to spill down my cheeks in steady rivers, and I'm honestly surprised I'm not dehydrated from the gallons I've cried this last week.

I stop breathing when he picks up the backpack I hadn't even realized he'd brought in with him, but instead of him taking it and leaving, the *zrrrip* of the zipper sounds and he pulls something out.

"I know it was my mistake that started this. I should have told you about Chrissy sooner, and I take full responsibility for that. Hell…" His free hand grips the back of his neck, and there's a lengthy pause before he continues. "Who knows, if I had, that whole fight and weirdness we had after all those damn Adam posts hit the Gram may never have happened."

No, it would have. It wasn't his past that was the problem in that argument; it was mine.

It's still mine.

You are your mother's daughter after all.

"Mason."

"Please, Kay." He crushes the black fabric in his hands, holding it to his stomach. "I'll do whatever it takes for you to trust me again, just please, *please* give us another chance."

Fuck!

I hate this.

I. Hate. This.

My sobs become uncontrollable, and I can already picture the newest memes I would inspire should anyone catch sight of me right now.

"I already told you, Mason." My words are stuffy from the snot clogging my nose thanks to my cry-fest. "I forgive you. This"—I bounce a finger between us—"is on me, not you."

He deserves the truth, but I still can't bring myself to tell him the details. I should just tell him what to google so he can see the articles himself. Yes, Jordan and her people helped bury them to the back pages of the search results, but they still exist. The internet lives forever.

"I love you, Kay."

See? My inner cheerleader tightens her high ponytail and glares at me. *He loves you, you love him. Stop being a fucking martyr and tell him. Tell him ev-er-y-thing. Maybe with him by your side, you can finally let it go.*

"We have class." It's a weak excuse, but it's the only one I have.

"Fuck class. We aren't leaving this room until you're mine again." Then without another word, he unfolds what's in his hands and holds it out to me.

Holy shit! Not him too.

A simple black cotton crewneck t-shirt stares at me. On the back, if you couldn't have guessed it, NOVA and #87 are stamped in red and white block letters. It's when he spins it around to show me the front—*My boyfriend owns the field, but I own his heart*, a red heart with football laces used in place of the word heart—that my knees give out and I fall to the floor.

#Chapter16

KAY'S BODY crumples in a way I've never seen a person who was conscious do before. It's like she completely collapses in on herself.

Seeing her cry tore at my insides like someone was taking my turf cleats to them.

This though? This unmoors me.

I'm at her side in an instant, ignoring the way my knees slam into the cold tile, and I pull her into my lap, cradling her to me.

Her body vibrates against mine she's shaking so hard under the weight of her sobs. This was not the type of reaction I expected, and I'm at a loss for how to help her.

I run a hand up and down her back, brushing my fingers through her hair in the way that can soothe her to sleep, but none of it seems to help; she only cries harder.

I did this. The thought whispers through my brain.

I do the only thing I can in the moment: hold her closer, resting my face on top of her head, breathing in the peppermint scent I've missed this last week.

"It kills me to see you this way, baby."

Nothing. No response.

The old me, the campus Casanova, wouldn't be caught

dead with an emotional woman while spewing his own feelings. But the new me, the one who knows he needs Kay, doesn't give a fuck. She is it for me, and given her love for comical t-shirts, I thought having one made about us was the best way to prove it.

I hate this. I thought it was painful to see how her shoulders would slump and she would tuck her chin to hide her face with each not-so-quiet whisper about us, but seeing her like this and not knowing how to help her…I've never felt so powerless in my entire life. Even my inner coach is silent.

"Do you want me to call E?" I doubt I'm her brother's favorite person right now, but I'll do anything if it means it will help her.

"I wouldn't." She finally speaks, loosening the knots that have formed between my shoulder blades. "I think he's spent this last week trying to figure out how to kick your ass through the phone."

"Fuck, baby." A bark of relieved laughter escapes me.

She still hasn't pulled away, and I'll enjoy the feel of her in my arms for as long as she'll allow it. Then, like she read my mind, she jackknifes in my hold and scrambles off my lap like a crab.

"Skittles." I reach for her, but she darts around the lecture podium, hiding behind it to keep away from my touch.

"Fucking jockholes." Her voice is scratchy from her crying jag. "Who are you all to think you can use t-shirts against me?"

Huh?

"Seriously, fuck you both." She slaps her hands against her thighs.

Both? What is she talking about?

Sure, my friendship with Grayson has cooled in the aftermath of breaking up with his best friend, but he would never try to move in on my girl—I don't for one second believe the people who have been saying that shit on the Gram.

I've never realized how much my actions were tracked. Why do people care what I had for lunch on any particular day? Do people really have nothing better to do with their time than try to stir up drama? I used to live for my status and the notoriety my football stardom afforded me around campus. Now, not so much.

My dogged determination to fix things with Kay has moved Grayson over to the not-fully-hating-me side of the line. He keeps me updated on how Kay is doing—or more accurately, how she's not—so why don't I know who else she's talking about?

"You know what?" she asks, aggressively digging through the messenger bag slung across her chest. "Here."

The muscles of my stomach contract from the impact of her fist punching it. Looking down, I see she has her own shirt balled in her grasp.

"I didn't think any of these existed anymore, but I guess I was wrong." The pressure to my gut increases as she digs her knuckles into me harder, until I work her fingers loose enough to free the white cotton. "You doubt I was bullied in high school? Think it was something I just made up for funsies?"

Her gray eyes are hard as steel, her glare unwavering. Bile crawls up the back of my throat at the cutting edge to her tone.

"Well, try going to school and seeing *hundreds* of people wearing those."

Her eyes narrow and drop to the shirt I hold limply between us, silently daring me to look.

Swallowing down what feels like a chunk of turf lodged in my throat, I pinch the material at the shoulders and let it fall open.

What is that?

Is that…

Fuck! Swollen eyes pinched closed, cheeks ruddy and wet,

mouth caught open in a wail—it's a giant picture of Kay's crying face with the words *Train-Wreck Crybaby* printed above it.

Who the fuck would make this into a shirt?

You really are a special kind of asshole, aren't you, Nova?

I look up, another apology on my tongue, this one soul-deep—but like she's been doing to me all week, Kay is gone.

#Chapter17

YESTERDAY I DID something I never do—I skipped class.

In my defense, I did have a mini breakdown, and if I'd stayed, I wouldn't have comprehended anything anyway.

Still, I ran—literally—from both Mason and the very real, very big feelings I still have for him. I love him. I love him the way Bette loves E, but unlike my amazing sister-in-law, I don't have the strength to weather the storm coming for us.

So, I did what I do best—run and hide.

First, I went to The Barracks. Of course I went to the gym. It's my second home, and I feel safe there. Plus, there are things to distract me there, to take my mind off all the things I don't want to think about.

Mason.

My broken heart.

Instagram.

Unwanted packages with reminders of a past I wish I could forget.

Calls and questions from Jordan about what to do about…*all* of it.

E freaking out.

JT virtually holding my hand.

Mason.

Mason.

Mason.

Why are you fighting him? He wants you back. He apologized, told you he loves you. Holy shit! *pulls shirt from behind back* Did you see this? Did you? Did you? *slides hand under the writing like Vanna White* This boy couldn't get you more if he were plucked out of one of Tessa's romance novels.

I look down and curse both my inner cheerleader and myself at the sight of the black cotton covering my chest. Yes, I'm wearing *the* shirt, the same one that brought on my breakdown, the same one that is like the antidote to the poison Liam dropped on my doorstep.

After tumbling until I almost couldn't move then joining in to help coach the Marshals, I came back to the Taylors'. Unable to be alone or anywhere Mason would know to look for me, I spent *hours* talking with both Taylor siblings.

As I drifted off to sleep, wearing *the* shirt, I had pieced together enough of the old Kay to believe I could do it, to believe I could be with Mason.

Then I woke and was reminded *exactly* why I need to stay away.

#Chapter18

TightestEndParker85: Hold up, time out. *stop sign emoji* Is this real life? @CasaNova87 are you really dating my sloppy seconds? #IHadHerFirst
side-by-side picture of Liam and Kay smiling from when they dated and a snapshot of Mason in his football gear during a game looking upset

UofJ411: *wide-eyed emoji* *mind blown emoji* #IHaveSoManyQuestions #CasanovaWatch #CasanovasGirl
***REPOSTED—side-by-side picture of Liam and Kay smiling from when they dated and a snapshot of Mason in his football gear during a game looking upset—
TightestEndParker85: Hold up, time out. *stop sign emoji* Is this real life? @CasaNova87 are you really dating my sloppy seconds? #IHadHerFirst***
@Lagerlefsebookblog: And the plot thickens #SomeonePassThePopcorn #CasanovaWatch #CasanovasGirl
@Lala_powergirl: Was the U of J just her safety school or something? Looks like @CasaNova87's girl has a thing for

Nittany Lions #WhereDoYourLoyaltiesLie #CasanovaWatch
#CasanovasGirl
@Lonniegallahan: I know ESPN is going to cover the game, but
does anyone think this might be better broadcasted on E!?
#ISmellDrama #ScoringMoreThanTouchdowns #CasanovaWatch
#CasanovasGirl

TightestEndParker85: Hey @UofJ411 I have so many stories
#ICouldWriteABook
***boomerang of Liam waggling his eyebrows with a smarmy
smirk***
@TheQueenB: This has GOT TO BE good #ImAllEars
@UofJ411: Do tell #WeAreListening

#Chapter19

"STILL NO PROGRESS on the Kay front?" Alex and I claim seats in the den as soon as we return from our walkthrough practice.

Snapshots from yesterday flash through my mind.

Kay trying to run away.

Kay telling me to let her go. *Yeah, right.* That is *so* not happening.

Kay crying, each tear like acid on my soul.

And the one that has haunted me through all my waking hours and followed me into my dreams: Kay crumpled on the floor.

"I talked to her yesterday." Sure, the conversation didn't go *at all* like I'd hoped, but after days of avoidance, it was one step forward before what feels like *all* the steps back.

"What did she say about the shirt?" Trav asks, and all I can think is, *Which one?*

Grayson was the only person I showed the shirt Kay shoved at me. I don't know why I haven't shared it with anyone else, but a part of me feels like I would be betraying her if I did so without her permission.

If the beaming smile on Trav's face is anything to go by,

he's feeling uber-proud of himself for having been the one to help me find the Etsy shop I used to commission the shirts I had made. Once I have Kay back, I *will* be making fun of him for even knowing about Etsy.

"She took it." It's not a lie. She did take the shirt, but they don't need to know about the reaction I received when I presented it to her.

My phone buzzes in my pocket, but I send the call to voicemail when I see it's Brantley calling—again. I don't need another pep talk about the game tomorrow. Last week was an anomaly. I may not officially have Kay back yet, but my head is on straight and my performance won't be affected by my broken heart.

"I get that your girl is all about her t-shirts and stuff," Kevin calls out, bending over to line up a shot at the pool table, "but I really hope you have more of a plan than that."

"Truth," Noah agrees, groaning as the eight ball sails into the corner pocket with Kev's shot.

More so now than before, I think as Kay's words from yesterday play back inside my mind. *"Fucking jockholes. Who are you all to think you can use t-shirts against me?"*

"All I'm saying"—Kevin's voice breaks me out of my memories—"is we need to make sure you have your shit together. I swear when I saw her on campus the other day, she left a Kayla-shaped cloud of dust in her wake when she ducked inside the library."

"Agreed," Alex adds, scrolling through the Madden menu with the game controller. "It's one thing for your girl to avoid you, but to avoid us? Not cool."

I want to be pissed at them for razzing me about something I take so seriously, but I can't. They have been amazingly supportive of my campaign to win Kay back.

There are times I wish she were talking to me so I could tell her about the guys and how they've been. I know she harbored huge fears of people trying to use her if they found out who her brother is, but with the exception of a handful of questions when the news first broke, the guys seem like they couldn't care less. They've been more concerned about not having their friend—Kay, not me—around.

"I don't think taking wooing advice from a group of bachelors is going to help me much," I say as I tap another call to voicemail. *Geez, Brantley is persistent tonight.*

"Dude." Alex snorts. "I can't believe you just said *wooing*."

"Whatever, bro." I shrug. "I love her."

Alex drops the taunting smirk, turning serious. "Respect, man." He holds out a fist for me to bump, which I do.

"Oh, bruh, this is *too* good," Adam chortles as he and two other Alpha brothers enter the den.

My hackles rise at the Cheshire-cat grin blooming on his smarmy face when he spots me in the room. I wish I could kick him out, but as an Alpha, he has as much of a right to be here as the rest of us.

"I think we should set up a whole wall of prop bets for the game against Penn State." He waves an arm at the back wall, which is coated in chalkboard paint, where the AKs keep odds for each week's games. "I have a feeling we're going to be able to tap into a whole new market with this." He points to something on his phone, and I force myself to ignore him.

I've just accepted a controller from Alex to join the Madden game when Adam butts in. "What do you say, Casanova? Wanna be our inside scoop?"

"What the fuck are you going on about?" I keep my attention on selecting my team; he doesn't deserve the politeness of eye contact.

Adam laughs again like he's some type of deranged hyena, and when I finally look over, he's rubbing his hands in glee. All he needs to do is put his pinky to his mouth to complete his Dr. Evil impression.

Before he can answer, the door leading into the den from

the hallway swings open with a *BANG!*, letting in a pissed-off Grayson.

Instinct has me instantly on alert and out of my seat.

"I know you have to leave for The Huntington soon, but can I borrow the Shelby?"

I was not expecting him to ask that. "Why?"

"Em was too impatient to wait for me to get out of practice, so now I need a way to get to Blackwell."

Why? Why would he need to go to Blackwell?

"What's wrong with Kay?" She's the only reason that makes sense.

Trav is the only one I've ever trusted to drive my baby, but it's not the Shelby that has my feet pepper-stepping, ready for action.

"Oh, this is great." Adam claps. Yes, the motherfucker claps.

"Shut the fuck up, Adam," Grayson snaps. I don't know if it's the curse or the uncharacteristic outburst from the power forward, but it doesn't matter—whatever it is causes Adam to listen. "She's fine. I just need to get to her."

She's fine my ass. I'm going to catch all sorts of hell from Coach Knight for this, but there's no fucking way I'm not going with Grayson.

"What. Happened?" I bite out, already pulling my keys from my pocket.

Except for the clenching of his jaw and his hand flexing around his phone hard enough I fear he might crack the screen from the force, he doesn't react.

"G?" Kay's name for him slips out. I don't usually call him by the shorthand, but I've also never seen him... so...volatile.

"It seems..." His jaw works side to side as he thinks over what to say. "All the posts about you and Kay have found their way to Penn State with all the 'you dating the enemy' bullshit hashtags floating around."

Fucking Instagram. I'm starting to see why my girl has such an aversion to it.

"What? Have more pictures of her cheering for E at his games surfaced?"

"Oh, shit. You don't know?" Adam's chuckles ramp up again, and I'm *this close* to putting my fist through his face. "Classic."

"You really don't know when to keep your mouth shut, do you?" Fire flashes in Grayson's eyes.

The atmosphere in the room grows charged as I rack my brain for what I could have missed. Brantley wasn't the only one I've been avoiding. Outside of checking to see if Kay texted me—she didn't—I haven't scrolled through my notifications.

"Grayson, what's going on?" Now Trav is up and at my side.

More silence, and this time I swear I hear a crack coming from the hand holding the phone, but the screen is fine when he holds it out for me to see the picture on it.

Similar to the last time I saw Kay's smiling face staring back at me from an Instagram feed, the sight has a red mist coating my vision.

Liam Parker. Liam mother*fucking* Parker is the one to post the shot, and then to add insult to injury, he has the fucking balls to call her sloppy seconds? He's dead. D-E-A-D.

"Oh, shit," Trav curses.

"What—ohhh," comes from Alex as he stands up from the couch.

Kevin and Noah close ranks, having similar reactions, and the four weeks until we play Penn State feels like an eternity.

"Trav, I'm going to need you to tell Coach Knight I had a family emergency, but I'll be at the hotel before curfew." I jerk my chin toward the door, silently telling Grayson, *Let's roll.*

"It's cute you think you're going without me." Trav claps me on the back, falling into step beside me.

"Seriously, Nova, it's like you forget we're a team," Kev says as the others agree.

I pause, meeting the eyes of each of those who are as much my teammates off the field as they are on it. Not even the bullshit Adam's still spewing registers. I'll deal with him later.

#Chapter20

"AREN'T you supposed to let me drink when I'm in crisis?" I complain, shooting a death glare at Carter when he exchanges the tequila bottle in my hand for a Smartwater. "Isn't it in the friend handbook or something?"

This is the second time in a week King has stopped me from drinking my troubles away. I'm not a fan.

"You can angry-eye me all you want, Dennings, but when you barely meet the height requirements to ride the rides at Six Flags, it *kinda* takes away the intimidation factor."

I roll my eyes and push off the counter. If he won't let me drink, he *better* let me eat some Ben & Jerry's.

"It is so refreshing to see someone *not* be intimidated by you." Wes attempts to hide a smirk behind his hand, but it's a massive failure. He's one to talk, though. King may be—well, the king of the Royals, but Wes is just as, if not more feared as the leader.

I was touched when they showed up. Sure, they came because JT asked them to check up on me, but the sentiment remains the same.

"You're not a very good monarch if you don't know not to replace her liquor with H2O." Em hip-checks Carter to the side and stretches across the counter to hand over a to-go cup with a familiar Harry Potter themed coffee logo printed on it. I must be in worse shape than I thought if they stopped at Espresso Patronum before showing up. I don't have it in me to tell her coffee from my favorite shop only makes me think of Mason.

King folds his arms across his chest, the sleeves of his black t-shirt straining around the tops of his biceps. His chin tips down to look at Em, eyes narrowing with a glare that has had men much larger than her peeing their pants. Except— God love her—all Em does is arch one of her perfect brows in a silent challenge.

The two of them have been around each other less than a handful of times, but the tension that builds between them whenever they're within a ten-foot radius is hot enough to get those around them pregnant.

"Hold up, Dennings," Carter commands when I try to make my exit. I stop but don't turn around, only angling my chin to look at him over my shoulder.

"I don't really want to talk about it, King." I let out a heavy sigh. I know what he wants to discuss, but I'm not in the mood. It's not even dinnertime and this already feels like the longest day on record.

I've freaked out.

Cried a few more buckets' worth of tears.

Talked Bette out of coming up *again*.

Had a meeting at All Things Sports with Jordan Donovan to keep E from blowing a gasket.

Then I got pissed.

Why can't Liam mind his own goddamn business?

I thought I'd grown. I thought I'd managed to put my life back together in a way I could handle. For the last couple of months, I struggled—and mostly failed—to come to terms with the unwanted attention on social media, but now that Liam is getting involved? It feels like my life is about to crumble around me like a house of cards.

"Dennings—"

"No, King." I whip around, slashing a hand through the air to cut him off. "I can't even begin to tell you how grateful I am for everything you did for me in high school. I know you're used to being the ruler supreme"—*Oops, did that come out too sarcastic?*—"and while the pull you have now extends outside of Blackwell, *this*"—I wave my phone in the air—"is something I have to handle on my own."

With that said, I spin on my heel, leaving Em and Carter to bicker, and head into the living room to drink my coffee, choosing the open spot next to CK. He doesn't ask if I'm okay or how I'm holding up; he simply drops an arm around my shoulders and lets me snuggle into his side, silently telling me he's here and has my back.

My gaze falls to my hands, the rainbow-jeweled bands adorning five of my fingers—*I really do need to find an emerald one to add CK to the fold*—a physical reminder of all the different people who have my back.

They aren't the only ones who would be there for you.

I don't appreciate my inner cheerleader bringing up Mason at a time like this. The more I think of him, the more the chances of me crying—again—increase. To stop the spiral over my decision to keep away from him, I thumb open the text I received this afternoon.

UNKNOWN: Oh boy! That UofJ411 SURE is interested in learning ALL the things there are to know about you. I wonder what I should tell them first? Or…maybe I should barter. Remember when E tried to get my scholarship pulled and I barely saw any playing time my freshman year because of it? I bet I could use them to dig up enough dirt on your precious Casanova to create a scandal big enough to have him fall in the draft. *thinking emoji* Oh the possibilities…

Like hell will I let that happen. I *refuse* to allow Liam to vilify Mason on social media before his career even begins. It would take a whole damn lot for a team to consider a player undraftable, but a problematic reputation and being seen as a potential public relations nightmare can have a player fall to a later round and cost him millions.

I don't want that for Mason. He has too much going for him, too bright of a future to let something—or someone—from my past taint it.

What does it matter if my heart stays broken if it means Mason's dreams will come true?

Chapter21

NOT PUSHING the Shelby to the max is a feat in and of itself. Thankfully, Trav isn't opposed to speeding to keep up, and we shave ten minutes off the drive to Blackwell.

"She's going to be pissed I brought you here," Grayson says as I find a parking spot two houses down from the one with Kay's Jeep in the driveway.

I don't waste time with a response, instead climbing out of my car and meeting the guys in front of what Grayson explains is the Taylor home.

"Listen." Grayson pauses, dropping the hand that was on the doorknob and turning to face our group fully. "This isn't going to be like lunch or the nights we would hang at Kay's dorm. This is damage control and keeping Kay from losing it completely. Everyone here is a *friend* to Kay. *Don't* start shit."

His eyes shift pointedly to the driveway, and it's only then I notice the matte black Corvette and Kawasaki Ninja parked next to Pinky. *This night just keeps getting better and better.*

He waits for us all to nod our understanding then, without knocking, opens the door and steps inside.

I'm the first in behind him, and I scan every face as quickly as I can. Em is the first to greet Grayson, and I see the rest of our group scattered behind her.

Tessa Taylor and her blonde friend each do this half-scowl, half-smirk thing as they watch from the kitchen, and I see those two Royal guys from the weekend eyeing our crew with speculation.

I double back, but still no Kay.

"Where is she?" I ask Em since she's the closest.

"Don't you guys have to be at the hotel soon?"

I shake my hands out in frustration. "Emma." My tone hardens and my voice drops an octave.

She sighs as if I'm being ridiculous. I might be, but I'm over all the obstacles trying to keep me from my girl.

"She's on the phone with E. Calm your jockstrap."

"Where?" I bark out.

"You need to chill, bro." The Carter guy moves to put himself between Em and me. It's a defensive move, and even in my less-than-rational frame of mind, I'm offended he can even think I would put my hands on her.

I'm out of my depth here. Without Kay, I feel like I'm floundering, and I can't see a way of getting her back until I get all the missing puzzle pieces together.

Other than the sound of a commercial for the latest Kevin Hart film playing on the television, nobody speaks.

Above us, the stairs creak as someone walks down them.

"Short Stack."

I whip around at my best friend's greeting in time to see Kay stopping on the final stair.

Her eyes are red and puffy, which is only emphasized by how wide they go at the sight of us. I'm getting fucking sick and tired of seeing her this way.

Her messy bun flops to the side as she tilts her head back to see Trav before he rushes her and pulls her into a hug. Kay's arms hang limply at her sides for a second before they wrap around him. They hold on a few seconds longer than typical, and when they finally separate, Kay cups his cheek. I can tell by the look she gives him she's having some kind of silent communication regarding what I told her about the whole Chrissy/Tina debacle.

I try hard—really I do—not to be jealous, but I am. At least I'm not storming over and ripping them apart like the caveman side of me wants to.

"What are you guys doing here? Isn't Coach Knight going to bench you for not being at the hotel?"

"Nah." Kevin waves off her concern, moving in next.

"He won't bench all his captains," Alex adds, taking his turn hugging her.

"We have a few hours before curfew anyway." Noah is the last to get her before her gray eyes land on me.

"Mason."

I don't know what I despise more, the fact that she is *still* calling me Mason or the defeated way she says it.

"You shouldn't be here."

I smooth a hand over the polyester of my hat. Again with this bullshit.

"The fuck I shouldn't." I close the distance between us in three long strides. "Wherever you are is where I'll be."

"You can't." She flails her hands about before finally shoving them in the pocket of the NJA hoodie she's wearing. *She shouldn't be wearing that—she should be wearing mine.* "I told you, I'm no good for you." She walks back, moving up another step.

I reach out to stop her retreat. The added height from the stairs makes her only a few inches shorter than me instead of the usual foot and a half. With both hands, I hold her face, resting my thumbs on the apples of her cheeks, and look her directly in her watery eyes.

"There is not one person on this earth who is better for me than you, Skittles." She sobs, warm wetness hitting the tops of my thumbs and sliding down the digits. "Stop trying to push me away."

"I'm not pushing you away. We're over. We're not a couple anymore. It's as simple as that."

Yeah, I don't accept that.

"Breaking up with you was the biggest mistake I've ever made."

I hear more than one person behind me agreeing, but I ignore them. Kay is the only one whose opinion on the subject matters.

"Your reasoning may have been wrong…" She shakes her head as best she can in my hold. "But it was the right decision."

"How?" My fingers flex, tangling into her hair. "How can you say that?"

"Because all the drama that surrounds me will bleed over onto you if we're a couple." A haunted pall falls over her expression. "The focus should be on how good of a football player you are, and how *any* team would be lucky to have you on their roster. Being with me makes you a target for a whole lot of other bullshit instead."

"Do you *really*, *truly* believe I give a shit what that asshat Liam Parker has to say?" She flinches at his name and I step in closer, moving until the tips of my sneakers hit the flat of the staircase.

"Honestly…" Her shoulders slump so much she shrinks an inch. "It doesn't matter what you think."

"Way to kick a man when he's down, Short Stack."

"Not the time, Trav," I mutter out of the side of my mouth.

"What I mean"—my girl rolls her eyes—"is *we* may not care what *he* has to say, but…" She pauses, inhaling the best she can through her stuffy nose. "There are people out there who *thrive* on what he'll try to stir up. I will not be responsible for putting a target on your back."

"Again, baby…" I tug her to the edge of her step, dropping my forehead to hers, bringing us closer. "I. Don't. Care about Liam Parker."

Another flinch.

"I get that, Caveman." Hope blooms at my nickname. "But *I* do. *I* know what he's capable of bringing down on us. *I* remember how others will take and twist and *use* the things *he* will say. I *can't* go through that again." That hope I felt shrivels and dies.

"Tell me."

She shakes her head. "I can't."

"Kayla." Her eyes snap to mine. "Tell. Me."

Pressure fills my hands as all her weight collapses in on itself—like yesterday—falling to the stairs as she curls up to hunch over her knees.

I don't know about you, Nova, but I'm over feeling helpless when it comes to Skittles. We need to come up with a game changer so we can stop feeling this way. I couldn't agree with my inner coach more.

Behind me, I hear Grayson ushering everyone else away, and I take a seat next to Kay, putting an arm around her back and tucking her against my side.

She may be physically next to me, but with each tick of silence, she pulls farther away.

From somewhere inside her sweatshirt, I can feel her phone vibrate, though it doesn't seem like she's even aware of it—or anything else, for that matter.

I look up at the sound of shuffling footsteps to see Tessa standing in front of us, fidgeting with her cellphone. Her eyes bounce between Kay and me, the skin around her lips bleaching white as her mouth pinches to the side.

"Kay?"

Kay's voice is slightly muffled, head still buried in her lap as she says, "It really freaks me out when you Taylors call me Kay."

The first spark of her sass has me letting out an almost startled bark of laughter. It's enough to have Kay lifting her head, her messy bun flopping around with the movement.

"Oh yeah?" Tessa folds her arms across her chest, leveling Kay with an expression that makes her seem older than her sixteen years. "And how do you think it makes me feel having to see you like this? I know I like to tell Jimmy I'm your favorite Taylor, but he was the only one able to help you when you were practically comatose."

What the what?

"That's a bit dramatic, T," Kay mumbles.

"Is it really?" Tessa puts her hands on her hips, staring Kay down as if to say *I dare you to argue.*

My gaze bounces between the two. "I don't care who, but someone better fucking explain."

Tessa's gaze flits back to Kay. When she remains silent, Tessa's shoulders roll back and she switches her attention me. "Whatever…she can be pissed at me later."

I assume the 'she' in this scenario is Kay, but my girl makes no move to stop her younger sister.

"When Uncle Mike died, Kay wasn't just depressed. She… shut down so fully it was like she was a walking zombie."

"You and Savvy need to stick to romantic comedies." Yet again, Kay's mumbled words are ignored.

"She didn't talk. She barely ate, and when she did, it was because we forced her to. She only slept when the exhaustion got to be too much." Again, her blue gaze goes back to Kay. "The worst was after days of being in bed, we finally convinced her to shower." Her head tilts back to look at the ceiling. "Everyone was in the midst of planning the funeral, so it was a few hours before anyone thought to check on her."

A lump the size of a football forms in my throat, a sense of unexplainable dread overtaking my body.

"She didn't try to kill herself," Tessa rushes to say, obviously having read my thoughts.

"Unlike what the press led people to believe." I whip around at Kay's hollow declaration. "I lost count of the number of stories—emphasis on *stories*—that were released about draft prospect Eric Dennings taking care of his suicidal sister in the wake of their father's death."

My eyes narrow. How is that possible? Yes, tabloids love to embellish, but their stories have to come from somewhere to avoid being sued for slander.

"Why would the paps care about a future NFL player's family, though?"

"I'm not just talking about the stalkerazzi." Kay shakes her head. "Every news outlet ran with the story because what E did, the way he stepped up for me, was human interest gold."

"Why didn't you sue to get them to issue a retraction?"

"Because 'a source close to the family' is where they got their information." Kay's mouth turns down in a frown.

"A source?" I arch an eyebrow.

"Liam." Kay buries her face in her hands, elbows braced on her knees, fingers digging into her hair. "We couldn't prove it, but after the breakup and the cheating was revealed, it was the best we could come up with."

Boy, this motherfucker just keeps digging himself in deeper and deeper. I crack my knuckles, imagining how satisfying the smash of his skin would be under them if I could knock him out when we play in a few weeks. Sure, there's a slim chance it could put an end to my career before it even starts, but I'm highly motivated to find an opportunity to fulfill this goal without being caught.

"Why?"

"Other than the fact that the dickwad loves drama?" I can't help but smirk at Tessa's choice of insult. "That day we convinced PF to shower, he showed up shortly after we pulled her out of it. It didn't matter to him that we realized she was in the shower for hours, letting what had turned to icy water pelt her as she sat on the floor, and I swear she was practically hypothermic—"

"I wasn't hypothermic," Kay cuts in, but Tessa continues like she didn't even speak.

"—by the time we pulled her out." Tessa's red ponytail swings with each shake of her head. "All he saw was that it was JT who got her out, that my brother saw her naked before she was covered with a towel. Even though he was dicking down most of the school's cheerleading squad, we believe he wanted to punish PF for his misguided belief that she was cheating on him with Jim."

"Dicking down? Really?" Kay asks.

"Just calling it like I see it," Tessa says with a shrug then walks away, leaving me with the pieces I hope to use to put my relationship back together.

Every bit of information I've been told only increases the murderous rage building in my gut, but one thing's for sure—I really like Tessa Taylor.

"Okay." I remove my hat, running a hand over my head before replacing it. "I feel like we're going around in circles here." I hook a finger under Kay's chin and turn her face to mine. "What does this have to do with us?"

"Mason—" A fresh round of tears starts as her voice breaks on my name.

"Baby." I take heart at how she nuzzles into my touch when I wipe to clear her cheek. "*Nothing* you can tell me will change my mind about us."

"With you being a better player—especially at the same position—Liam is going to use your connection to me to try to hurt your draft potential."

"I highly doubt—"

"That's because you don't understand." Her previously small voice finds strength so it can talk over mine.

I love this woman, but she frustrates the fuck out of me. I'm trying to understand, but I keep feeling like even after we hashed all this stuff out, there's still so much she's not telling me.

"Then explain it to me."

"I gave you the t-shirt, and I'm sure you've seen his post on Instagram." Her chin rises, but instead of looking *at* me, she stares off at a spot just past my shoulder, and I get that not-getting-all-the-information impression again. "He's stirring up the hornets' nest. I barely survived back then, and that was only with overwhelming panic attacks and isolating myself from anything and anyone that wasn't The Barracks. You…"

The muscle of my pec jumps as the flat of her hand presses over my heart.

"…have the potential to have a huge career. Being linked to me—a person who sometimes throws up at the mere idea of being the focus of media attention—I'm only going to hold you back." *Why the fuck do I feel like she's not telling me everything?* "Like I told you…I'm no good for you, Mason."

Abruptly, she stands, brushing imaginary dirt off her delectable ass. Too bad it's covered by the hem of her hoodie.

"So please just go. Kick Nebraska's ass tomorrow and forget about me."

Without giving me a chance to stop her, she turns and runs up the stairs, out of sight.

She wants me to go? Fine, I can do that.

Beat Nebraska? Might as well put the win in the Hawks' column now.

Forget about her? Never going to happen.

This was my third attempt at talking some sense into her. It's a good thing I play football instead of baseball and I have another down to play.

#Chapter22

UofJ411: What's with the new seats? #MusicalChairs #CasanovaWatch #CasanovasGirl
picture of Mason and Kay sitting in separate rows in class
@Bellebookblog: I saw them talking before class so this confuses me #Confused #CasanovaWatch #CasanovasGirl
@Bestiesandbooks: Has anyone figured out what happened between them? #WhyTheDistance #CasanovaWatch #CasanovasGirl

TightestEndParker85: Aww @CasaNova87, I know you were able to hold on to the football this weekend, unlike when your little birdies played Iowa. Too bad you can't hold on to the girl. #ShesNotThatGreatAnyway
***REPOSTED—picture of Mason and Kay sitting in separate rows in class—UofJ411: What's with the new seats? #MusicalChairs #CasanovaWatch #CasanovasGirl**
@UofJ411: Oh shit! #GrabThePopcorn

Chapter23

"HEY, T, you cool to head to The Barracks early?" I call out to Tessa as I round the banister of the staircase at the Taylor home.

"Sure." Her red ponytail swings around as she turns from the open refrigerator. "I'm good to go when you are."

I take the water bottle held out to me and grab Pinky's keys from the rack on the wall. "Let's roll."

T barely sits still on the drive to The Barracks, the excitement of me helping coach the Marshals' practices these last couple of weeks not having waned at all. Getting to spend extra time with her is a side bonus of trying to keep my mind off things by picking up every extra shift at the gym that I can. Plus, her easy joy helps ease some of my heartbreak.

I thought the first week after the breakup was hard, but *damn*, it had *nothing* on this one.

Why can't Mason leave me alone? Did he not listen to *anything* I said last week?

No, the stubborn fool keeps trying to talk to me, and Em says he's come around our dorm looking for me more often.

Most of the school is still speculating on Instagram regarding the status of our relationship, and when I asked him if he could denounce us on his page, he responded by posting a picture of a red jersey-style t-shirt that read *I have no life. My boyfriend plays football.* In between the two sentences was a big cheerleading bow with a large 87 in the middle.

Mason laughed in my face when I confronted him about it.

"What?" He shrugs. "I didn't post your picture, or say your name. Hell, I didn't even write a caption. It was vague-booking at its finest."

I slapped him across the face, and even now the memory of the sound being loud enough to be heard over the din of students hustling to class is enough to have my lips twitching. Then the jerk had to ruin it by chuckling when I stormed off. He even had the gall to wink at me when I chose to take a seat in a row different from our usual spot and between two other classmates so he couldn't sit with me.

"Should I be afraid you're gonna kick my ass from one end of the blue mat to the other tonight?" T points to the *Repeat after me: YES COACH* tank I have on.

Shoulder-checking my locker shut, I sit on the bench and tie my cheer shoes. "Remember how earlier, you were all gushy and calling Mason the 'perfect book boyfriend' like one of those romance novels you devour?"

T visibly swallows, and I can't help but smirk, which only has her blue eyes widening.

*Can we mess with her? Just a little bit? *pinches fingers together* She's been bombarding us with all her lovey-dovey, hopeless romantic stuff—which I think you should listen to, but who am I, right? *holds hand up* Let's have some fun with the little sister.*

I ignore the dig about letting myself be with Mason but ultimately let T off the hook, jerking my chin toward the locker room door. She has been too crucial of a person in keeping the overwhelming depression and panic from winning and pulling me under fully like it did back in high school.

"Fine." T slings an arm around my shoulder as we walk

across the mat to find a space to stretch. "But while I'm icing whatever new bruises I end up getting tonight, we"—she bounces a finger between us, as if I could misunderstand who she's referring to—"are watching *A Cinderella Story*."

I groan. Of course she picks a movie where the hero is a football player.

"Kay." Coach Kris steps out of her office onto the gym floor, and I'm instantly on alert because she didn't use my nickname. Then when she turns to reenter the office, every hair on the back of my neck stands on end.

I hastily follow her in.

"A courier delivered that a few minutes ago." She points at a black, white, and green Peter Pan gift bag with a stunning rendition of my tattoo on it. "Has your name on it."

My breath catches at the sight. I don't need to see the card to know exactly *who* it's from, but Coach's smile has me suspecting she has looked at it.

Mason strikes again.

Why can't he just let me go? Did I not slap him hard enough?

You should have kneed him in the balls. *demonstrates how to do the defensive move* Men tend to get the message loud and clear when you go after their junk.

"OH MY GOD!" T squeals in my ear. "Is that what I think it is?"

She knows all about the shirts, but this is about to be the first time she's witnessed me receiving one.

I dig my knuckles into the ridge of my brow. This is the perfect storm to bring out Tessa's teenybopper side. I nod because I can't seem to find my voice.

T traces the outline of Peter down to Wendy, captivated by the illustration. "Wow," she says breathily. "This is gorgeous, PF. Maybe you should think about adding some green shading around your tat."

"Funny, T. Can we focus on something else please?"

Dammit, Mason.

I bring a hand to my ear, rubbing over the area where I'm inked. I never even told him the full significance of the tattoo and yet he still knew to use it…what? Against me?

I think maybe he might be conferring with T on the side. His romantic gestures are only getting better.

"No way, sis. You *have* to open this now."

Grrrr. I *hate* when she pulls the "sis" card, because 99.9% of the time it gets her what she wants.

"No."

"Oh come on," she whines, peeking through the tissue paper sticking out of the bag.

"No way." I need to stand firm on this.

Unfortunately, she's too used to dealing with me and continues to paw at the gift.

"OH MY GOD!" T screams then jumps up and down.

I'm almost afraid to ask what garnered such an animated reaction, but we all know I must.

"What…is…it?" I struggle to get the words out.

T turns to me, hands over her heart, stars in her eyes.

"There's a *ring* box in there." She whispers the words like she's afraid the item will disappear if she speaks too loudly.

My brain shuts down, my whole world stopping like Zack Morris called timeout to the camera.

No.

No way.

Just no way.

There's not a ring box in that bag. Even if there were, there is *absolutely* no way it *means* what Tessa thinks it means. I need to shut this down—now.

"It's *just* a ring box, T. No need for the dramatics."

"But what if it's—"

"It's not." I'm quick to cut her off before she can finish her thought.

"How do you *know* it's not that?"

"I just do."

"How?"

"Tessa." My voice takes on a warning tone.

"Kayla," she deadpans, crossing her arms. Dammit, why does hearing my real name from the Taylor siblings break me so easily?

I throw up my hands and huff. "You mean *besides* the fact that it's *crazy*?" One of her perfectly sculpted red brows rises, as if saying *Yeah, not good enough,* so I try again. "This isn't one of your books, T. Not everyone gets a happy ending."

"Why not? Art imitates real life."

A growl escapes before I can stop it. These damn Taylors are too stubborn for my own good. "Fine." I cross my arms, mirroring her stance. "How about the fact that we only dated for like two months?"

"So? Doesn't E say he knew Bette was the one the moment they met?"

Son of a bitch. This is the problem with being friends with people your whole life—they know *everything.*

"Fine. How about we're still in college?"

"Again, so were Bette and E."

Another growl. "It's not the same, T, and you know it."

"Fine. If it's not an engagement ring, *what* are you so afraid of? Open the bag."

I don't want to—I *so* don't want to—but as I look between Tessa and Coach Kris, I see curiosity from the former and concern from the latter reflected in their eyes. If I *don't* open it now, it'll only intensify.

Holding my breath on a deep inhalation, eyes closed, I reach into the bag. My fingers wrap around *the* box, my breath rushing out on contact. I pull it out and set it next to the bag, not ready for it quite yet, and reach back inside for the shirt I know is there.

There's a piece of paper folded inside the cotton, but I put it aside to deal with later.

Pinching the shirt between my fingers, I see it's not the one from his Instagam post, this one is a white long-sleeved scoop neck with black and red lettering and football elbow patches. I hold it up to read: *My boyfriend SCORES more than yours.* Bracketing the word "My" are two hearts, and the "O" in scores is a football. The lettering is black, and the hearts and football are red. And, obvs, the back bears a bold NOVA and #87.

"Oh my god." T squeals and snatches the shirt from my hands. We are starting to reach critical levels here with the amount of *Oh my god*s she's dropping. "Dude, this is like the shirt you had made for G." She strokes the elbow patches.

"I'm pretty sure that's where he got the idea from."

I never did get to wear my basketball patch shirt since the day of the U of J/University of Kentucky basketball game was the same day everything changed.

"Enough stalling. Time to open the box." T holds it out in the flat of her hand.

I shake my head. "I don't wanna."

"Come on, Kay. What's in the box? *What's in the box?*" she cries out, Brad Pitt in *Se7en* style.

I pick it up to shut her up.

My gaze flits from the box to T, back to the box.

With a deep, fortifying breath, my eyes squeeze shut and I flip the lid open.

Cracking an eyelid the barest of millimeters, I see something sparkly nestled inside black velvet.

Oh, thank god.

I was right. It's not an engagement ring, but two new eternity bands wink back at me, one a deep emerald, CK's birthstone—*How the hell did he know that?!*—and the other a gorgeous peridot. The light green gems of the peridot are an almost perfect match to Mason's eyes.

The shock of what this means causes me to drop the box as if burned by it. *Holy shit! Holy shit! Holy shit!* I don't know if I can handle this; it's too much. I need JT, and I *need* him now.

Pulling my phone from my pocket, I tap on his contact in my favorites, and with a shaky hand, I hold it up to my ear. My entire body trembles as I wait for him to answer; when his voicemail clicks on, I mumble a curse and hang up.

T, having retrieved the fallen ring box, is bouncing in front of me in excitement. She's also holding out the folded note I've yet to read.

"Here, don't forget this."

I stare as if it's a cobra waiting to strike. It isn't until Tessa forcibly places the card into my hands that I take it.

The rings are bad enough. I'm not sure I'll survive the note.

> ***Skittles,***
>
> *I borrowed a little inspiration from the shirt you showed me you had made for Grayson to add a little flare to this one. Don't tell him, but I think the footballs work better than basketballs.*
>
> *Originally I was only going to get you a ring for me, but I remembered how CK gave you crap that first time you came to the AK house and figured I'd do my boy a solid, finally get him added to the fold. I know I'm going to need all the allies I can get to convince you we belong together.*
>
> *I did do one thing to set mine apart from the rest, though that should come as no surprise. If you do decide to bestow upon me the honor of being added to the representation of those who are most important to you, know I had it sized to fit your left ring finger.*
>
> *Why, you may ask?*
>
> *Rings worn on this finger typically have a bigger meaning to them, and I'm hoping this can hold my place until I replace it with something more official down the line.*
>
> *I love you, baby, so much.*

<3 Mase

Oh my god! Oh my god! Oh my god!

Shit! Now my inner cheerleader has officially turned into T. I'm done.

There's absolutely *way* too much for me to process.

I whip my phone out again and text JT.

ME: 911!!

Breathe.

I need to remember to breathe, because I am currently not doing so.

In.

Out.

In.

Out.

Okay, that's better. It's a fact that the brain needs oxygen to think, and I desperately need to think.

My eyes dart around the room in a frenzy, searching for answers.

The sound of a FaceTime ringtone cuts through my panic, and I pull it out to accept JT's call.

"Hey, sorry, we're warming up before the game," he says in greeting.

Damn. I forgot he had a game tonight.

"Kayla, what's wrong?" All the happiness bleeds out of JT's voice, my face and lack of response broadcasting how hysterical I am.

Like always, my full name coming from a Taylor is all I need to snap out of it. Still unable to find my words, I shift the camera to show the open ring box in T's hands.

JT blows a whistle through his teeth. "Damn. I take it one of them is Mase's birthstone."

Camera back on me, I nod, too in shock for the use of the

short version of Mason's name to have the usual painful effect it's had of late.

"Wow. Ballsy."

Another nod.

"What do you need, Kay?" my best friend asks, zeroing in on what he's deemed the most important part to tackle first.

"You." This is why I can't be with Mason. I can't handle drama without using my best friend as a crutch. I love my other friends dearly, but JT is the one I lean on.

"You have me. Any chance you can catch a flight down here?"

"I gotta check."

"I've got you booked on the seven fifty-five flight out of Newark tonight," Coach Kris calls out from her desk.

"What?" I look up, confused.

"Go home. Pack. See your person."

See? Everyone knows JT is my person. Shouldn't my boyfriend be the one to fill that role? Just more proof not getting back together with Mason is the right thing to do. Now if only I could convince my heart.

"But...what about practice?" I ask the first thing that comes to mind while my brain tries to play catch-up.

"Please..." She waves me off. "You're no good to me like this. Take the weekend. Get your head on straight, and we'll get back to it Monday night."

"I don't understand." I hate that I'm missing something. I feel like I'm trying to add two plus two but coming up with five.

Coach Kris comes around her desk, joining me at my side so she can see JT on the screen as well. "I bought her a ticket. She'll be there in a few hours."

T spins me around and starts pushing me toward the door. "I'll have Carter pick me up after practice."

I stop, pulling T then Coach Kris into a hug.

"Thank you," I whisper.

"Always."

#THE GRAM

Chapter24

UofJ411: You forgot a caption @CasaNova87 #ExplainPlease #CasanovaWatch #CasanovasGirl

REPOSTED—picture of a shirt that reads: "I have no life. My boyfriend plays football.—CasaNova87:

@Cheril2412: What does this mean @CasaNova87 ? #WhatsWithTheVagueBooking

@Christyhearsbooks: Are you the boyfriend this shirt is talking about? #AreYouSingleOrNot

@Cmd427: Is this a cheerleader bow with your number in it? #KaylaDenningsIsACheerleader

TightestEndParker85: Oh this is cute @CasaNova87, but I have a better shirt I could show you if you want @UofJ411

REPOSTED—picture of a shirt that reads: "I have no life. My boyfriend plays football.—CasaNova87:

@TheQueenB: I feel like we NEED to see this. Don't you think @UofJ411?

@UofJ411: I think I have to agree with @TheQueenB on this one

#Chapter25

A FEW HOURS after rushing around to pack and get to the airport in time for my flight, I'm standing outside of JT's dorm with my fist poised to knock.

The whole trip here, I tried to focus on getting to spend three uninterrupted days with my closest friend when in fact that's not what this is. I'm running—from my problems, from the drama, from all the things pushing me toward a complete breakdown. If only I could have left my broken heart behind too.

Knock-knock.

The door opens and I'm met with a very muscular, very naked chest. My eyes travel up the planes of said chest and come to a stop on an equally attractive face that breaks into a smile.

"Well, hello, love," says Harry, JT's British, soccer-playing roommate.

"Hey, Harry."

He swings the door wide for me to enter, calling over his shoulder, "JT, someone's here for you, mate."

JT gave me a virtual tour of his dorm during one of our video chats, but seeing it in person allows me to appreciate its size and how nice the space is.

Unlike my own dorm back at the U of J, theirs opens directly into a galley kitchen space with the living room completing the rectangular shape, both rooms serving as the center of the suite.

JT and Ian's—another member of the Blue Squad— bedrooms and a full bath branch off to the right, with Harry and the fourth roommate, Spencer's, rooms and bath to the left.

Being guys, the large flat-screen on the wall in the living space comes as no surprise, as does the extensive gaming setup underneath. I am impressed with how nice and homey the space feels given four males live here, with the three-person couch, end tables, large armless chair, and blue, white, and black area rug.

A door in the right branch opens and out steps my best friend, still drying his hair with a towel. Next thing I know, I'm scooped into JT's arms and squeezed against his damp chest in a G-like bear hug.

The towel gets dropped over my head, and by the time I free myself from the terrycloth, JT is pulling a shirt over his own. "I see you officially met Prince Harry."

"She's charmed, I'm sure." Harry lives up to his British-roots-inspired nickname by bowing with a flourish.

Ignoring the bro-dude insult sparring that has commenced, I root around in my bag until I find Mason's note and slap it against JT's stomach, eliciting an *oomph*. "I swear to god, if you don't let me drink tonight, I'm revoking your best friend card."

Deep laughter fills the room. "Carter and I only stopped you from drinking on the nights when you had to work the next day. So sue us for wanting to prevent you from getting sick should you be tossed around in the air."

I roll my eyes, hating how logical his reasoning sounds when all I want is a little liquid oblivion.

"What's this?" JT asks as he bends to retrieve the white paper from the ground.

"The straw." I put my bag in the room he indicates is his.

"The straw?" He arches a brow.

"That broke this camel's back." I point to myself.

Why is it when I was first faced with the gift bag and its contents, I felt like running around like Macaulay Culkin in *Home Alone* when he discovers everyone is gone, but in JT's presence I can instantly fall into joking about it?

He opens the note, and I watch as he reads it. He runs a hand down his face when he's done, blowing out a deep breath. "Damn. Respect."

I huff and cross my arms. "Whose side are you on?"

"Yours." He steps around me and heads for the fridge, retrieving two bottles of Patrón Silver, a bag of limes, shot glasses, and a salt shaker then places them on the counter. "Always."

"Okay." I take the chilled bottle from him and clutch it to my chest lovingly. *Salvation.*

"Ian!" JT shouts down the hall and pulls out a chair at the small four-top table between the kitchen and the living room.

"What's up, man?" Ian's face is focused on his phone so he doesn't see me when he walks out of his bedroom. When he finally does look up, he smiles the instant he spots me. "PF." He rushes me and picks me up into a hug, a common greeting thanks to my short stature.

"Hey Ian." I take a seat at the table.

"Did you know she was coming?" he asks JT, pulling out the chair to my right.

"Yeah. I didn't want to say anything until I could talk to the whole squad." Pain-filled whiskey eyes meet my grays. I hate that he's still beating himself up over how my identity was outed. "PF being here needs to stay on the DL as much as possible."

"Got it." Ian rubs his hands together gleefully. "So...tequila?" I nod. "Sweet." He smiles then calls out to Harry where he sits on the couch. "You in, *Your Highness*?"

"Shut up you wanker," Harry retorts, claiming the last seat at the table. "I had to be named after the prince," he grumbles.

"I guess it could be worse. You could be named William." I try to offer some comfort.

"True. My brother does get it worse than me."

"Wait…" I make the timeout gesture with my hands. "Your brother is really named William?"

"Oh yeah."

"Oh man," I say with a laugh.

"Mum and Dad just *had* to move us to America." He gives me a wink. "At least I'm not a ginger like your mate here."

I don't know about you—*nudges my side*—but I think he's even more charming in person, and I could listen to him talk all day.

JT gives him a scowl, but I reach out and fluff his thick red locks. "To be fair, he's not as much of a ginger as the prince. His hair is a few shades darker."

My defense gets the first genuine smile from my bestie, and the tension he seems to have in his shoulders lessens. I hate that he feels he has to stay on alert in case I lose it. It's one of the many things that make him such an exceptional friend, and because of it, I'm comfortable enough to let go and be the PF he refers to as my true self.

"Alright, we need some tunes," Ian declares, and Jason Aldean's voice comes through the speakers. Born and raised in Kentucky, he's a country boy through and through. With his black hair and matching black eyes, he is the definition of tall, dark, and handsome. Beside Rei, JT's flyer, he's probably the person I know best from the squad.

"Alright, ladies." I clap my hands. "Enough chitchat. It's time to drink."

"She's feisty. I like her," Harry says.

I pour out four shots and distribute them, each topped with a slice of lime. Lick my hand between my left thumb and pointer finger and shake salt onto the spot. Holding up my glass, I toast the guys, lick the salt, and toss back the shot, feeling the warm burn down my throat. I suck the juice from the lime slice and grin around the fruit.

It's going to take more than one shot to get me to the mind-numbing level I seek, but it's a start.

I pour out and down a second one before any of the guys have finished their first.

"Damn, Spence is gonna be mad he missed this," Harry comments as he grabs the Patrón to refill his glass.

The guys talk about their missing roommate's plan while I slide the bottle over from Harry and toss another shot down the hatch. Swallowing down the tangy juice, I keep the lime pinched between my teeth and confess, "I slapped him."

Three sets of startled and confused eyes blink at me from around the table before Ian asks, "Spencer?"

I laugh around the fruit in my mouth, finally removing it with a shake of my head. "No. Mason."

"Like a playful 'oh you're so silly you big hot football player you' type smack?" JT asks, doing his best airhead impression.

"That voice you just did"—I circle a finger in front of his smirking face—"*better* not have been intended to be me."

He gives me an eyebrow waggle, both brows bouncing up and down on his forehead like he's a freaking cartoon character. I meet it with an exaggerated eye roll.

"Keep being a smartass, *James*"—I take immense pleasure in the scowl his full name pulls from him—"and I'll be more than happy to give you a demonstration." I wiggle the fingers of my right hand.

"And what, pray tell"—JT rests his elbow on the table and props his chin on top of his fists—"made you slap your dear sweet Romeo?"

"Casanova," I mutter under my breath, but the curl to my best friend's lips tells me I didn't say it soft enough. "And I slapped him for vague-booking."

"Oh, yes. I bet Tess broke the speed of light with how fast she sent us the screenshot of that beauty." He barks out a laugh.

"*Beauty?*" I screech.

"Yes…beauty." He pours out the next round of shots and holds my glass out for me to take. "Anyone with eyes can see lover boy realizes he made a mistake."

"So I'm just supposed to forgive him because he buys me a few gifts?" I bite into the lime with way more aggression than it deserves.

JT snorts then groans as tequila shoots out of his nose. "No. Besides, you would *never* be swayed by trinkets. What I'm saying is—think of all the things he has done since he pulled his head out of his ass."

All of my attention falls to my now empty shot glass, and I spin it in slow circles. Long fingers enter my field of vision as he counts off each of Mason's romantic gestures.

"He risked his life showing up at King's—"

"Dramatic, and he doesn't know the Royals' reputation."

"Fine." He huffs at my sarcastic retort. "He risked his life asking Em to help him." He arches a brow and cocks his head as if to say *I dare you to tell me that's not true.*

I concede with a nod, because Em sure does have one hell of a fierce protective side.

"Then there's the first shirt he had made that was *so* perfect you slept in it." *Dammit! Why do I tell him everything?* "And the vague-book one? Yeah, that was a damn good one too. How much you wanna bet the back has his name and number on it too?"

I'm sure it does. The caveman—

I sputter into a coughing fit at the nickname slipping into my subconscious.

"My personal fave, though…" He slips a hand under my left, running a thumb back and forth over the aquamarine birthstone I wear for him on my forefinger before dragging it over the amethyst band on the middle then stopping on my naked ring finger. "He didn't just get one of these for him. No…he remembered some offhanded conversation he over-heard you having with CK and made sure to include him too."

I scowl at the finger now tapping the bare thumb on my right hand. Cool liquid splashes above JT's touch, and I lift my narrow-eyed stare to see overflowing shot glasses weaving under our noses as Ian attempts to break the tension. I grab one and down it just to shut up my inner cheerleader, who's agreeing with JT about taking Mason back.

Hours pass as we continue to down shots—me out-drinking all the guys because, one, my mission is to get drunk, and two, they all have some form of practice tomorrow and I don't.

Done with the heavy stuff for the night, we settle into the most entertaining game of *Would You Rather* I have ever played in my life. Before I know it, it's closing in on two in the morning.

I stumble a little getting up, my brain just the right amount of fuzzy, and I giggle in the way only a happy drunk can.

"PF." Is it just me, or did JT drag out the *Pffff* in my name to eight hundred syllables?

"Achievement unlocked!" I shout, throwing my arms up in the air and doing a happy wiggle dance to celebrate my buzz.

The door to the dorm opens during my performance, but we're too busy ribbing each other to pay it much attention.

"Impressive showing, love." Harry compliments how well I hold my liquor.

"Seriously, PF, you pack it away like a champ, especially for someone under five feet." Ian hooks an arm around my neck, pulling me into a hug.

"I'm over five feet." I push off him and stumble back into JT, who tucks me against his side for safety.

"Please." JT snorts. He's right, damn four eleven. *Couldn't give me one more inch, huh God?*

"Hey!" I bend my head back and feign displeasure. "You're supposed to be on my side."

"Always." He kisses the top of my head. "Time for bed." He pushes me in the direction of his room.

"Buzzkill."

"Yeah, yeah. You'll thank me tomorrow."

"Damn. If I knew you guys were having a party, I would have stayed here and saved some money." A deep, deep voice cuts through our laughter.

I peek around JT's arm and see another muscular, tall, hot guy.

Geez, is it like a requirement to be good-looking to live in this dorm? Because dayum. It may be the tequila talking, but I'm inclined to agree with my inner cheerleader.

"Oh heeeeeeyyyy, you must be the ballplayer," I say with a drunken wave.

The brunette cutie gives me a flirtatious smile, and if I wasn't so hung up on Mason, I might return it with interest. Instead, all I can offer is the grin of a happy drunk.

"Yup, I'm Spencer. And who might you be, gorgeous?"

"Nope." JT pushes for me to continue toward his bedroom. "Time for bed, PF. Say good night."

"Good night boys," I singsong.

When I step inside JT's room, he leaves me to change into my pajamas. I strip off my tank and reach for the t-shirt I wear to bed, but when I pull it out of the bag, I almost drop it when I realize it's Mason's football shirt.

Son of a bitch.

I must have grabbed it on instinct. There's no way I can wear this to bed.

Twisting the fabric in my hands, I open the door. "J."

He whips around at his shortened name, all the earlier apprehension returning full force. "PF?"

I pinch the shirt between my fingers and hold it out in front of me like it's a sweaty gym sock. "I need a shirt to sleep in."

His shoulders drop away from his ears as he eyes the gray cotton, all perceived threats assessed and dismissed. "Because, what? That's a pair of pants you're holding?"

One downfall to the type of closeness we share is we're not afraid to call each other out on our shit.

"Hardy-har-har," I mock. "I know *this*"—I shake the top— "is a shirt, but after I burn it, I'll be down one pajama top."

Ooo, I hate it when he uses my eye roll against me.

"As the son of the Blackwell fire chief, I feel like it's my duty to talk you out of your pyro urges."

"Don't ruin my buzz by being all responsible like." I toss the shirt at him, but because of my inebriated state, it lands about seven feet to the right of him. "You're already on my shit list for taking the side of the *enemy* earlier."

"Whatever you say, sis." Hands cup my shoulders and I'm steered back inside the bedroom, where I'm promptly handed one of his UK cheer tees.

With him too busy laughing *at* me, the door doesn't close all the way, and snippets of conversation filter in through the crack in the door.

"Damn, JT. You've been holding out on us. Your girl's hot," says the deep voice belonging to Spencer.

"Careful. PF's practically my sister, Spence."

"Wait...*that's* the friend you've been helping through a breakup?"

"Yeah."

"So she's single then?"

"Bruh. Seriously?" A warning note enters JT's tone.

"What? She's a smokeshow."

"Listen, man, she may *technically* be single right now, but that's only until she figures out how to get out of her own way and takes the guy back."

Is that really what JT thinks? That I should be with Mason? Is that what all that championing was earlier? He needs to get his punk ass back in here so I can kick it.

Okay, that might be the tequila talking more than anything else.

"Plus—and trust me on this—you don't want to get in her guy's crosshairs. He's not someone you want to mess with."

I can't listen to any more of this. There will be no members of Team Mason allowed inside my brain space.

On that note, I pull back the covers on JT's bed and snuggle into my spot, letting the buzz from the tequila lull me to sleep.

Chapter26

CAUTIOUSLY, I crack one eyelid open, slowly taking stock. To be honest, I probably feel better than I should—only a mild headache and slightly sluggish—given the amount of tequila I consumed last night.

The events of the last eighteen hours pop up in my memory like a game of whack-a-mole, and I pull a pillow over my head in an effort to hide from them.

Isn't alcohol supposed to help you forget?

Girl. My inner cheerleader twirls the end of her ponytail with her fingers and tilts her head at me. *Haven't you learned by now there's no forgetting Mason Nova? *holds out left hand to admire a ring on it* Talk about an epic grand gesture.* She flips her hand around and wiggles her fingers at me.

I'm going to need caffeine if I have to deal with my own subconscious plotting against me.

I'm not the only one. Did you already forget about all the things JT said last night?

Tossing the pillow to the side, I reach for my phone and take note of the water bottle and Advil next to it.

CTG BFF JT: Text me when you're up. Also, there's chocolate milk in the fridge and a greasy bacon, egg, and cheese sandwich waiting for you.

And that right there is why this man is my bestie. Everyone needs a person in their life who will put together a hangover care package for them.

I down the Advil and roll to my back to text JT.

ME: You are the BEST best friend EVER!!! *trophy emoji* *gold medal emoji* *clapping hands emoji* *blue heart emoji* *crazy face emoji*

ME: I can even forgive your Judas tendencies with this gesture.

CTG BFF JT: I know *kissy face emoji*

CTG BFF JT: And please, you'll be thanking me soon enough.

I'm grumbling to myself as I type out my next message.

ME: When will you be back?

CTG BFF JT: Later. I'm on my way to practice now.

ME: Okay. I'm going back to sleep then *zzz emoji*

CTG BFF JT: Nope. Get your lazy ass out of my bed and dress for cheer practice. Coach knows you're here and asked me to ask you to help choreograph mine and Rei's partner stunt routine again.

I shouldn't be surprised by the request; I did the same for them last year. The final approval on their routine will come from Coach Ramos, but having spent my whole cheer career partnered with JT, I'm an expert on what stunts he excels at.

ME: Do you really think me stunting with your squad is a good idea? That's what started this whole mess.

CTG BFF JT: It'll be fine. I already told everyone no taping of anything and not to post about you being down here. Stop stalling and hustle up, buttercup.

ME: *GIF of Anna Kendrick saluting*

I should have suspected it wouldn't take JT much time to arrange for me to get in some form of cheering while I'm here. Ironically, nothing makes me feel more centered than being tossed in the air. Who knows? Maybe it will help me figure out what to do about the added threats from Liam.

Goose bumps dot my arms when I crawl out from beneath the warm covers, the slight chill in the room reminding me it is November. Rummaging through my bag, I search for a hoodie, only to realize, just like with my sleep shirt, I subconsciously packed Mason's.

Was it really subconscious? Why won't you just admit you want to be with him already?

Fucking hell.

Throwing the garment like it was the one that offended me and not my own conscience, I stomp over to JT's closet and rip one of his blue UK hoodies down with enough force to cause its hanger to bounce off the bar and fall onto the floor.

I need chocolate milk and coffee stat.

"Stupid fucking football player. Why can't you just leave me alone?" I mumble, attempting to pull the sweatshirt over my head. "I should just have E tie you to a block dummy and let the O-line take care of you."

"You're kind of violent for such a tiny little thing."

I let out a scream worthy of a horror film. With my head

still stuck inside the oversized hoodie, I wasn't aware anyone was in the kitchen.

"Sorry." My head finally pops out from its cotton confines. "Didn't mean to scare you." Spencer sends me a sheepish smile over the rim of his coffee mug.

"No, it's fine." My memory is a bit fuzzy thanks to my tequila buzz, but I do remember meeting him, however briefly, before his conversation with JT last night. "I just didn't expect anyone to be home."

"Ah, I'm not in season yet. Taking the rare opportunity not to set an alarm."

"Preaching to the choir on that." I shuffle over to the fridge and pull out the half gallon of chocolate milk, chugging straight from the container.

"Guess it's a good thing I don't play football, huh?"

I give a noncommittal shrug, unwrapping my breakfast sandwich and placing it in the microwave to warm.

"I take it it's more a particular player than the sport you have a problem with?"

Someone is too intuitive for me to handle before noon.

I bite into my sandwich with a nod, choosing to eat right at the counter.

"You staying the whole weekend?" Another nod. "Sweet."

By coming here, I know I'm falling into old habits of running away, but I don't really care too much. Besides, I get the impression JT is going to continue to go all big brother on me and force me to confront all the things that have me running to begin with.

Spencer and I make small talk while I eat and he has his coffee. He's a constant flirt, but unlike Adam, who is a total skeeze, Spencer's efforts remind me more of D's.

Ooo, you know who would go all caveman on Spencer if he were here?

Shut up! I shout at my inner cheerleader. This weekend is a Mason-free zone.

snorts Good luck with that.

"Excuse me," Spencer says politely when there's a knock at the door.

Two-thirds of my hangover cure done, I spin to make the essence of life—coffee.

"Dante."

"Spence."

Based on the sounds I hear, the two of them are doing the whole bro-hug, back-slapping thing.

"JT isn't here," Spencer says.

"Oh, I know." D chuckles. "I'm here for something *much* better-looking."

The smile I hear in his voice tells me without his older brother here to keep him in check, his flirtations will reach epic levels this weekend.

"KayKay." I barely have time to put my mug on the counter before I'm lifted into a familiar Grayson bear hug, this one complete with being swung around like a rag doll.

"You can put me down now," I say, hitting his shoulder.

"Whatevs. Let me have my moment. Unlike G, I never get any quality Kay time to myself."

With me too busy enjoying D's gregarious personality, it takes longer for the thought to hit. "You *can't* tell him I'm here, D," I implore, giving him my best puppy dog eyes.

"Don't worry, your guard dog already gave me the speech." A giggle escapes at his description of JT.

"You good to wait while I shower?" I gesture toward the bathroom with my mug. "I need to wash away the last of this tequila haze."

"Want someone to wash your back?" D waggles his brows.

I roll my eyes. I don't know if it's D's ridiculousness or the fact that I put seven hundred miles between me and my issues, but I feel a little bit lighter as I grab my bag and disappear inside the bathroom.

#Chapter27

CHECKING my phone has become something I've started to do with embarrassing frequency. I do so hoping Kay will finally text me, but all I have are notifications from Instagram.

I admit, my vague-book post falls into the type of thing Kay likes to avoid, but I did it with the hope that by declaring my relationship status, it would help shut down the speculation ones that have been trending.

Did it work? Sort of.

*Sort of? *smacks hat against thigh* Do I need to put it up on a whiteboard or something? Write it in Xs and Os? You did see all the comments your post got, right? Don't even get me started on that fuckwat. It's a good thing it's a bye week, because you, sir, need all the extra practice time if you're going to have a winning season when it comes to Kay.*

My inner coach likes to talk a lot of shit, but I don't see him coming up with anything good in his playbook.

"You have a game plan for this weekend?" Trav asks as we make our way out of the athletic center after our morning workout.

"Go to Blackwell, go to The Barracks, go to wherever Kay will be and not leave until we're an official couple again." I shove my hands inside the pouch of my hoodie in deference to the cold wind.

"I take it you mean *official* official and not the bullshit Gram post you tried the other day?"

The post was a power move. Granted, it was one that got me reamed out and slapped by Kay and razzed by the guys, but I was looking to shut down some of the more persistent #CasanovasGirl comments.

If it weren't for how stressed it makes Kay, or you know, the fact that social media is the main obstacle in getting my girl back, I wouldn't care.

"Isn't that that King guy with Grayson?" Trav points to where Grant is leaning against a matte black Yukon talking to, sure enough, Carter King.

"I think so. He and his friends do seem to have an affinity for that paint job." We change direction. I still haven't decided how I feel about the guy, but maybe keep your friends close and all that jazz.

Grayson is the first to spot us, greeting Trav enthusiastically while Carter eyes me speculatively.

"I can't tell if what you did was stupid as shit or ballsy as fuck." He holds his phone out, displaying my Instagram.

Trav loses it and cackles like a freaking witch beside me while I bump Carter's outstretched fist.

"Didn't realize the U of J was part of your kingdom." My hands wrap around the strap of the duffle bisecting my chest as I brace myself with my feet spread apart.

"You joke"—the corner of Carter's mouth kicks up—"but Jackie O loves to discuss the reach of my monarchy."

"Can you *please*"—Grayson clasps his hands in front of his chest—"call Em that in my presence later?"

"I would, but do you think it's smart to mess with her without Kay around?"

"Eh." Grayson waves off the concern. "Tiny Taylor will be there. She'll play royal guard while Smalls is gone."

"Why would you call Em Jackie O?" Trav asks.

I snap my fingers to bring the Three Stooges back around and focus. "What do you mean by 'without Kay around'?"

"Tessa called me for a ride home from The Barracks last night, and she and my sister spent the whole ride trying to come up with new plans because Dennings couldn't play chauffeur for them this weekend anymore.

"Why not?" Kay always makes sure to be around for Tessa if needed. What the hell would keep her from that?

"Don't know." He slips his hands into the pockets of his leather jacket and shrugs. "All I do know is I haven't seen her Jeep around town, and now I'm responsible for picking up the Troublesome Twosome from school."

My mind reels, trying to figure out what all this could mean. Sure, I said I'd spend the next three days essentially stalking anywhere Kay could possibly be, but from what I'm hearing? It sounds like that's going to be a bigger task than I once thought.

"What's your deal with my girl, anyway?" I don't give a shit about the technicality that Kay isn't mine; like hell am I going to refer to her as anything less, especially when it comes to some dude I basically know nothing about.

"True that." Trav rocks back on his heels beside me, adopting a laidback facade. "We've heard things about your sister from Short Stack, but not you."

"Yet"—I continue, picking up Trav's train of thought— "you sure seem to be around a lot and know a surprising amount about her."

"You trying to move in on my boy's girl? Slide in there as a rebound?" Trav has his charming smile fixed on his face, but I hear the threat simmering underneath the question.

Grayson spins to face the giant SUV behind him, but the bounce of his shoulders gives away his laughter. Carter shoots him a chilly glare when he mumbles something that sounds suspiciously like "wrong cheerleader", but with his back to us, it's too hard to make out.

"For all intents and purposes, Dennings and I are friends." He lifts a hand at the twin questioning expressions Trav and I give him. "She doesn't really *do* the whole *friend* thing, but that's the best way to describe us."

What is he talking about? Kay has tons of friends—Em, Quinn, Grayson, CK, Tessa, JT, me, and the guys. I start to list everyone, but again, Carter holds up a hand.

"With Dennings, you fall into one of three categories: family, NJA family, or an acquaintance. I'm in this weird middle ground between family and acquaintance because I'm really more JT's friend than anything else. But"—a strange softness overtakes his features—"even if I wasn't, I would have her back for her always being there for Savvy."

"Why?" I ask, still not convinced of his motives.

"I may not have legal custody of my sister the way E does with Kay, but I'm the one who has raised her most of our lives. Kay has always been one of the people to help smooth things over with Pops when Sav would spend multiple school nights sleeping at the Taylors'."

It makes sense. Whether Kay realizes it or not, she breeds loyalty from those around her. Look at how invested my teammates have become in me fixing my fuckup.

"Alright." I nudge Trav with an elbow so he knows to stand down, and then I reach out to give Carter a bro-shake that says *We're cool*. I don't have time to waste on macho-posturing anyway. Kay is all that matters. Now the real question is: where the hell is she?

Chapter28

I DIDN'T REALIZE how much I missed the anonymity of being just another student at the U of J until we walked back to JT's dorm after working on his partner stunt routine with Rei.

Yes, there are a number of students from Blackwell Public that attend U of J, but they, as well as everyone else, didn't seem to care until Mason started showing interest in me.

The whole thing is stupid, if you ask me, but I guess a bunch of people in their late teens/early twenties aren't as mature as one would hope.

"You guys are still coming to the basketball house tonight, right?" D asks after we all finish gorging ourselves on Chinese food. He and Rei came back to JT's earlier and have been hanging with us and JT's roommates since.

"If you're all going to a party, does that mean I get dibs on the TV?" I lean back against the couch, trying to find a comfortable position with the food baby stretching the limits of my leggings.

"Nuh-uh, KayKay. You're coming too."

I shake my head. "You should know better than most, D— how many times have I told G I'm not into the whole frat scene? I'm good drinking right here."

Last night—with the exception of the detour into hey-

Mason-is-doing-dreamy-things   territory—was   perfect:
hanging out, taking shots, playing nonsense drinking games.
I would like to repeat those events for the next two nights
until I have to return home and face reality.

"I think it's a great idea," JT chimes in.

My eyes go wide and I give him a *What the fuck?* glare.

"Don't give me that look." I narrow my eyes to slits. "It'll
be good for you to get out and be social."

"I'm social." I fold my arms across my chest defensively.
I've been social all day. Did I or did I not spend time with the
Blue Squad? What more does he want from me?

"Not so much." He gives my ponytail a tug. "Plus, it's the
basketball house, not a frat. It'll be mostly guys from the
team, the cheer squad, and significant others. Think of it more
like a Royal Ball."

Damn him for always trying to push me out of my bubble.
It irks me that I can't even use my issues with school cheerleaders as an excuse, because he knows full well I like his
squadmates.

"It'll be good practice for you." The gleam I see twinkling
in his whiskey eyes does *not* give me the warm fuzzies.

"Practice for what?" I ask out of the side of my mouth.

"Dealing with uncomfortable social situations."

I don't want to ask him what he means by that. I *really*
don't—but I can't *not* ask.

"*Whyyyyy?*"

"For when you take lover boy back." The every-single-
tooth-on-display smile he flashes me is too *You know I'm right*
for my liking.

"I hate you." Not really.

"No you don't." *Dammit.* "And you don't hate him either."
Fucking hell.

The room goes silent enough you could hear a mouse fart,
or in this case, D's whispered, "Oh shit."

"I didn't pack anything I could wear to a party." I toss out the excuse as a last-ditch effort, ignoring the commentary on the future of my romantic life. JT knows about the…for lack of a better word, threats Liam has made. We're going to have to talk about *that* at some point this weekend.

"I got you, girl. We're basically the same size," Rei offers, sealing my fate.

Glancing around the room, I see six *Checkmate* expressions looking back at me.

Whoo! Party! Party! Party! My inner cheerleader starts to do the running man.

Guess I'm going to a party.

#Chapter29

I PUT hella miles on the Shelby today. I knew the chance of finding Kay at home after what Carter told me was slim, but I still drove past the Taylors' before swinging by Kay's family home. The first was easy to rule out because there was no pink Jeep in the driveway, but at the latter, I spent twenty minutes ringing the doorbell and creeping around looking through the windows like some sort of peeping Tom.

After that, I drove around town for an hour searching for a familiar flash of pink. When that came up empty, I started to make my way back north to see if she was at The Barracks—she wasn't—then decided to swing by my house. It was a long shot, but I was hoping maybe the twins had extra practices or clinics booked with Kay this weekend.

They didn't, and unfortunately for me, Brantley was home and got his chance to pin me down about my "public image". As he droned on and on about how being seen as marketable and drama-free will help me be a cut above the rest come draft time, I tuned him out until he said, *"I'm not so sure this girl is the best thing for you."*

I snapped to attention after that.

"Come again?" I choke down the rush of protectiveness, reminding myself this is my stepdad I'm talking to.

Hell, Brantley's been the only father figure I can remember having in my life since my biological dad died when I was two. After Mom, he's the biggest supporter of my NFL aspirations. I've followed his advice on anything that can help give me a leg up—like joining Alpha Kappa—but Kay is a no-go area. She is mine, plain and simple.

"I know you think you love this girl, bu—"

"It's not a thought. It's a certainty." I cut him off before he can finish whatever asinine comment he was about to say. I swear there are moments I wonder if deciding to use him as my agent was the best plan.

As much as he was pissing me off claiming Kay's family drama could hurt me negatively, it was that comment that had things clicking into place for me.

Family! She would go to family.

Bette was up two weeks ago to make sure Kay was okay after the breakup. From all the stories she told me about E and Bette changing their lives for guardianship, the last thing she would want is for Bette to do what Kay would feel like was putting her life with E on hold again.

With my inner coach cracking up over how I'm a dead man when I get there, I embark on the almost-four-hour drive to Baltimore.

I make excellent time, shaving off thirty minutes from my estimated travel time, but as I look at the gates in front of E's home, I can't decide if it's a good or bad thing.

I'm feeling a little bit like I'm a prince in one of those Disney movies my sister Livi loves and E is the dragon I have to face to get my princess. I should have asked Grayson how homicidal E has been feeling toward me these last two weeks before heading straight to his lair.

With a deep breath, I gather my courage and push the intercom button.

"Mason?" Bette's voice sounds from the box.

I look for the camera that must be there and give a small wave when I spot it. "Hey Bette."

The gate buzzes and swings open. I take that as a good sign.

Heading up the paved drive, I park near the front door, where she waits in the open doorway. She's wearing a faded Penn State football t-shirt, knotted at the side. Based on the size, it must be one of E's. My Hawks' pride urges me to make a crack about wearing something from a subpar football program, but I'm probably in enough trouble and wisely keep my mouth shut.

Herkie rushes to greet me, and I bend down to love up on Kay's favorite canine. I can't help but notice Bette is giving me the disappointed mom look I'm familiar with from one Grace Nova-Roberts.

I hope you're okay calling an audible, because I don't think this is going to go how you were expecting it to, Rookie.

"Eric, get your ass down here," Bette calls out after motioning for me to follow her into the living room.

"Damn, woman. What's with the Eric-ing?" E jokes, running down the stairs. The smile on his face falls the instant he spots me.

Shit!

"What's *he* doing here?" The fact that he directs the question to his wife and not me is another strike against me.

"Not sure. We haven't gotten to that yet." Bette reaches out a hand for him to join her.

I look around for Kay but don't see her anywhere.

"I haven't seen anything new on your Instagram, so tell me"—E crosses his arms over his chest—"what did you do to Kay now?" The snap in his voice is expected, but the question itself confuses me.

The post he's referring to was from two days ago, but the rings...

Those were delivered *yesterday*.

Kay left The Barracks suddenly...yesterday.

Wouldn't she have told them when she got here?

Should I take it as a good thing that he was internet-stalking me instead of driving four hours to kick my ass? Or is Kay hiding somewhere waiting to see how I handle the third degree?

"You're more concerned about me vague-booking than the rings I gave her?"

His hands clench into fists at his sides. Bette, reading her husband's emotions flawlessly, puts an arm up when E takes a step in my direction.

"You gave Kay rings?" she asks calmly while her husband grinds his teeth.

"Yes?" I ask more than say.

Shouldn't they know this?

"If you think you can propose—even if it's supposed to be some grand romantic gesture to fix your colossal fuckup—without asking me for permission first, you're insane."

If the growly way E laid down his declaration is any indication, I guess it's a good thing Kay *hasn't* told them about the rings, or the corresponding note. I may not have actually proposed, but I did insinuate that I plan to one day.

"Why don't we sit down?" Bette gestures to the couch, bringing E with her and draping an arm behind his back.

"Okay." He leans forward, resting his elbows on his knees. "Rings—go."

I swallow thickly, once again looking around for Kay and coming up short. This is about so much more than the rings, but they are as good a place to start as any. All my attempts have failed. I'll take all the help I can get. I *need* Kay in my life.

I tell them everything, starting with the birthstone bands and Tarantino-ing back from the night I tracked her down to Carter King's party. The two of them listen without comment, but there's no missing the concerned looks they share when I mention the times Kay shut down.

"I know you have no reason to help me…" I mirror E's position and meet his narrow-eyed gaze unflinchingly. "But I love your sister very much."

My heart rate kicks up as he remains silent, not giving any hint of his feelings.

Bette looks from E to me and back again. "She loves you too."

Hope soars like one of Trav's beautiful spiral passes, and I latch onto it like it's a Hail Mary to win the game. "You really think so?" Vulnerability bleeds into my tone.

"Without question."

The breath I didn't realize I was holding escapes in a rush, and I sag back into the couch. I've held on to the belief that Kay loves me, but it means something to have it confirmed by her family.

"Why are you here?" E asks.

Isn't it obvious?

"For Kay." I lift my hand to stroke Herkie's head when he jumps onto the couch. Are they going to let me see her? Do I have to pass a test before I'm granted access?

"While I can respect that you wanted to have this discussion in person…" E shifts, the defensiveness of his posture easing. "Doesn't driving all the way down here take away from the time you could spend with my sister?"

"I figured as long as I could convince you to *not* kick my ass when I showed up, I'd get to see Kay sooner if I was where she is."

"Wait." Bette holds up a hand. "You think Kay is here?" She points to the floor to indicate the house.

"Yes?"

"She's not here." There's a self-satisfied curl to E's lips that tells me he's taking great pleasure in delivering this information.

Herkie lets out a sigh of pleasure as I absentmindedly stroke one of his ears in an attempt to digest what this could mean. If Kay isn't here, where is she? Where else would she run off to?

I relay the telephone-esque game of details that had me driving almost four hours. A headache starts to form at the base of my skull, and I grip the back of my neck to alleviate the pressure.

"King picked Tessa up from practice yesterday?" I nod at E's question. "This was after you sent her the birthstone bands?" I nod again. "And he said T and Savvy had to make new plans because Kay wouldn't be around?" I'm not quite seeing the significance, but Bette sure does. She has me recount each of my gestures and Kay's reactions.

The helplessness from witnessing Kay fall apart is so visceral that even now I feel like I'm drowning in it.

Bette sits up suddenly, her back straightening like she's a marionette and someone pulled her string. "I know where she is."

"Where?" My keys are already in my hand, desperate to get to her as quickly as possible.

"She's gotta be with JT." She turns and speaks more to E, as if searching for confirmation.

Another memory surfaces, this one of Tessa telling me something along the lines of how JT was the only one able to get through to Kay when she broke down heartbreakingly after her dad died and the bullshit Liam put her through. The color leeches out of my knuckles as I ball my hands into fists. Even an indirect thought of that asshole Parker has a wave of rage assaulting my sanity.

"Okay." I switch my keys out for my phone.

"What are you doing?" Bette studies me closely.

"Looking up flights from Newark to Lexington. The flight itself is about two hours, and I'm just trying to figure out which one I can take given my drive back to Jersey first."

For as poorly as I reacted to the picture of Kay and JT when I first saw it, I would never begrudge my girl her friends. I respect them for their unwavering support of her through the years; I just want to be the person she runs to from now on.

"Aww." Mama bear Bette seems to give way to a romantic.

"Before you do that"—E shifts a few inches closer—"you need to ask yourself if you can handle the full weight of Kay's insecurities."

Why does everyone think I'll run because things aren't easy? I do play football, a full-contact sport. I'm made of tougher stuff than most.

"Don't try to tell me you think she's right in saying she's not good enough for me, because I'll tell you the same fucking thing I told her." I'm not even aware I've stood up until I feel the soft press of Bette's hand keeping me back from being toe to toe with her husband. "There is not one person on this earth better for me than her."

"You've got that fucking right, Romeo." And now we're back to arms crossed, death-glaring E.

"It's actually Casanova."

"Do you *really* think it's a good idea to remind me of the nickname you earned by being a manwhore?" E cuts me a sharp look.

"Just trying to lighten the mood." I shake my hands out to dispel the tension pumping through my veins. Getting into a fight won't earn me any favor with Kay when I get to her.

"What my *over*protective husband"—Bette sends E a *Behave* look—"is trying to articulate is that Kay may never be able to handle being in the spotlight that follows you. I get and can appreciate what you were trying to do with your Instagram post, but would you really be okay if you had to keep your relationship out of the public eye?"

I don't care about any of that. The validation I used to derive from my social profile has lost its appeal. It started

with seeing Kay get stressed out when we would trend, and
after learning the—too few—details of her past, I understand
her reactions better.

"My relationship with Kay is nobody's business except
ours. If it helps, I'll delete my accounts right now."

Bette and E share a look I can't decipher beyond it being
some type of silent communication.

"Look." Bette places her hand over mine and gives it a
squeeze. "When Kay talks about—and when she's with you—
she's more like her old self, her *true* self than we've seen in
years."

She isn't the first person to say something along these
lines, and I hope and *pray* it's true.

"Then why is she working so hard to convince me she's no
good for me?"

"Because," E cuts in, "being with you leads to things that
prey on Kay's insecurities, and *they*—among other things—
can lead to her falling apart. In her mind, by *not* being with
you, she's protecting you."

"I don't need her to protect me. I just *need* her to love me."

I've said it before, but I'll say it again—Kay is my girl,
plain and simple.

E takes my measure, his head tilting to the side as he does
so. "Okay." He reaches for the iPad on the coffee table and
starts swiping across the screen. "We have to move quickly,
but there's a flight out of BWI in just over an hour. Let's go."

Everything happens in a rush after that. I grab my
overnight bag from the Shelby then pass the keys off to Bette,
the three of us climb into her Range Rover, and my boarding
pass is downloaded onto my phone.

Bette leans over the center console. "Any idea how to find
Kay when you get there?"

"I'm going to have Grayson pump his brother for
information."

"Good plan," E agrees, taking the turnoff for the airport.

"JT won't give away anything about Kay, but D"—he nods as if answering himself—"he's the weak link."

I pull out my phone.

ME: I need your help.

GRAYSON: What do you need?

Chapter 30

I STILL HAVE my doubts about attending a house party, but I know when I've been outvoted. Here's hoping that earlier anonymity will extend to tonight, because JT refuses to even let me wear a hat.

He thinks I don't see it, but I know what he's doing; this *knowing a person as well as they know themselves* thing works both ways. JT wants me to see that I can handle the possibility of being recognized in a less pressured atmosphere, like away from the U of J.

"Stop worrying." JT puts his hand over mine to stop it from picking at the top of the thigh-high boots Rei lent me to wear. The rest of my outfit is pretty casual—a simple white tank top and stonewashed skinny jeans—but I couldn't resist the shoe porn suede boots. They called to me.

The Ubers come to a stop in front of a large UK-blue-sided house. Unlike the AK house, the Kentucky basketball house is less mansion and more classic American suburban family home with its wide white trim, tan wooden pillars, and wrap-around porch.

The lawn and landscaping are manicured and well maintained, and even with a few people dotting the porch, it's not littered with empty beer bottles or Solo cups.

"We're gonna go in there"—JT points at the house as the rest of our party files out of their respective vehicles—"drink some beer, and have a good time."

"But—"

"What we aren't going to do is worry about any of tonight ending up on social media," he continues, without giving me a chance to offer an objection.

D leads the way, and as the door opens, I am surprised by how much this does remind me of the nights we attend Carter's Royal Balls.

There's music, the volume enough to be heard but not requiring to be shouted over. The sixty or so people in attendance are scattered around playing NBA 2K, talking, dancing, and congregating around a beer pong game.

From those I recognize, it's mostly the members of the Blue and White Squads, the basketball team, and a sprinkling of others.

The knots in my shoulders loosen a tad at the realization. For as bad as my history is with cheerleaders who aren't from NJA, JT certainly fell in with a good group here.

"KayKay, play pong with me." D reaches out to pull me toward the table.

"Hells no," I say with a laugh. "The last place I'm playing beer pong is in a basketball house."

"Why?" D gives me a pout and bats his unfairly long lashes at me. Naturally, I roll my eyes at him.

"You guys drill free throws for a living."

"That's big talk coming from a football queen." D may be teasing, but it doesn't prevent me from checking to see if that raised any interest. No one is paying us any mind, but it's a hard habit to break.

D goes full-on puppy-dog-eyes on me to convince me to play. Not gonna happen.

"What about a game of flip cup?" I point toward the kitchen.

He looks over my head, an easy feat for him, scoping out the empty table sticking out into view. "Works for me." He drops an arm around my shoulders and turns back to the room. "Anyone who wants to help me kick KayKay's ass in flip cup, we'll be in the kitchen."

Enough people break off from various rooms at D's bellow to play a game of eight-on-eight.

With each flip of the cups, my earlier apprehension drains like the beer down my gullet. It's a good thing beer is such an appetizing beverage because it should pair well with the crow I'm going to have to eat when I admit to JT he was right to drag me out tonight.

We trash-talk and laugh almost more than we actually play, and it's the most fun I've had in two weeks.

Our teams are pretty evenly matched, trading off who comes out the victor. Rei and I fall onto each other in a fit of giggles at the guys' attempts at victory-dancing in such a confined space. Let's just say a man closer to seven feet than six should *not* try to running-man without warning his neighbor.

I roll my eyes as JT shoots me an *I told you so* grin and reaches for the blue pitcher to refill for our next game. I'm concentrating on making sure the beer hits the fill line two inches from the bottom of the cup when the hairs on the back of my neck stand on end.

#Chapter31

BY THE TIME my flight lands in Lexington, Grayson has come through for me with a text saying his brother is at a party at the basketball house. Personally, I have my doubts that Kay will be at this house party, but Grayson seems more than confident.

He had to guesstimate the address from an old visit since asking Dante for it would raise suspicion. If Kay *is* in attendance, I don't want anything to spook her before I get to her.

Thankfully, it's easy to ascertain it's the correct house by the handful of people milling about and drinking on the front porch.

My hands worry the strap of my duffle as I pause on the sidewalk, staring at the house as my Uber drives away. I made a promise to myself that I wouldn't leave here without Kay. Looking down, the gray cotton of my U of J football hoodie mocks me. My attire sure isn't going to help me stay incognito, but I didn't have anything else to work with since this was an unplanned trip.

I sure hope Grayson is right and Kay is here, because I'm unsure how my presence will go over otherwise.

"Aw, shit," says the guy closest to the door as I make my approach. "You're Mason Nova."

I'm used to strangers knowing who I am, and it's not from ego—it's fact. I've had more plays on the ESPN highlights reel than any other college player in the past few years and have been featured on the cover of *Sports Illustrated* with other players speculated to go in the first round of this year's draft class.

"Hey, man." We exchange the typical dude hand-clap-shake-bump. I have a reputation for always being gracious when meeting fans, and hopefully this time I can use it to my advantage.

"What are you doing down here?" His own hoodie declares his status on the basketball team, so I'm even more certain I'm in the correct place.

"My girl is down for the weekend. I decided to come and join her." I point to the door behind him. "Is it cool if I just head in?"

"Oh, yeah. Door's open." He steps to the side and motions to the strap across my chest. "Everyone drops their shit in the room to the left if you wanna ditch your stuff. It'll be safe."

Offering my thanks, I head inside and take him up on his suggestion.

A smidge less recognizable without my sweatshirt, I proceed unimpeded as I make my way through the downstairs. This party is a lot more low-key than Alpha parties and reminds me more of how things are in the den with a few people dancing and others playing video games.

Not seeing a familiar rainbow-streaked blonde in the mix, I continue through the house and into the dining room. Kay also isn't among those playing beer pong, and I decide to add Dante and JT into my search. Between the former's towering height and the latter's red hair, I'm hoping one of them might be easier to spot. Kay is so short she tends to get lost in the shuffle.

A cheering sounds from the next room, I hit pay dirt,

seeing Dante and JT among those playing flip cup. I don't see Kay yet, but she can't be far if they're both here.

Dante shifts to the left, and there she is.

Fuck! She's a sight to behold.

I drink her in like the starved man I am.

The curls I love to run my hands through tumble around her shoulders and down her back to her waist.

Her toned muscles and luscious curves are displayed in all their mouthwatering glory in a tight white tank top, the deep U of the neckline showcasing the generous swell of her cleavage.

As hot as the upper half is, the bottom sure as shit holds its own. Her jeans look painted on, and I can't wait to see what the back view looks like. Those sexy-as-fuck boots bring to mind all the ways I can get them wrapped around my hips.

My favorite thing about her in this moment? It's the first time her eyes haven't been rimmed in red in weeks. I hate that she ran, but at least being here seems to have done her some good.

I can't stop my mouth from tipping up at the corners when I notice I'm not the only one cataloging the other's appearance. Kay's molten eyes are like a physical caress as they travel across my chest and down to where my black t-shirt clings to the muscles of my stomach.

The disbelief is clear to see on her beautiful face. My gaze drops to her mouth as she pulls her bottom lip between her teeth. I know exactly what she tastes like, and I can't wait until I'm the one doing the nibbling.

Without giving her a chance to object to my presence, I cross the space between us in a few long strides, bend down, put my shoulder to her stomach, and toss her over it in a fire-man's carry.

Mine.

Time to show her I'm still her Caveman.

#Chapter32

I BLINK MY EYES REPEATEDLY, sure I'm hallucinating, but nope, he's real. Looking hotter than should be legal in dark wash jeans filled out by his muscular thighs, a black t-shirt molded to his washboard stomach, and a backward black ball cap is Mason Nova.

What the hell is he doing here?

Like a flower to the sun, my body turns to follow his as he walks around people and the table to me. Without a word, I'm suddenly lifted from the ground and hanging upside down over his shoulder, causing me to let out a screech.

When he turns to take us away from the group, I brace my hands on his ass—*Why do I have to notice how amazing it is?*—to peer up at my best friend, who's *supposed* to have my back but is standing there unmoving.

"You're not going to stop this?"

"Nope," my supposed bestie answers.

"*Seriously?!*" My voice pitches.

"Go talk to him," JT advises calmly.

"Why would I do that? And why are you so okay with this?" I try to gesture to the fireman's carry I'm in.

"Don't act like I haven't made my stance on the situation perfectly clear." He toasts me with his Solo cup.

I huff in frustration. "You are *so* not my best friend anymore. You are now Undesirable Number One to me."

"Oh you must be mad if you're using a *Harry Potter* reference, but you messed up there, babe, because you just referred to me as Harry—*you know*, the good guy?" He pretends to fluff his red hair, and I bounce on Mason's shoulder with his laughter. "I've always fancied myself more of a Weasley."

"Yeah, like Percy Weasley—book *five* Percy Weasley," I spit out, super annoyed to still be hanging upside down.

"Now that's just mean." JT ignores me and speaks to Mason. "Good luck, man. She's pissed." He claps Mason on the shoulder and turns back to the flip cup table.

Confident JT isn't going to follow and kick his ass—much to my disappointment—Mason carries me out the back door and onto the wraparound porch.

Once outside, he shifts me from his shoulder to pin me between the side of the house and his body. Tingles follow in the wake of his touch, his hands skimming up the backs of my thighs to wrap my legs around his hips before cupping my butt.

I try to hold on to my mad, remembering how hurt I was when he broke up with me and all the reasons he needs to stay away from me. It doesn't work. With our bodies pressed together in such a familiar way, every defense and objection I have flows out of my brain, one after the other.

It doesn't help that JT is right and he's had me teetering closer and closer to the edge of giving in and taking a chance on love.

Bitch please. *eye roll of all eye rolls* Who are you trying to kid? You know you were planning on taking back Mr. Tightest End— hehe, see what I did there?—when you got home.

Yeah…well…

Fuck! I can't even argue with myself properly with Mason close. Is it really too much to ask to have gotten the two other days I thought I would have before I had to face him?

His exquisite seafoam green eyes bore into me with all the love I've been craving. How am I supposed to keep my distance when he looks at me like that?

Goose bumps break out across my skin, but I don't know if it's from the chilly November air or from being so close to Mason.

Memories of each pregame good luck kiss trickle into my brain, my back pressing into the hard siding as Mason shifts to balance me with his lower body.

An involuntary moan passes through my lips as the hard length of him hits my center. My senses are overwhelmed by the flex of his muscles around me, the scent of his fresh soap filling my lungs, and the body heat warding off the worst of the chill.

My hands fall to his heaving chest, the cotton of his shirt warm under my touch.

Oh, how I've missed this, missed him.

I'm not sure how long we stay there, staring at each other, both our hearts pounding—he's so close I can feel his too—JT's words bouncing around my skull, encouraging my heart to take a chance.

"God, Kay," is all he says before his lips are on mine.

This kiss.

Oh my god.

It's all-consuming.

He doesn't just press his mouth to mine—he devours me.

His hands cup my face between them, his long fingers threading through the curls at the base of my skull, tugging on them and tilting my head for a better angle.

My arms find themselves looped around his neck.

I feel *everything* in this kiss, all the apology, the pain, the longing, the passion, the love Mason has to give—and, most of all, hope.

#Chapter33

THERE'S SO MUCH I want to say, so much I *need* to say, but I can't concentrate this close to Kay. It's been too damn long since I've had her body wrapped around me like this, and it dissolves my self-control. I crave her like an addict. She's my drug of choice, and all I want to do is overdose.

I take her face in my hands, tilting it to mine, and seal my mouth over hers. Her slender arms wrap around my neck, and after a few seconds, she starts to kiss me back.

I know we need to talk. *Technically* speaking, we are currently broken up, but I couldn't *not* kiss her right now. It's a compulsion, an inherent need to communicate my feelings on a baser level.

God I missed this.

We lose ourselves in our kiss, as so often happens with us. I explore her mouth with my tongue, and not even the bitterness of the beer she was drinking can take away from her intrinsic sweet taste.

I swallow down her moan, only managing to drag myself away enough to separate our mouths and rest my forehead against hers.

This close I can appreciate the finer details of her face. Her makeup covers the freckles I like to count on her nose and cheeks, but it makes her eyes appear larger, the flecks of blue slightly more prominent inside the swirls of gray.

Every inhalation brings with it hints of both the peppermint of her conditioner and the vanilla on her skin.

"*God*, Kay. I'm sorry. So *damn* sorry."

Yes, she's told me she forgives me, but all this started because I false-started.

"For kissing me?" Her voice cracks.

"No." I shake my head. "*Never* for that."

My fingers flex around her nape, her dark gray orbs broadcasting a tormented pain I yearn to take away.

"I'm such a fucking idiot." A self-deprecating laugh breaks free before I can stop it.

"Mason—" She tries to cut in, but I don't let her.

"No, please. Please let me say everything I *need* to say to you."

I pull back, maintaining eye contact, and stroke her cheeks with my thumbs. I think the action soothes me more than it does her.

"I know I let other people influence me, but I'm *never* making that mistake again." I place a finger over her lips to stop what I know will be her next rebuttal. "You"—my finger drags across her bottom lip—"are the *best* thing that has *ever* happened to me. *Nothing*"—I push enough to drag her lip down—"can make me think differently."

The thin black choker necklace she wears bobs with the movement of her swallow as she digests both what I'm saying and what I'm not.

"I love you, Skittles. So *fucking* much."

"Oh, Mase."

Fucking finally! I resist the urge to do a touchdown dance at her calling me Mase.

One of her hands glides up my chest, curling around my neck and toying with the hairs exposed under the brim of my hat. My heart stutters, the fear that our relationship is irreparable pulsing through my limbs.

"Mase." She cups my jaw, and I nuzzle into the touch. "I love you too."

My body goes boneless at her words and I almost drop her before I readjust to keep us both upright.

"But..." My spine stiffens at her *but*. I hate that word right now. "I'm *scared*."

"It's okay to be scared, babe." I blow out a breath, her bangs fluttering from the force. "I just need you to believe I'll always be here to hold you through it."

Even with her skin riddled with goose flesh, it's still soft as silk as I skim my fingertips along her forearm. I circle the wrist of her left hand and pull it between us. The grooves of her birthstone bands scratch across the pad of my thumb, making the nakedness of the ring finger all the more noticeable.

If the distance from the last few weeks has taught me anything, it's that I am 100%, totally, completely, head over heels in love with Kay.

"You're it for me." I pinch the bare digit.

"You can't know that." Curls brush my jaw as she shakes her head. "It's only been two months."

"I don't care if it's been two months or two *hundred* months. From the moment I saw you...something told me you were made for me." I bring her hand to my mouth and kiss her ring finger. "Every day since then has only driven the point home more."

"Mase." A tear leaks from her eye, and I wipe it away. "I'm a mess. I don't know how to cope with all the things that come with your future career."

"We'll learn together."

I already plan on spending part of my time down here with JT—he's the expert when it comes to helping Kay through the worst of things. If there's anyone who will be able to coach me into being able to do the same for my girl, it will be him.

"I will do anything you need me to do to feel secure in us. All I ask is that you be mine."

"You don't—" She drops her gaze to focus on our linked hands. "There are—" She sucks in a deep breath, her voice turning small. "There are things...*important* things you don't know about me. What if...what if you change your mind because of them?"

My gut clenches. I have suspected she's been withholding from me. I'm so far gone over her, though, I honestly can't think of what could make her fear come true, if anything like that even exists.

Hooking a finger under her chin, I push until her now watery gray eyes meet mine again. "Whenever you're ready to tell me, I'll be here, but know this"—I smooth a finger over her jaw—"nothing you can tell me will change my mind. Whatever has happened in the past has helped make the woman in front of me now, and I love her."

She sucks in a startled breath, her lips parting slightly with the shock.

Good. If I accomplish anything this weekend, it will be that she will unequivocally believe the depth of my feelings for her.

"How did you find me?"

The question catches me off guard. It's almost hard to believe this is the third state I've been in today looking for her.

"Well...after taking a tour of Jersey, I continued my road trip to Baltimore."

"You *went* to my *brother's*?" Her eyes do a quick scan of my body like she's checking me over for injuries.

"I'd go anywhere for you."

Bleh. You've turned into a cheesy character from a romantic comedy. My inner coach can fuck off because the smile that blooms on Kay's face has the biggest one I've had in weeks spreading across mine.

"Oh, put those away." She pushes a finger into one of my dimples, which only has me grinning harder. She's always telling me my dimples can make a girl go stupid. Telling her as much gets me a playful slap to the shoulder.

"Does this mean you're going to admit you're mine again?" I nip at the tendon running along the side of her neck, and her answering moan makes me want to find the nearest flat surface so we can make up properly.

"You're such a caveman."

I can't help but smirk against her skin. "You know it, baby."

The eye roll she gives me when I pull back is all the answer I need.

Chapter34

I'M DOING THIS. I can't believe it, but I am.

I just hope it doesn't all end up blowing up in my face.

"Can we get out of here?" My scalp stings when Mase's fingers tangle deep into my hair as he asks the question.

As conflicted as my feelings have been during our time apart, the only way I can answer is with a yes.

It's insane that he went to E's trying to track me down. My brother may be a teddy bear with me, but he can be down-right grizzly to anyone he feels has wronged me.

It shouldn't surprise me that E thought Mase was good enough to pass muster; he's been fighting for me—for us—for weeks.

I have to trust in Mase's declarations. Instinctually, a part of me believes if anyone can handle the things I'm too scared to face, it will be him.

"Have any place in mind?"

Going someplace private is the smartest decision. It's actually a miracle nobody has stumbled upon us already.

"Yup." That devilish smirk that never fails to make me feel weak in the knees makes an appearance. Without further explanation, he lowers me to the ground, allowing my body to slide along every inch of his on the way down. Those damn dimples deepen in naughty promise.

The flip cup game is still in full swing when we return to the kitchen. I rub at my arms in an effort to chase the chill away, unsure if it's lingering from being outside for an extended period of time, or if it's because of the number of eyes now trained in my direction.

Warmth and calm infuse me as Mase steps up behind me, looping his arms around my middle and tugging until my back is flush to his front. A sigh of contentment escapes at how easily he is able to center me.

Why did I try to run from this?

"We good here?" JT asks, circling a finger at us.

Lips ghost over the soft spot behind my ear with a whispered, "Mine." I should roll my eyes at this additional display of Mason's caveman antics, but after spending weeks thinking I wouldn't get to experience them again, I can't bring myself to do so. His possessiveness is one of the things that got me to love him the way I do.

Besides…this has nothing on how he barreled in here, tossed me over his shoulder, and carried me away like those he is aptly nicknamed after.

"We're good." I nod, placing my arms on top of Mase's, in no rush to move.

"Does that mean I get to be Ginny again?" JT drops down, shuffling closer on his knees in an over-the-top display of pleading. There are days I wonder about his sanity.

"She is definitely the most badass Weasley." Approval shines in JT's eyes at Mason's comment. "The movies don't do her character justice the way the books do."

"Oh, man." JT slaps the floor before jumping back to his feet. "He's a Potterhead too? He's perfect for you, PF."

Tilting my head back, I catch sight of Mase's smug expression. After weeks of me telling him I'm not good for him, I'm sure he's *loving* being told otherwise.

There's a kiss to the top of my head, and his chest expands behind me with a deep inhalation, breathing me in.

I feel the loss of him the instant he steps away, my heart only settling when his fingers thread their way between mine. "Our Uber is here."

How did I miss him ordering one? Also, who cares? With promises to meet up with JT and the others tomorrow, we make our goodbyes.

As soon as the door to the hotel room clicks closed behind us, Mase lifts me in his arms. My legs automatically wrap around his waist and hook at the ankles. He devours my mouth like a starving man let loose at an all-you-can-eat buffet, pressing my back into the wall by the door.

If I thought the way he kissed me at the basketball house was hot, that was a small campfire compared to this raging inferno.

His tongue licks inside my mouth, and I meet it stroke for stroke. Grateful for all the years of tumbling experience, I use my thigh muscles to grind onto the erection pressing against his zipper. My panties are instantly ruined, my body remembering exactly what he is capable of doing to it.

My hands slip beneath the hem of his hoodie and t-shirt, skirting across the dips of his abdominals. He's hard and hot all over, and I tug until I pull both tops off and drop them to the floor along with his hat, which gets knocked off in the process.

Someone sign this man up for an underwear endorsement. He is H-O-T, hot, hot, hot, my inner cheerleader declares.

He doesn't give me long to appreciate his hotness before his mouth is attacking mine again. He sucks on my bottom lip, the bite of his teeth making me weak in the knees in a way that would have me melting into a puddle on the floor if I were standing.

Speaking of puddles, my bladder chooses this moment to remind me of all the beer I consumed playing flip cup.

What a clam jam. My inner cheerleader isn't the only one pouting as my head thunks against the wall in frustration.

"What's wrong, babe?" Mase asks, one of his dimples peeking out.

"I have to pee." I cringe as I say the words. Talk about breaking boundaries.

His other dimple makes an appearance, clearly entertained by my admission. The frosty look I give him has zero effect as he sets me on my feet, the smack on my ass when I turn for the bathroom only proving this further. Even through the thick wood of the door, I can hear his deep rumbling laughter after I slam it in his face to take care of business.

My eyes rise from where I'm washing my hands to meet passion-dilated ones in the mirror. I'm not sure if I should be disturbed or not that my boyfriend was obviously listening to me pee outside the door, but I can't find it in me to care as he stalks in my direction.

His body blankets mine, bending me over the counter as his tattooed arm reaches to twist the tap, cutting off the running water.

"What are you doing?" I watch as his hand presses to my stomach, the warm olive tone of his skin all the more striking against the harsh white of my shirt.

"You were taking too long." He grinds his hard-on into the upturned curve of my ass.

I roll my eyes. "I've been in here for *literally* one minute."

He ignores my logic and uses his free hand to push my hair to the side then drags his lips over the exposed skin, starting at the soft spot behind my ear and traveling down my neck to bite the juncture where it meets my shoulder. A moan slips past my lips as he licks away the sting.

I'm transfixed by our reflection as he continues his trail of kisses. His fingers hook under the straps of my tank and bra and slowly, teasingly lower them until they are stopped by the bend of my elbows braced on the counter.

Breathing becomes difficult under the weight of my lust as his hand trails a path from my throat, down my sternum, and disappears below the neckline of my shirt. Without the resistance of the straps, both articles of clothing fall away and my breasts are exposed, my nipples beading against the chilly air.

With a rumble in the back of his throat, Mase latches onto my neck again, this time hard enough that I know it will leave a mark.

Arms crossing at the wrists, he fills each of his large hands with the opposite breast, the pink of my nipples visible between his fingers as he pinches and twists them. My already soaked panties flood more, and the counter in front of me becomes my sole support.

"*God, Kay.*" I push onto my toes, oscillating my hips, each squeeze and pluck on my breasts a direct line to my clit.

"*Mase.*" His name falls from my mouth like a broken cry.

"I need you." Stubble pricks along the sensitive skin of my back with his kisses.

I crane my neck around, searching, seeking, until I capture his lips with mine. My doubts when it comes to us never stemmed from the physical. Here, we excel. Nothing else can get between us here. It's just me and him.

"Take me." I speak against his mouth, our lips brushing with each desperate word.

Permission granted, a hand presses between my shoulder blades, bending me fully over the counter, the tips of my toes barely maintaining contact with the floor beneath them.

Deft fingers undo the button on my jeans and the hiss from the zipper echoes in the acoustics of the bathroom. Cool air hits my overheated skin as he peels my jeans over my ass and down my legs until the tops of my boots prevent them from going below mid-thigh.

In the mirror, I see his eyes flare and his Adam's apple bob with a swallow as he takes in the sight of my propped-up ass bisected by the flimsy piece of white lace that is my thong. *Thank you cheerleading conditioning and your countless squats.*

With one last squeeze, his left hand releases my right breast to travel down the length of my body, my stomach contracting with a sharp inhalation at the feel of his calloused fingers. Pleasure sparks with the abrasion of the lace of my thong when he traces the outline of my pussy lips through the material.

"You're *soaked*, baby." Mase groans, his fingers pushing into my slit with my underwear.

Tingles, shivers...each sensation almost painful in its intensity.

I have no words, my brain consumed by the pleasure he is bringing to my body.

His hand cups my butt cheek, squeezing and lifting, letting it go to watch it bounce. His finger slips under the strip between my cheeks, traveling from the waistband down to where it disappears. On his trip back up, he gives a tug, pulling the front triangle tighter against my clit, and a whimper escapes my mouth.

"Mase—don't—tease me." It's a struggle to get my words out.

His eyes flash to mine in the mirror. Using both hands, he slowly and—*dammit*—teasingly rolls my thong over the curve of my ass, the material releasing from my aching center with a pop it's so wet, down my legs to rest on top of my jeans.

Then his tattooed arm hooks back around my body, the black tribal ink and olive skin a stark contrast to my pale milky complexion, anchoring himself once again with his hand possessing my right tit, and without warning, he thrusts two fingers inside me. I cry out from the intrusion, not in pain

—I'm far too wet for that—but from the unexpected pleasure. I'm two seconds away from coming, and he's barely started.

His fingers curve in that way that finds the sweet spot inside me and I'm coming, all over his hand, my cries of pleasure bouncing back to me off the walls.

He continues to work me over until I'm coming a second time. My body might be ready for an orgasm coma, but Mase is clearly just beginning if the way he's undoing his own jeans is any indication. When his hands release me to undo his pants, my body sags against the counter, the hard granite digging into my belly.

His firm length nestles in the cleft of my ass then he's pushing it through my wetness, coating himself with my juices.

He lines himself up with my entrance but doesn't push farther. "Watch," he commands, his breath brushing the shell of my ear, waiting for me to lift my head from where it's resting on my fisted hands.

Once my dazed eyes lock onto his blazing green ones in the mirror, he grips my hips, and in one powerful thrust—the possibility of which a true testament to how wet I really am—he seats himself inside me to the hilt, his balls pressing against my thighs, each of us groaning in unison.

We both still for a moment as he lets my body adjust to his size. Once he's sure I'm ready, he starts to piston in and out, and I send a silent prayer of thanks to the inventor of the birth control pill for allowing me to experience each drive without the barrier of latex.

Mase snakes his left arm between my bent elbows to find purchase on my chest once again, his right looping around my hip to press on my clit. He's over me, covering as much of me as physically possible in this position, and the simultaneous attack on my major erogenous zones is almost more than my body can handle.

"Watch, baby." His command comes after my eyes start to

drift closed again. "Watch me take you. See how good we are together."

His words have as much of an effect on my body as his touch.

"I love fucking you this way. The way your ass presses against me and the way your back arches is the sexiest thing I've *ever* seen." His words are more growl than speech. "But as much as I like it, I don't get to see your beautiful face when you lose it."

His fingers stretch up to graze the underside of my jaw, the affectionate move a contradiction to the animalistic way he's claiming me.

"Now I'm kicking myself for not thinking about fucking you in front of a mirror sooner. *Best* of both worlds, baby."

Another orgasm rips through me as he continues to play me with both his body and his words. After our time apart, I'm not sure how much more I'll be able to take before *actually* passing out from pleasure.

"And, *god*, the way you look in your reflection, your mouthwatering tits squeezed together resting on the counter, as if served up on a platter for me, your arms pinned by your top while you're bent over for me to take...*hottest. Thing. Ever.*" He punctuates the last three words by pulling out to the tip and slamming back home each time.

"Mase...I can't." I struggle to put together a sentence under the onslaught of pleasure.

"I know, baby." He places a kiss to the side of my neck, leaving his mouth there as he speaks, the words rumbling through me. "Let go for me one more time. I've got you."

The stimulation on my clit is almost too much to take, but the countertop is keeping his hand trapped against it, his nimble fingers continue their teasing pattern. There's no way to stop what's coming, and honestly I'm not sure I want to.

"Come on, baby. Let go. Come all over my cock. I've got you."

His words serve as the catalyst for the biggest, most epic orgasm of my life. I feel him release inside me and we ride out our pleasure together.

He's careful to brace himself with his elbows on the counter to keep from crushing me as we catch our breath.

Able to read how absolutely wrecked I am, he scoops me up into his arms and carries me to the king-sized bed in the middle of our room.

In my daze, I'm mildly aware of him removing my boots and stripping my clothes the rest of the way off my body before doing the same with his own. He lifts me like I weigh no more than a feather and arranges us in the center of the mattress, pulling the covers around us and spooning his body around mine.

His whispered "I love you" is the last thing I'm conscious of before sleep claims me.

#THE GRAM

Chapter35

TheQueenB: Look @UofJ411 at what it couple from @TheUofJ I spot canoodling in the background. #IHaveTheScoop #CasanovaWatch #CasanovasGirl
screenshot of a picture of a UK basketball player and his girlfriend with the image of Kay wrapped in Mason's arms circled in the background

UofJ411: Thanks for the update @TheQueenB #WeHaveEyesEverywhere #CasanovaWatch #CasanovasGirl
REPOSTED—screenshot of a picture of a UK basketball player and his girlfriend with the image of Kay wrapped in Mason's arms circled in the background—TheQueenB: Look @UofJ411 at what it couple from @TheUofJ I spot canoodling in the background. #IHaveTheScoop #CasanovaWatch #CasanovasGirl

TightestEndParker85: Yeah this won't last @CasaNova87 #TakingBets #OverUnder #YouShouldCutYourLosses

REPOSTED—screenshot of a picture of a UK basketball player and his girlfriend with the image of Kay wrapped in Mason's arms circled in the background—TheQueenB: Look @UofJ411 at what it couple from @TheUofJ I spot canoodling in the background. #IHaveTheScoop #CasanovaWatch #CasanovasGirl

UofJ411: Oh shit! You're not going to let this slide, right @CasaNova87? #DefendHerHonor #CasanovaWatch #CasanovasGirl
screenshot of post by @TightestEndParker85: Yeah this won't last @CasaNova87 #TakingBets #OverUnder #YouShouldCutYourLosses

Chapter 36

WAKING up with a naked Kay in my arms is hands down my favorite way to start the day. After spending the last couple of weeks afraid I would never get to experience this again, I allow myself a few more minutes to properly appreciate it.

My big spoon is wrapped tightly around her little one, my body doing its best to figure out the math on how to get the entirety of its six-five frame to be touched by her four-eleven one. The length of Kay's body is suctioned to mine from neck to knee, the plump curve of her ass cradled against my groin in the matching bend of our hips.

The scent of peppermint wafts from the riot of curls spread over my arm, my shoulder pillowing her head, my arms banded around her, refusing to let her go even in sleep.

"*Mase,*" she says on a sigh. I don't know what's sexier, the gravelly, sleep-roughened sound of her voice or that she's back to calling me Mase.

"Morning, baby." I nuzzle into the back of her neck, nosing her hair out of the way for a trail of kisses. My muscles tense and stretch around her, the leg snaked between hers hooking around her ankle and pulling her closer.

"I'm not having sex with you," she mumbles into her pillow.

A chuckle breaks free at how grumpy she sounds. *Oh, my little anti-morning person.* It doesn't surprise me that morning sex isn't at the top of her list of favorite things, but I'm confident I can bring her around to my way of thinking.

"What if I do all the work?" I drag my teeth down the shell of her ear, grinning at how she squirms against me in response.

"I'm too sore."

I shouldn't smile, but I can't help it. It's common for Kay to be sore after sex given that I'm double her size, but if she's calling a timeout on the sexy times, it means it's much more than normal. We were rather *enthusiastic* last night—all three times.

Look at you finally living up to your MVP status. Good job, Nova. You earned a water break. Looks like my inner coach is feeling cheeky after last night as well.

"So you're saying you're going to be walking funny today?" I nip at her bare shoulder. The idea of there being a visual representation of how she was owned by me, how she's *mine,* is one hell of an ego boost.

"You're such a caveman." I swear I can hear her roll her eyes, and I love it.

"You love me anyway." I knead the breast my hand is cupped around, thumbing her nipple until it's pebbled against my palm.

"Will you *stop* that?" She tries to wiggle away, but my hold on her is resolute and causes her to huff in frustration. "It's halftime for my vagina. Go entertain your dick in the shower if it can't wait until tonight."

My girlfriend, ladies and gentlemen—always so full of snark for me. She's damn lucky I love her.

You're so full of shit. Weren't you the one trying to convince me that it's because she's different and doesn't fawn over you like the jersey chasers?

I hate when my inner coach is right.

With one last kiss on her head, I roll away and climb out of bed—by myself.

I'm reaching for my phone on the nightstand when Kay's lights up with a text next to it, and the contact coming up as UNKNOWN has me pausing to take a closer look.

UNKNOWN: It really is a shame you deleted all your social media accounts, because if you look hard enough, you can find pretty much ANYONE on there. Did you know your Casanova and his quarterback bestie used to date the SAME chick in high school? Oh the stories she could probably tell me...

Who the fuck is texting her? Better yet, why do they give a shit about Chrissy? Other than her playing my best friend and me, there's not a story there to tell.

Is it...

Could it be...

Is Liam Parker texting her? Wouldn't she have his number blocked?

Rage slams into me at the possibility. The urge to wake her up and demand answers is strong, and I've already taken a step toward the bed before I stop myself. Getting all up in Kay's face about this without thinking it through could have an adverse effect on everything we accomplished last night.

The last thing I need is for Kay to revert back to the whole *I'm not good for you* bullshit she tried to spout. I just got her back; no way in hell am I going to let anything try to take her away from me again.

You're gonna need help for this play.

My inner coach is right—again. I quickly type out a text to JT, giving him our hotel and room information and asking him to come.

I was really hoping to have Kay to myself without any drama. So much for that.

After toweling off, I pull the only non-U of J apparel I packed —a white long-sleeved Henley and black joggers—not trusting myself to resist crawling back into bed and trying to convince Kay to call an end to her halftime if I walk out in only a towel. A man's self-restraint can only take so much, and keeping away from a naked Kay is a test I'll fail every time.

Sure enough, she's in the same position I left her in, the colors peeking out from her blonde hair against the white bedding. I stand at the foot of the bed, marveling at how damn tiny she really is lost in a sea of bedding on the king-sized mattress. It amazes me that she chooses to be with such a brute of a man like me. There have been times I've been afraid to crush her, but it's like there's an instinct inside my DNA that prevents that.

A quick check of the time tells me JT is going to be here shortly. Risking bodily harm—an acute possibility with Kay— I move to play alarm clock, brushing hair off her face and kissing her temple. "Come on, Sleeping Beauty. Time to wake up."

A disgruntled *harrumph* greets me as I avoid the arm swung back to bat me away. *So adorable.*

"Though your aversion to mornings is cute…" Safe from rogue limbs, I lean back over and place a string of kisses across her cheek. "I need you to get up and put some clothes on."

"Since when do you try to get me to put clothes *on*?" she mumbles.

"Baby…" Man, what I wouldn't give to be able to explore her naked body right now. "If your best friend wasn't on his way over, I wouldn't care if you stayed naked. In fact, I would insist."

"JT's coming here?" She finally rolls to her back, twisting to face me, hands balled to rub the sleep from her eyes.

"Yes." I search the floor for last night's discarded shirt, scooping it up when I find it and tossing it in her direction at the same time there's a knock on the door.

Gray eyes go wide before she scrambles to pull the black cotton over her head. I need a moment to appreciate her. I don't care that she's all wild sex hair, leftover makeup smeared in the corners of her eyes, and beard burn across her neck; she's never looked more beautiful to me.

Knock-knock.

Oh, that's right. JT is here and we've got shit to handle.

Kay makes no move to get up, so I answer the door.

"I would have bet good money she wouldn't be up before noon today," JT says as I let him in.

"Yeah, well, my boyfriend is a pretty annoying alarm clock." Brows scrunched, eyes closed, jaw to the floor, one arm bent to cover her mouth and the other raised above her head, Kay lets out a full-body yawn.

"You woke her up?" JT directs the question to me while sliding a cardboard carrier of coffees and a paper bag onto the low table in the small seating area in the room. When I nod, he reaches out a fist for me to bump.

Kay continues to shoot us both sleepy death glares from the bed. I know better than to say so out loud, but whenever she tries to act tough, I think it's the cutest thing. She attempts to be fierce but only ever makes me think of those memes about Baby Groot when he is mad.

"I brought you a coffee." JT hands Kay a paper cup, which she quickly cradles to her chest.

"You're my favorite." Her lips purse as she blows across the lid, my dick twitching inside my pants at the sight. Damn her for calling halftime. The three orgasms I had last night mean nothing when I'm trying to make up for weeks without her. Never mind that getting hard in front of her best friend isn't appropriate. I find when it comes to Kay, the rest of the world can just fuck off.

Isn't the rest of the world the reason you asked JT to come here?

I nod to myself at the reminder from my conscience. I don't give a flying fuck what anyone else has to say about me, Kay, or our relationship. And while Kay doesn't either, it still affects her. My job is to protect her and to learn the best methods to help her cope.

Which brings us back to JT...

"Do you wanna shower, baby?" I hook a hand under the strap of the duffle JT brought with him. I couldn't convince her to shower with me, but maybe she will feel inclined to do so now that her own things are here. Plus, it'll give me a few minutes alone with JT to discuss strategy without having to worry her unnecessarily.

"Sure." She slips from the bed, my shirt falling to her knees as she stands, and my eyes automatically go to the bare expanse of leg on display. Again, my dick twitches as I remember how good those legs felt squeezing my ribs during our third bout of lovemaking.

Her fingertips brush across the back of my hand as she takes her bag from me, sparks shooting up my arm from the touch. It doesn't matter how simple or innocent the contact; I will always react viscerally to Kay.

Neither JT nor I move until we hear the snick of the lock, each taking one of the wingback chairs bracketing the table. I keep my mouth shut, not quite sure how to begin this particular conversation. The last time I talked to JT at length, he was doing his best to encourage me to make things right with Kay, a fact that only makes me feel like more an asshole given that I suspected my girl was cheating on me with him when I jumped to conclusions.

"How bad is she going to freak when I show her this?" I

hold out Kay's phone with the text message displayed. "More importantly, is this Liam, and how do I help her deal with it?"

I loathe that I'm not, and don't know how to be, what Kay needs during her times of crisis. I'll be *damned* if I don't learn.

"You mean…" JT leans back in the chair, crossing a foot over the opposite knee, draping his arm over his bent leg. My only clue he's pissed is the vein pulsing at his temple. "Is she going to start back on her bullshit about how she can't be with you and it's for your own good?"

I bark out a laugh. It is clear to see how this guy became best friends with my girl.

"Yes. I would very much like to avoid *that*."

JT rubs his chin in thought, the silence stretching between us. My pulse is erratic and I rub my damp palms along the tops of my thighs for no other reason than to have something to do while nerves course through my system.

"She'll probably freak over that more than these." It's his turn to hold a phone out to me, and he directs me to flip through screenshots he saved to his camera roll. Instagram after Instagram post flies by with each flick of my thumb: UofJ411, TheQueenB (whoever the hell that is), more UofJ411, and finally…Liam motherfucking Parker. "And yes, that's Liam who sent her the text."

With a calm I'm not even close to feeling, I hand him back his phone before I send it flying across the room and into a wall. "Why doesn't she have him blocked?"

"She does. We're only assuming it's him because the text said things that make it pretty clear it is him. We also assume he's using burner phones, because each time he has texted her, it's been from a different number."

A buzz starts underneath my skin. "This isn't the first time he's contacted her?"

"No."

"I'm gonna need a little more than that."

My hackles rise as JT glances over his shoulder, checking to make sure the door to the bathroom is still closed before shifting to lean forward, his elbows braced on his knees, coffee cup held between his hands.

"He's been making veiled threats about trying to hurt your chances in the draft."

Brantley would *freak* if he heard that.

"That seems highly unlikely," I say.

"Agreed." JT nods. "But you see...PF isn't necessarily the most logical person when it comes to you."

She's not the only one, my inner coach murmurs, tossing in his two cents.

JT falls silent, and when he finally speaks again, I'm not expecting the subject change. "I can't believe you went to E's." If I'm not mistaken, there's a gleam of respect in his eyes.

"What makes you think that's how I found out she was here?" He's correct, but learning the thought process that led to drawing that conclusion might help me understand more of their family's dynamics.

"I was on the phone with him when you texted me."

I start to tell him about what happened during my short time in Baltimore but cut myself off at the sound of the bathroom door opening. Everything else around me goes fuzzy as Kay steps out and becomes my sole focus. How the hell can she look so good fresh from the shower?

Her long curls are pulled up into a high ponytail, the strands still damp, leaving water spots behind on her *If CHEERLEADING were easy they'd call it FOOTBALL* tank. I can't help but think the shirt is a dig at me. The wink she gives me when she sees my amused smirk only confirms my suspicion.

"What are you guys talking about?" Kay asks as she settles herself in my lap.

Home. The thought flits through my mind, and as crazy as it sounds, it's true—Kay is my home.

The earlier anger over our bubble being popped by outsiders returns. Needing a distraction, I start to trace the large stars printed in the panel of NJA blue camouflage running down the side of her leggings.

"It seems someone at the U of J finally found their confirmation that we are, in fact, still a couple." I figure I'll start with the easier of the two issues, and I offer her my phone to scroll through the Instagram feed. As she looks at the posts, the sight of the purple and blue jeweled bands circling the fingers of the hand holding the phone only broadcasts the absence of the light green one I tried to add.

Will she wear it? Will she deem me worthy of being added to the collection meant to represent those closest to her? Should I take heart that she's also not wearing the emerald one I got her for CK? Or is that just because I was the one who got it for her?

"I'm so sorry, Skittles." I curl myself around her to speak softly into her ear, her body expanding with a deep inhalation. "I know this is the type of thing you hate."

Her hair tickles my nose as she shakes her head. "It's not your fault."

I wish that were true. The only reason the busybodies at school are interested in her is because she's my girlfriend. This is my doing. It's my responsibility to fix it as much as I can.

"It is." I ghost a kiss to her cheek. "But please don't run from me." I can't go back to feeling the way I did these last couple of weeks.

She doesn't say anything—not a word.

My gut clenches with uncertainty. Why isn't she saying anything? Shit, what is she going to say when I show her the text from Liam? Am I about to lose her again?

Any lingering hope I held on to ticks away like seconds on

a game clock as she rises from my lap and walks across the room, still silent.

I swallow down the bile in my throat as I watch her reach for her bag. *This is it. She's leaving me for good.* The thought flattens me harder than any linebacker.

I shift my gaze to JT, but he hasn't made any attempt at getting up. No, instead he looks like he's settling into his seat more, drinking his coffee like he doesn't have a care in the world. *The fuck?*

It's then that I notice Kay isn't pulling the strap of her bag over her head but tugging open the zipper. Unable to see what she's doing with her back facing me, I hold my breath, praying like I do when the game is on the line and Noah is about to attempt an unheard-of-long-distance field goal to win.

Pain-filled eyes find mine when Kay turns around. The slim column of her throat works as she struggles to swallow and her lashes fan over her cheeks as she drops her gaze to whatever it is she has cupped between her hands.

Again I look to JT, but he's still not giving anything away.

Kay's feet shuffle along the carpet until the blue cotton of her socks touches the tips of my white Nike Uptowns. I focus on her adorable compulsion to match her wardrobe, too afraid of what I'll read on her face if I meet her gaze.

"Mase." Her soft voice soothes me like Gatorade after a game. "Mase, please look at me."

As if my eyelids have kettlebells hanging from them, I struggle to lift them to do as she asks.

"I'm not running." She fiddles with the object she's holding, and I finally notice it's a ring box—a *familiar* ring box. "Quite the opposite." Her thumb slips into the seam, and I can't help but notice her nail is also painted blue as the lid opens with an audible *snap*.

The sight of the peridot ring nestled inside the black velvet has me sagging back in my chair.

She kept it.

She has it with her here.

My breathing grows erratic, not wanting to get my hopes up only to have it fall short like an incomplete pass. "You brought it with you?"

"That's not the only thing of yours she brought with her," JT says.

"Aren't you supposed to be *my* friend?" Kay whips around to face JT only to find him looking at the ceiling in an effort to play innocent.

"What else of mine did you travel with, Skittles?" I reach out to take her hand, linking our fingers together to bring her attention back to me. Her body turns, but the floor once again becomes her focus.

"Oh, you know…" A singsong lilt enters JT's tone. "Only your t-shirt, your hoodie…"

"Oh, *really*?" I should probably curb my instinct to smile, but I can't help myself.

"Don't gloat. It's not attractive." Kay's ponytail flops forward as she drops her head. "And you"—she thrusts an arm out, pointing an aggressive finger at JT—"*so* aren't my favorite Taylor anymore."

"Lies," he says with confidence.

"I'm not gloating," I claim, only to receive an eye roll. "Okay, maybe a *little*." I pinch my thumb and forefinger together. "And I'm *always* attractive."

Kay makes that face where she can't decide if she wants to hit me or kiss me. You know the one: lips pursed, mouth moving side to side, nose twitching like a bunny. God I love her.

While she debates what to do, I liberate the box from her grasp, taking out the emerald band and slipping it on the thumb of her right hand then freeing mine.

As I take her left hand in my right, her jaw drops, eyes flaring wide as my thumb runs along her bottom knuckles.

Placing the ring in front of her finger, I don't blink as I slide it home. We still have a long way to go in terms of how to handle the ongoing social media attention and Liam Parker, but like when she wears my hoodie to my games, knowing she will allow me to claim her in this way is enough for now.

#Chapter37

WHEN I LEFT Mase and JT alone earlier to shower, I had legit worries about the two of them coming to blows. They are two of the most important men in my life, and they're both alpha and fiercely protective. It was a tossup how things would play out.

I wonder what Mase would say if he learned JT was actually his biggest advocate these last couple of weeks. Hell, even I'm surprised by how adamant JT is that Mase is the right guy for me.

Now, with those light green eyes looking at me with awe and a kind of love I've only ever witnessed between E and Bette, all the broken pieces of my heart start to fuse together. I'm still not convinced I'm the best person for him, but if Mase wants to love me, I'm going to be selfish enough to let him.

Leaving my hand in his, I spin and settle myself back across his lap. The automatic way his arm comes around to tug me a few millimeters closer brings an instant smile to my face.

"I know the whole reason I'm down here is to see you"—I glance at my best friend, a look of approval on his face as he watches the subtle ways Mase and I interact—"but why are you here? I figured we'd meet you at the gym later."

With there being no game on the schedule for the Blue Squad, our plan today is to finish up choreographing JT and Rei's routine.

"I asked him to come," Mason answers, holding out my phone, and this time, the sight of a text from an unknown number freezes me in place. "I wanted him to be here when I showed you this."

Those all-too-familiar doubts start to creep their way back in. *Can I do this? Can I really?* The back and forth of Mase's thumb over the band representing his place in my life grounds me in the here and now.

"I heard *everything* you and the others said to me." He releases my hand to cup my face, his thumb now brushing along the apple of my cheek. "I want to be the one able to help you when you get overwhelmed by the bullshit. Who better to teach me than the expert?"

"I do so enjoy being recognized for my expertise."

I roll my eyes at the smug expression on JT's face and the way he's buffing his nails against his University of Kentucky Cheerleading sweatshirt for effect.

Doesn't Mase see? He's already turning into that person. There's no panic churning in my gut or cold sweat breaking out along my back at the fact that the bubble of anonymity I thought we had being in Kentucky has popped. I'm not drawing away or running to hide and put as much distance between us as I can. No, instead I try to get as close as possible, my body nuzzling into his.

There's still so much we need to discuss. I need to lay all my cards on the table for him. After he knows all the gritty details that could come out, then it will be up to him to decide if I truly am the one he wants to be with. Maybe if I offer to bring Jordan and ATS in to handle his public image, it might be enough of an incentive to ignore any fallout on him come draft time in April.

JT likes to tell me I'm being melodramatic, and maybe I am, but it's still not a risk I want to take.

#Chapter38

TheQueenB: First our king of football @CasaNova87 chose a Nittany Lion supporter for a girlfriend. Now said girlfriend is… what? Trying to convert him to a University of Kentucky fan? Have you seen this @UofJ411? #WhoDoYouCheerFor #SplittingLoyalties #CasanovaWatch #CasanovasGirl
screenshot of Mason hugging Kay from behind, surrounded by people cheering in University of Kentucky gear

UofJ411: Is that why we haven't seen @CasaNova87 around campus or the AK house? #LoversGetaway #CasanovaWatch #CasanovasGirl
REPOSTED—screenshot of Mason hugging Kay from behind, surrounded by people cheering in University of Kentucky gear—TheQueenB: First our king of football @CasaNova87 chose a Nittany Lion supporter for a girlfriend. Now said girlfriend is…what? Trying to convert him to a University of Kentucky fan? Have you seen this @UofJ411? #WhoDoYouCheerFor #SplittingLoyalties #CasanovaWatch #CasanovasGirl

TightestEndParker85: Hey @CasaNova87, spending your bye week wasting it on Kay Dennings' whims to visit that bestie @CheerGodJT of hers isn't going to help you beat me and my boys in a few weeks #HawksAreGoingDown #FeedingFrenzy
REPOSTED—screenshot of Mason hugging Kay from behind, surrounded by people cheering in University of Kentucky gear—TheQueenB: First our king of football @CasaNova87 chose a Nittany Lion supporter for a girlfriend. Now said girlfriend is...what? Trying to convert him to a University of Kentucky fan? Have you seen this @UofJ411? #WhoDoYouCheerFor #SplittingLoyalties #CasanovaWatch #CasanovasGirl

UofJ411: Anyone else counting down the days to the last game of the season for our @UofJFootball? #LetMeHearYourHawkCry #CasanovaWatch #CasanovasGirl
screenshot of @TightestEndParker85: Hey @CasaNova87, spending your bye week wasting it on Kay Dennings' whims to visit that bestie @CheerGodJT of hers isn't going to help you beat you and my boys in a few weeks #HawksAreGoingDown #FeedingFrenzy

Chapter 39

THIS WHOLE DAY has been like a rollercoaster with its constant ups and downs.

Up: Waking up cuddling with a naked Kay.

Down: The invasion of Liam Parker's text messages and Instagram trolls.

Up: Kay putting on my ring.

I will say this; most of the day has been on an upward swing. One of the other highlights for me was getting to watch Kay help create JT and his partner Rei's cheerleading routine. Being both a football player since the age of five and having a sister who cheers, one would think I would have spent my fair share of time watching the cheerleaders, but that would be incorrect. Don't get me wrong, I've obviously seen them do their thing on the sidelines during games and have been to a handful of Livi's bigger competitions through the years, but nothing compares to the up-close-and-personal view I got today.

With the few tricks Kay and JT did in demonstration, it is *undeniable* why they were champions. JT lifted Kay with one foot in each hand, only the slightest shake to his arms as he held them fully extended overhead while she explained something to Rei. Then after counting off, Kay flipped backward and landed hand in hand with her legs stretched up in the air in a handstand. Before anyone had time to appreciate the flawlessness of the stunt, JT bent his elbows and Kay popped back around to her original standing position overhead.

I can't tell you what's more impressive, the effortless way JT flipped her over his head and into the air or how Kay landed each trick as steady as if she were landing on the ground and not in his hands.

Even with all that, nothing compared to watching Kay coach them. With the easy way she commands attention and respect from everyone, it's no wonder she chose not to cheer in college—coaching is her *calling*.

My pint-sized smartass even chose to add Biz Markie's "Just A Friend" to their practice playlist.

We had another up in attending JT's roommate Harry's soccer game—oh I'm sorry, *match*—but the celebratory dinner we went to after brought us to our current round of downs.

It was obvious JT didn't want to show Kay the posts, and I respect him for actually showing it to me first as a buffer, but it didn't do much to soften the blow.

It's one thing for UofJ411 to use info about Kay and me for the bulk of their content, and it's another for someone else to be actively tagging them with updates. Now we have to deal with Liam Parker jumping in on the CasanovaWatch and CasanovasGirl hashtags.

Since handing JT back his phone, Kay hasn't said a word.

The door of our hotel room beeps, and the tumble of the locks disengaging is almost deafening in the stilted silence, which has only grown since we left dinner. It now feels like a physical entity, hovering around Kay and me like a fog.

The top of her ponytail brushes along my inner arm as she moves past me into the room. My feet shuffle as I hesitate to follow, unsure what to say. Kay has enough insecurities of her own; I don't need her trying to take mine on as well.

She's already withdrawn into herself, so now I need to keep her from pulling away from me again.

As I swallow down the lump of fear in my throat, the soles of my sneakers drag along the carpet until I come to an abrupt halt upon seeing Kay standing in the middle of the small seating area. There's a steely determination lurking behind those stormy eyes of hers that I wish I could get a bead on.

"Babe..." My feet melt into the floor as I stand transfixed by the sight of the white of her teeth digging into the red flesh of her plump lower lip. Then...

She starts to shed her layers.

Gone is my hoodie.

Her slim arms cross over her stomach. Slowly, inch by inch, her tank top starts to rise above her toned abdominals, over the swells of her breasts pushing against the material of her sports bra with each rapidly accelerating inhalation.

Her elbows point toward the ceiling, and in one fluid movement she peels it over her head, the fabric falling to the floor like a leaf from a tree. Eyes, now brimming with confidence, lock on mine again the instant she's clear of the garment.

Me? I remain rooted to the spot, my dick hardening, tenting the front of my joggers.

This woman, whose head doesn't even reach my shoulders, *commands* me.

There's a *rrrrip* when her foot skitters over the back of her sneakers as she toes them off, kicking them to the side.

Less than three feet separate us, but it feels like miles as I wait for her to close the distance. I don't blink, not willing to miss a step. My lungs scream from holding my breath in anticipation of her next move.

She doesn't disappoint...

One of her tiny hands—the same one with my ring winking at me—presses between my pectoral muscles. The gentle flex of her fingers is like the hardest shove, and I fall into the wingback chair behind me.

The hesitancy from earlier is gone, replaced by a satisfied smirk that has my balls tingling.

Hands braced on the arms of the chair, her mouth presses to mine, my tongue parting her lips to tangle with hers. I'm rock hard in an instant.

"Baby..."

She kisses across my jaw, the scrape of her teeth audible along my stubble. Warm suction envelops my earlobe and precum leaks onto my boxer briefs.

Her pulling away has me emitting a groan of frustration, though it's quickly replaced by one of pleasure when her hand snakes underneath the hem of my shirt and hoodie, her fingertips skimming along the grooves of my abs, the muscles twitching in the wake of her touch.

Her torso pushes my knees apart as she bends and lowers herself between my now spread legs.

Fuck me she's a vision kneeling before me.

Her lashes fall to her cheeks as she focuses on slipping beneath the waistband of my joggers and briefs, tugging them down only enough for my dick to pop out like a mother-fucking goalpost.

Down, down, down her hands continue to travel until they curve around my knees, anchoring us together as her eyes take in my cock from root to tip. She accuses me of being the possessive one, but this? The intensity in the way she studies every inch of me? It's like a goddamn tangible caress of ownership. It's so fucking hot it almost has me coming on the spot.

Her palms spread on top of my thighs, the heels of her hands digging into the tight muscles. Her lips part, warm breath puffing across my sensitive head, sending shivers skittering up my spine.

She continues her upward trajectory, slipping back under

the hem of my shirts and shoving them as high as her arms can reach. With each inch they rise, Kay's head lowers until, without warning, she takes my cock in her mouth.

"Fuck, babe…" I push through gritted teeth at the feel of her throat contracting around me. "Don't you have a gag reflex?"

My life before Kay entered it was filled with more blowjobs than I could probably count, but this? This is head unlike any other.

It's been only seconds, but already my balls draw up tight, readying for release.

"Skit—" *Doesn't she need to breathe?* I think as she maintains her position for one last swallow, the walls of her throat constricting around my length and making the edges of my vision blurry.

Finally, *finally*, she starts to move.

Up and down her head bobs. Her cheeks hollow with suction, lips flaring out with each drag back up my length, tongue tracing every vein and ridge. There is *nothing* teasing in the way she works me over; she's pure intent.

"Babe…*fuck*." My hands spear into her hair, the tie holding her curls snapping as I fist the strands tightly. I worry I'm being too rough, but her hum of approval tells me it's for naught.

Her hands search for purchase on my eight-pack, pushing down for stability as my hips drive upward. Cum boils deep in my balls and I warn, "I'm gonna come."

Instead of heeding the warning, Kay redoubles her efforts, pushing in closer, deep-throating my dick until the soft petals of her lips make contact with the skin at the base. She swallows—I explode. Ropes of cum shoot from my dick and coat the back of her throat.

She doesn't release me until she has taken every last drop I have to give. Only then does she settle back, her ass resting on her heels and one hell of a self-satisfied expression on her gorgeous face.

"Damn, baby." I'm pretty sure the top of my head is somewhere across the room.

I'm not sure how long we sit here—me with my heart pounding against my ribcage, breaths sawing in and out of my lungs, and her with lips swollen, pink flush covering her from face to chest—before I move. First I toss my hat to the ground, and I quickly follow it with my sweatshirt and Henley. Tucking myself back into my joggers, I shift forward, hooking my hands under Kay's armpits, and reverse our positions.

Her skin is hot to the touch as I skim along the dip in her waist up to her sports bra, my gaze automatically falling to the pink tips topping her now freed and bouncing breasts. I rid myself of the distraction with a shake of my head, divesting her of her leggings and draping her legs over the armrests. *Perfection.* That's what she is. Completely naked, spread out like my own personal buffet ready to be devoured.

Except…

That's not what I do.

Kay squirms as much as the position allows—which isn't much—as I ghost my fingers up the length of her leg, starting at her ankle and ending in the crease where her thigh meets her groin.

My hands curl around her hips, my thumbs meeting at the top of her pubic bone and dragging through her slit from top to bottom. *Holy fuck, she's soaked.* Feeling how turned on she is from giving me pleasure has my dick stirring to life again.

Her swollen clit is on full display with her pussy lips spread open, begging for my attention.

"Eyes on me," I instruct, leaning forward, holding my position just over the bundle of nerves until those graphite irises reveal themselves to me. The second they do, my lips surround her clit, teeth scraping along the oversensitive tissue as I tug it into my mouth.

Ambrosia. Sweet, addicting, tempting ambrosia is what she tastes like.

"*Mase*," she pleads, back arching, shoulders pushing into the chair, searching for enough leverage to lift her center closer to my mouth.

I use my tongue to draw figure eights, lapping up every bit of her until I find her weeping center and thrust inside, mimicking what I plan to do after I have her coming all over my face.

My scalp burns as she yanks and twists my hair, her nails raking across the skin at the back of my neck.

"Come for me, baby," I command when I feel the walls of her pussy flutter around my tongue. It takes considerable effort not to plunge my fingers inside her to push her over the edge, but if she's going to be sore again tomorrow, it's going to be from my cock.

The sound of her pleasure bounces off the walls when I bite down on her clit one more time and she tumbles into orgasm.

Her body doesn't even get the chance to go limp before I'm shedding my pants and reclaiming the chair with her straddling my lap.

I cup her at the nape and pull her in for a crushing kiss, entering her at the same time our lips touch. The sound she makes as I bury myself inside her to the hilt is almost carnal enough to make me come.

"God, baby." I pump my hips relentlessly, spurred on by each audible proof of her pleasure. "You feel so good." She's not the first to tell me she's on the pill, but she's the only woman I've actually taken bareback. Every time I get to have her without a barrier between us is better than the last.

"*Mase*." Her voice hitches.

We pick up the pace, both chasing our oncoming orgasms.

With a final slam of my hips, I come with a roar as she soaks me to the balls.

"I love you." I breathe the words into the curve of Kay's neck as she slumps forward, completely spent.

"I love you, too."

I take heart in the fact that she didn't hesitate in the least to return the sentiment. There's still much to discuss to keep this—the Mase and Kay we are in private—safe from the outside world, but we can worry about that tomorrow. Tonight is for us.

#Chapter40

LEAVING Kentucky is going to be difficult for me for a handful of reasons. For starters, I'm going to miss JT terribly. No amount of video-chatting can truly recreate what it's like to hang out together in person. Also, it means returning to the place where the attention on Mase and me is a bajillion times greater.

God! I can't even imagine what things are going to be like around campus tomorrow.

You know what? That's a problem for future Kay. For now, present Kay is going to enjoy being wrapped up in the drool-worthy arms of her hunky boyfriend.

Enjoy? Guurrrlll...I don't know about you, but that feels like too tame a word to describe what this feels like.

It's not often my inner cheerleader and I are on the same page prior to coffee consumption, but she might be onto something this time. The way Mase holds me makes my heart flipping sing. It's like even in sleep, he needs to assert his dominance. All his long, sinewy limbs coil around me like he never plans on letting me go.

Will he always feel this way? I squeeze my eyes shut against the negative thought hard enough to have spots dancing behind my eyelids. I can't think like that. Mason said he doesn't care what others have to say—*we* are the only two people in this relationship.

I want to believe him. I *need* to believe him. These last few weeks without him, I wasn't living; I was merely existing. It was damn close to being a repeat of four years ago, and *that* is unacceptable. It may have been a silent one, but I made a promise to *never* put E and Bette through that again, and *dammit*, I intend to keep my word.

Not running away from Mase and what we share is the first step.

The obsidian ink of the tribal tattoo decorating the arm under me stands out in stark contrast against my paler skin. My fingers start to trace the lines and swirls down to his wrist.

"*Mmm.*" The contented sound rumbles in my ear. "I love when you do that, babe."

A pleased smile curves my lips. "Good." It is by far one of my favorite things to do. "Because I don't think I could resist even if you didn't." I twist to place a kiss on the bicep under my head, the muscle jumping at my touch.

"You'll get no complaints from me." He squeezes his arms tighter around me, the scuff on his jaw setting off familiar sparks between my shoulder blades as he starts his own series of kisses. "Shower with me?"

How can I say no to that?

It is morning though…

As if hearing my internal thought, he shifts, slipping an arm under my knees and another behind my back, lifting me from the bed bridal style and carrying me to the bathroom.

I'd be annoyed if I wasn't so damn happy. That's why, instead of getting an eye roll, a sleepy smile is all he sees as he stretches to turn on the taps, waiting for the water to warm before stepping inside the shower with me still in his arms.

He lets my body glide down his as he lowers me to my

feet, the warm spray covering us both from the rain shower head above.

One of the best perks of having a hairstylist for a sister-in-law is getting to use the shampoo station installed in her home when I'm down for a visit, but none of those washings have anything on when almost six and a half feet of naked Adonis perfection is the one doing it, though. Sorry, not sorry, Bette.

The feel of Mase's fingers working my hair into a lather is blissful. "You are *so* hired," I moan.

His deep chuckle surrounds me as he hooks a finger under my chin to tilt my head back, rinsing the suds from my curls. "You're saying if football doesn't work out, I can have a career as a shampoo boy?"

My spine stiffens. I know it's a joke but, *fuck*, I don't like it.

"Babe," he soothes, placing a gentle kiss on my forehead. "Stop worrying."

I wish I could.

"I'll never be able to smell peppermint without thinking about you," he says, popping the top on my conditioner bottle. "Christmas should be interesting this year."

We're still two weeks out from Thanksgiving—why is he bringing up Christmas?

"Why's that?" I ask as his deft fingers work to untangle knots as he encounters them.

"I'm afraid I'll get a semi any time I come across a candy cane."

"You're ridiculous." I giggle.

"You know you love me."

"I do." Really, I do—even more so because he knows exactly how to distract me and get me out of my head.

Since Mase is too tall for me to successfully wash his hair, I grab the loofah and get to work washing his body instead.

And what a body it is. My inner cheerleader scans Mase from head to toe. She's not wrong; it's like a freaking work of art. The pop of his traps, the round balls of his shoulders, biceps as large as my head, corded forearms, strong wrists, and all that dark ink decorating it.

Give me a Y. Give me a U. Give me an M, M, Y. YUMMY!!

Mentally, I roll my eyes at myself. Only Mason is able to make my inner cheerleader forget the fact that we were never the type to actually cheer like non-club teams. Though, she's not wrong.

I watch the soap suds wash down his body, following their path along the cuts and ridges of his washboard abs, into the V at his hips.

"Careful, baby," he cautions when I kneel down to soap up the tree trunks he calls legs. "Don't start something you don't plan on finishing."

My teeth bite down on my bottom lip at the sight of his manhood at eye level. It starts to lengthen under my attention, but he's right—I'm sore once again.

I nod, rise from my crouch, and poke him in the side. "Turn around so I can do your back."

He does as I ask, and I make sure to give it the same proper attention I gave his front. The magnificent bubble of his ass is even better to look at naked than it is in his tight football pants. He twerks it at me when I squeeze it before turning around to face me.

The loofah is snatched from my hands, the purple puff looking comically small inside his massive hand. The flashing of his delectable dimples is all the warning I get before he sets to work turning the tables on me.

Brushing a few errant curls over my shoulder, he starts at the curve of my neck then drags the puff down my arm.

Water droplets cling to the dark fringe of lashes surrounding his eyes, and like every other time, I can't look away from the captivating seafoam color. My skin feels alive under both the exfoliating weave of the loofah and the warmth of his stare following in its wake.

The thick, soupy air inside the shower fills my lungs as I struggle not to hyperventilate from stimuli overload.

He continues his washing, paying extra special attention to my breasts and between my legs. I whimper, unable to fight the sensations that have me on the verge of coming. "You need to take your own advice, Caveman." The breathy quality of my voice negates any real authority.

He continues to tease until the water starts to turn cold.

#Chapter41

"LISTEN, BITCH..." I can't stop the twitch of my lips as Em drops into the chair next to mine in the library. The narrowing of her eyes underneath her perfect, *perfect* eyebrows tells me she doesn't find my amusement at her frustrated term of endearment funny.

"Yes, Emma?" I lean forward, resting my chin on my palm and blinking at her with wide-eyed attention.

"Don't be trying to full-name me, missy."

Ooo, someone *is in a mood.* I snicker at my inner cheer-leader, and the murderous glare I get from Em tells me it's probably a good thing I'll be sleeping at home tonight and not the dorm.

"Want to tell me what has your panties in a bunch?" I ask, clicking the top of my highlighter in and out.

"Oh good." A flurry of movement follows in the wake of Q's declaration as she takes the chair on my other side, the legs lifting and slamming back down with a bang. I wince, thankful I chose a table on the more deserted third floor. "You found her."

I close the lid of my laptop and slide it to the side. I get the impression my study time is over if the expectant looks on my two friends' faces are any indication.

"Wow." I feign boredom, the *pop-click, pop-click* of my highlighter only adding to my nonchalance. "You two are in rare form today."

Q beams at me, her ass bouncing around in her seat in her typical ants-in-the-pants excited fashion. But not Em. Nope, she's making this pinched expression that has me wanting to offer her a glass of prune juice.

"You're lucky I love you like a sister, because otherwise I'd kick your ass right now, Kayla."

My brows fly up toward the edge of the ball cap I have pulled low over my face. I lay my arm across the table and reach for Em's hand. "Talk to me."

Her shoulders rise as she takes a deep breath in, turning her hand enough to link fingers with mine. "I miss you."

The walls I keep around me turn into jelly at her admission. This last week since returning home from Kentucky has been insane.

Sunday I slept at home to spend time with Bette since she drove up to bring Mase his car.

The next day E showed up. He said it was to bring Bette home, but since he followed it by spending his entire off day in Blackwell and having meetings with Jordan Donovan, I know what he was really doing—hovering. That didn't stop me from sleeping at home another night so I could see him.

If it were just those two nights, it wouldn't have been a big deal, but…this weekend is NJA's first competition. Instead of working three days a week, I've worked every night, making sure our stunting is solid across the board.

This is where the missing thing comes into play.

I've essentially turned into a commuter, sleeping at the Taylors' at night because they are closer to The Barracks and spending every other second of my free time in the library to keep up with my course load.

"If you think she's bad"—Q waves a hand at Em—"you should hear the guys bitch at Mason about you still not being back at lunch." She scrunches her arms up and pinches her fingers together, miming playing the world's tiniest violin. My gaze shifts to Em and we lose it, collapsing onto the table, our heads knocking together in a fit of giggles.

Minutes pass before we're able to compose ourselves enough to speak, and again, I'm happy we're tucked away upstairs; otherwise a librarian would be lecturing us on keeping the noise down.

"How about this…" I sit up, wiping the tears from my eyes. "Tomorrow's game is a night game"—which I'll be missing as well.

Since Mase and I have been confirmed as a couple again, things have leveled off on the school's Instagram, but I can only imagine the speculation my absence is going to stir up.

"Why don't you both come to Blackwell tonight?"

"Slumber party?" Q perks up like Herkie does when I open up peanut butter. Seriously, best addition to our group.

"What season of *Gossip Girl* are the girls on in their millionth binge?" Em asks, knowing of T and Savvy's obsession with the show.

"I think season three, but whatever—I'll take all the Chuck Bass I can get. It's better than being forced to suffer through *every* movie with a football player as the hero."

A divot forms in the middle of Em's cheek. I appreciate how she's biting back her laughter, but not as much as I do her letting me bitch about T's backhanded support of Mase during our breakup. Sisters.

"Why are you even on campus?" Em asks. "It's Friday."

"I promised Mase I'd meet him after the team's walk-through. Wait…" I hold up a hand, a thought suddenly occurring to me. "*How* did you even know I was here?"

"The Gram," Em and Q answer in unison. *Of course.* I may have said things have leveled out, but they didn't stop. I doubt they ever will.

MASON

#Chapter42

THE ONLY THING that stops me from chucking my phone across the room when the alarm blares early on Sunday morning is knowing it's waking me up so I can see Kay. Fuck I miss my baby. It doesn't matter that it was at my coaxing that she didn't come to yesterday's game—the Hawks kicked Michigan State's ass, in case you were wondering—I still felt her absence.

Kay was going to rearrange her entire schedule to be able to sit in the stands and cheer me on. And yes, I wanted nothing more than to see her there, my name and number on her back, doing just that. But after hearing about everything she needs to handle for a competition, I pulled on my big boy jockstrap and told her to skip the game.

All week, she made seeing me a priority among her hectic schedule. She thinks we're not seeing each other until tonight, but little does she know, she's in for one hell of a shock. All it took was one phone call.

"How do I get a ticket for this thing?" I ask Livi, her hair up in a high ponytail, blue camouflage bow still in place from practice.

"Are you coming?" Her hope and excitement are so strong I can feel them through my phone's screen. Typically, if I make it to a

competition, it's one of the bigger ones that happen during my offseason.

"Trav!" Livi shouts, startling my best friend into dropping the game controller in his hand as he sits next to me.

I swivel the phone so he can see my little tyrant—er, sister—on the screen. Why did Mom have to go and have more kids? I may be the oldest sibling, but the twins are the ones who really run the show. "What's up, Livs?"

"Are you coming too?" She blinks, putting the full weight behind her puppy dog eyes. If my sister has me wrapped around her finger, Trav is practically tattooed on it.

His answer is automatic. "Anything for my favorite girl."

See what I mean?

"Hold up." Noah, never one to know how to mind his business, cuts in. "Where's our invite?"

Trav takes the phone from me as I lean over and roll my eyes in a way that would make Kay proud. "You wanna come to a cheer competition?" I ask in disbelief.

He shrugs his shoulders as if to say Sure, why not?

"Hot girls in tight skirts?" Alex rests his pool cue on the ground and uses it to support him as he leans forward. "Who wouldn't want to be surrounded by all that?"

Kevin high-fives him and Noah holds out a fist to bump. There are days I question why I'm friends with these idiots.

"You do know the majority of those girls are jailbait, right?" These guys act like there isn't a plethora of pussy at their disposal on the reg. Given the bye week bash stories I heard when I got back from Kentucky, this certainly still holds true.

"Doesn't mean we can't enjoy the show," Kev asserts, and they are back to blowing it up with their fists.

What started out as me pumping Livi for information on the competition so I could surprise my girl evolved into a field trip for our whole crew.

"No fair." Noah smacks the back of his hand on the *Cheer*

is her world and she is mine written in white across my chest.
"Why does yours get to be different?"

I level him with an *Are you for real?* look. Noah has *Official
Cheerleader Bodyguard #NJA* printed on his blue camouflage
tee, as do Kev and Alex.

"Come on, No." Kev ambles down the stairs with a
swagger only he can manage. "You know Nova is still trying
to woo his girl. Let him have his moment." He claps me on
the shoulder, the force behind the action enough to have me
taking a step forward. There are days I swear that dude
doesn't know his own strength.

We hang out by the front door, waiting for the others to
join us. With the team playing a night game, the victory party
didn't really get underway until after midnight, so most of
the house is still asleep recovering.

"Man…am I glad I'm no longer a pledge," Grayson says,
kicking his way through the Solo cups littering the floor. The
Alphas are known for having the nicest house on Greek Row,
but that's never the case the morning after a rager.

"Aw, *man*." Noah throws his hands in the air, coffee
spilling out the lid of his to-go cup and onto the sticky beer-
covered floor. "Why do *you* get a different one?"

Grayson chuckles, plucking at the collar of his *Sorry dudes,
the cheerleaders are with me* shirt. "For one"—he lifts a finger—
"I was already going to this thing before y'all decided to join.
And two"—he ticks off another finger—"Smalls got me this
one last year for when I flew down to see her teams compete
at Worlds."

The old staircase creaks as Alex thunders down with the
same speed he exudes on the field. "Let it go, Mitchell," he
advises Noah. "I don't want to listen to you bitch the whole
way down."

"For reals." Trav bites back a huge yawn as he walks a
pretty co-ed to the door. "You trying to hurt my feelings or

something? I thought I was clever as fuck when I was ordering these babies."

"Fuck you, McQueen." Noah shoulder-checks Trav as we make our way out the door.

Trav yucks it up, taunting Noah with his *Don't you wish your sister could cheer like mine?* tee. Kay isn't going to be the only one to freak when she sees our shirts. Livi is going to lose it when she catches sight of the *Livi's 'Brother'* written on the bottom of Trav's. "When you find the Etsy shop, you can pick the design. For now...deal with it."

As much as I love driving the Shelby, today she gets a break to accommodate us all.

"Just wait, No," Grayson shouts over to Noah before he can get in Kev's SUV with Alex. "CK has a special one from Smalls, too."

Trav chortles as the three of us load into his truck to Noah flipping us off. Time to take this shit-show on the road.

"I've never seen so many bows in my life," Alex comments as we follow the flow of people into the arena hosting the UCA Northeast Championships.

"This is nothing. You should see what it's like at Nationals," I say, thinking of when the family all flew out to Dallas to see Livi compete with her old gym a few years ago.

"Cheerleaders *eh-ver-ee-where,* as far as the eye can see." Trav holds up his hands, spreading them out as if to indicate a billboard reading *Take a look at all the cheerleaders.* "Thousands and thousands of them."

"Why haven't we come to one of these things sooner?" Kev asks, taking in the scene around us with wide eyes.

"Because the most time any of us have actually spent with cheerleaders before this year was limited to the bedroom,"

Noah states proudly. Unlike myself, most of the guys have sampled from the cheerleading waters.

The competition is already underway, one of the lower level teams for another gym performing on the blue mat when we step inside the arena. Only about half of the three thousand seats are filled, but I know from experience they will be full by the time they get to the higher level teams.

Grayson scans the stands for Em and Quinn—the two of them came down with Kay and NJA—motioning for us to follow when he finds them. It comes as no surprise that they each sport their own funny t-shirt. Who they are sitting with, however, is a shock.

My mom rises, running a hand down her shirt, smoothing down the silk before leaning forward into our row in front of them to pull me in for a hug. "I'm so happy you came." She pulls back, cupping my cheek in that way only a mom can. "The twins haven't stopped talking about how excited they are since you told Livi your plans."

I wonder what Grace Nova-Roberts would have to say if she knew the real reason you chose to come is to earn you bedroom brownie points.

I ignore my inner coach. Shocker. Yes, the decision might have partially been made in the hopes that my girl will show me how happy she is that I am here in the form of one of her mind-blowing blow jobs, but it doesn't take away from the twins' happiness. As long as they didn't say anything to Kay about my plans, we are all good.

Trav pushes me to the side, causing me to stumble on his way to scoop Mom into a hug. The asshole is such a suck-up.

Introductions and greetings are exchanged by all, and I'm extremely grateful to note Brantley is not in attendance—though it's not like we expected he would be. Not gonna lie, a tiny part of me was afraid he would come if for no other reason than to nail down another chance to talk to me.

There's no way to miss the hard blue eyes studying me as

I pull my seat open. The man is around Mom's age, and based on the fit of his *I'm a proud DAD of a freaking awesome CHEER-LEADER* shirt, he keeps himself in shape. My mouth feels like the Sahara and I have difficulty swallowing when everything clicks into place on *who* he is—Pops Taylor.

*Aw, shit! *chuckles behind clipboard* You thought having to see E or JT was bad? This guy is a firefighter. They'll never find your body.*

My shoulders square. I can do this. I apologized, fixed my mistakes, fought for the girl, and got her back. Jackass in my head may be taunting me about E and JT, but they are good with where Kay and I stand. Why should this be any different?

Resolve in place, I hold out a hand to shake and say, "Mr. Taylor?"

Both my questioning greeting and hand hang there, sweat trickling down my spine as I wait.

"Just so you know…" I wince when he finally takes my outstretched hand, his grip punishing. "If my son and younger daughter hadn't told me about the lengths you went to in order to win my baby girl back, well…"

Did I say sweat was trickling down my back? Nope, now it's a straight-up river. Fuck me, this guy is scary.

"I love Kay very much, sir." The intensity of his glare softens marginally at my admission.

"So I heard." My knuckles protest under the increasing pressure around the hand he still hasn't released. "Just remember…" Another squeeze. "I know *exactly* how hot a fire needs to be to make a body disappear."

Around us, the guys lose it. Full-on bent over, leg-slapping guffaws at my expense. I look to Mom for support, but she instead chooses to sit there in silence, as if her oldest son's life wasn't just threatened.

Looks like someone has dropped in the favorite child rankings, Nova.

They all continue to razz me as we watch the competition, the girls explaining the intricacies of scoring and the jargon associated with competitive cheerleading. With each NJA team to take the floor, the cheering and hooting and hollering from the guys increases. By the time the Marshals are announced, I'm shocked we haven't been asked to leave.

All thoughts of my out-of-control friends fade when I see Kay walk out with two other NJA coaches for the senior teams. God*damn* my girl is fine as fuck.

Even from up here, I can see how good her ass looks in those painted-on dark wash jeans, and I can't help but smirk at the army boots on her feet. I don't need her to say it to know she chose them because the NJA teams are all named after different roles in the military.

COACH PF is written in rhinestone-encrusted white block lettering on her back, and even though I prefer it to be my name and number there, I can admit she works the hell out of her coach's jacket. The stretchy blue camouflage material hugs her curves, and all I want to do is run down these stairs, put my hands on the black panels on her sides, and lift her into my arms.

An ear-splitting whistle sounds behind me, and when I look back, Pops Taylor, Savvy, Grayson, and Em are on their feet, each stretching their pinky and thumb out in the *hang loose* gesture and shouting Tessa's name.

Down on the mat, she is returning the gesture, and when I slide my gaze back to Kay, I see she's doing the same. The guys notice we've captured Kay's attention and jump up, tugging and pointing to their shirts while yelling my girl's name.

Not to be outdone, I pop up as well, and when Kay's eyes flare wide at the sight of all of us making fools of ourselves, I let loose the biggest, shit-eating, dimples out in all their get-yelled-at-to-put-them-away glory.

The unfiltered awe on Kay's beautiful face when she realizes who all came to cheer her teams on is like a punch to the gut. She can be so fucking raw with her emotions, and it slays me every time she lets the vulnerability shine through.

Music starts and Kay whips around to face the mat, breaking away from our stare-down. Throughout the two-and-a-half-minute routine, I can't help but shift my attention to Kay. Her pride and excitement is plain to see. Every time the Marshals hit a stunt, she's shouting, clapping, arms thrown in the air, jumping up and down, shimmy dancing and bumping hips with the other coaches. I can't even handle how fucking adorable she is.

"Damn." Quinn blows out a breath after the Marshals clear the floor and the next team is announced. "They keep performing like that, there's no way they don't repeat at Worlds this year."

"That's *nothing*," Savvy says, crossing her arms and leaning back in her seat like she has a secret. "Wait until you see the Admirals. The stuff Kay has helped them come up with to take back their title is *insane*."

My enthusiastic agreement on Kay's talents when it comes to coaching earns me the first smidge of an expression of acceptance from Pops, and I mentally fist-pump. What I witnessed down in Kentucky was impressive, and I can only imagine what she is capable of coming up with for a whole team. I'm so damn proud of her. I hope one day I can shout it for the whole world to see.

#THE GRAM

#Chapter43

QB1McQueen7: We know we look good, but what we really wanna know is WHICH ONE was her favorite?? *laughing face emoji* *shirt emoji* #Don'tLieMineTotallyIs
picture of Trav, Mase, Kev, Alex, Noah, G, and CK showing off their shirts
@LacesOutMitchell5: Flag on the play. You didn't give any of US a chance to pick a custom phrase! *angry face emoji* #YouCheated #WardrobeOverhaul
@CantCatchAnderson22: OMFG @LacesOutMitchell5 didn't we tell you to stop bitching? #BeLikeElsa #LetItGo
@SackMasterSanders91: ^^What he said
@CasaNova87: Keep dreaming. #SheLikesMineBest
@TheGreatestGrayson37: All you idiots are wrong. MINE is her favorite. #MyTshirtGameIsStrong #Besties

CasaNova87: Cheering on cheerleaders *football emoji* *bow emoji* #MyFavoriteCheerleader #PutMeInCoach #NJAForTheWin
picture of Mase hugging Kay into his chest so only the back of her COACH PF jacket shows

#Chapter44

I RUSH AROUND the dorm making sure I have everything I'll need for the long weekend.

"You and the girls still coming down tonight?" Bette asks. I should feel bad that I'm not looking at her during our video chat, but when I glance at my open laptop, she's just as busy prepping tomorrow's Thanksgiving meal as I am packing.

"Yup. We'll leave straight from the rally, swing by King's to pick up T, then continue on down the turnpike to you guys." That reminds me...

I spin around to make sure Em and Q left their bags and spot them on the floor by the door. *Perfect.*

"Are you excited for tonight?" Bette pauses to lick a streak of mashed potatoes from the side of her hand.

"Yeah." In honor of rivalry week—aka when we play Penn State—the school puts on a big pep rally for the football team. Last year, I opted to skip it to spend more time with my family, but this year I'm going to support the guys.

For as hesitant as I was about letting the football set into my life, I have really grown fond of Mase's teammates. They are ridiculous and genuine and treat me as if I'm just one of the guys. When the bomb dropped that Eric Dennings is my brother, I was afraid I would lose all that.

I shouldn't have been. Not once have they brought up E to me.

"What I want to know is—" There's a *smack* followed by a squeak from Bette, telling me E slapped her ass before pushing her out of the camera's view. With a final zip of my duffle, I lean back against the bed and meet my brother's smirking face. "Am I going to be seeing your boyfriend mugging it up for the camera with you on my newsfeed later?"

*Ooooh, shit! Look at big brother making jokes. Can I ask you something though? Am I the only one shocked he didn't freak that you allowed Mase to post a picture of you two on his Instagram? *holds up hands* Now before you start with the whole you weren't facing the camera thing, your name was, and I would have put money on E losing his shit.*

"I thought you approved of that?" I really hope he's not changing his mind, because as much as saying yes to all the posts the guys made after the cheer competition—where NJA swept the small regional—was scary, I can't find it in me to regret it. Even Pops cracked a smile as each of the guys read their comments out loud as they typed.

"Oh I do." E nods so enthusiastically he looks like a bobblehead. "You keep taking those baby steps."

My head joins his in its up and down motion. I may not be ready to be fully out for the public to see, but as I reach for the new black U of J football hoodie Mase gifted me, I think, *Yes, baby steps.*

My head pops free of the thick cotton when there's a knock on the door to the dorm.

Who could that be? I'm meeting G at the AK house.

I say a quick goodbye to my family and jog down the hall to answer the door. When I do, I'm greeted by the sight of an attractive but unfamiliar brunette. "Hi?"

My greeting may have been awkward and sounded more like a question than anything else, but still, she doesn't return it. Instead she scans me from the top of my head, pausing on the hawk stretching across most of my torso, and down to the tips of my black and white Chucks. I take it from the way her mouth is twisting to the side she's not impressed. Actually... the face she's making kind of reminds me of Bailey's the first time I met all of my roomies.

"Can I help you?" I ask when she continues to stay silent.

Her head swivels left then right before coming back around to face me. "Do you mind if I come in?"

I blink then blink again. I don't know this girl. The only reason I step to the side to allow her in is that more than one resident is sending questioning looks in our direction as they walk past.

There's a gasp when I shut the door, and when I turn to face her again, I can tell her eyes were locked on the bold NOVA #87 printed on my back.

Keeping close to the door, the knob within easy touching distance, I ask, "Who are you?"

She squares her shoulders, determination gleaming in her eyes. "I came to offer a little friendly advice."

Oh-kay...not what I asked.

"That's all well and good, but seeing as I have no idea who the hell you are, I'd say we're *far* from friends." I make a rolling motion with my hand. "Let's try this again."

"I came to warn you."

Oh my god. Again with this? What is with this chick trying to be all ominous?

"Okay, well that's great." I clap my hands in front of me. "But you see, I have somewhere I need to be"—I jerk a thumb over my shoulder—"so I'm gonna have to cut this short."

"You're going to see Mase?"

My hackles rise at her saying my boyfriend's name. Sure, I'm not the only one to call him by the shorthand, but it's the familiar way it rolls off her tongue that rubs me the wrong way.

"I don't see how that's *any* of *your* business. So again…" This time I'm grabbing the doorknob when her next words freeze me on the spot.

"I'd be careful." Her tone takes on an almost syrupy sweet quality. "He doesn't always take no for an answer. I should know."

My blood boils and my muscles seize, a haze of red forming at the edges of my vision. Her identity becomes as clear as the football field under the stadium lights.

"Chrissy? Or do you prefer Tina?" Her body jolts like she was electrocuted upon hearing I know about her duel identities. "I need to know which name to curse if you're really insinuating what I think you are trying to insinuate."

"Why are you so quick to assume I'm lying?" She folds her arms over her chest defensively.

"Because"—I mirror her stance—"I find it hard to believe a guy who asked permission to sleep beside me in only his boxer briefs is a rapist. *Especially* of his own…*girlfriend.*" I spit out the last word, her duplicity making her not worthy of the title.

"Wow." Her mouth holds an O shape a few seconds longer than necessary. "Going right for the R-word."

I roll my eyes, annoyed.

"You know…" I take the two steps needed to eliminate the distance between us, the cloying scent of her perfume invading my senses with each breath I take. "A person accusing another of the crime should really be able to *say* the word."

This time I'm the one scanning her in disgust. Sexual assault and rape are serious issues. So many—*too* many—victims never get justice. There's a stigma associated with reporting the crime, too much victim shaming and blame placed on the wrong party. So when people make false accusations—and my gut screams at me that Chrissy/Tina is one of them—it only hurts those who truly deserve justice.

"Why now?" I ask. "Why come to me instead of saying anything back then?"

She visibly swallows, her eyes darting to the left before answering. "Brantley paid me off to protect Mase."

I bob my head, humming a soft *mmhmm* like we're on the same page. Sure, the money Brantley *obviously* comes from given the mansion Mase's family lives in would be more than enough to pay off a teenage girl and not even feel it. It wouldn't even be the first time a coverup happened to protect a promising athlete. But what I have a hard time believing...

"And, what?" I release my arms, holding them up in an *I'm clueless* gesture. "He laid out the terms for it to be possible for you to come forward the first year his stepson is eligible for the draft?"

Something smells fishy, and it's not the leftover tacos we gorged ourselves on last night.

Chrissy/Tina shifts on her feet, her earlier resolve returning, her jaw tensing.

"Fine." She blows out a breath. "Liam said there was a chance you wouldn't believe me"—ice fills my veins at the mention of my ex—"so he wanted me to ask you what you think the *press* will think."

Sonofabitch. Is this his next step? His texts and internet trolling aren't getting the results he wants so he's trying this? I just wish there wasn't a part of me rioting at the possibilities.

"The press would *crucify* you when the truth came out," I counter.

She shrugs as if it's no big deal. "What's a little bad publicity when your bank account is flush?"

"Liam paid you?" I shouldn't be surprised. His family is loaded too. I never understood why he went to Blackwell Public instead of Blackwell Academy.

"Yup. He DMed me on Insta and made me an offer I couldn't refuse." She does her best—and by best, I mean terrible—impression of a mobster. "He even said he would throw in a bonus if I could time it right with the draft."

I spring back and hurl the door open, grabbing this bitch's arm and throwing her out of my dorm.

Fuck me! This was why I tried to stay away, tried to use the breakup as a clean break. It's too late now. My heart will never be whole without Mase.

My head bangs against the wood of the door, my eyes closing as I take a deep, *deep* breath.

The stories about Mase might not be true, but the ones Liam could tell about me are. We just gotta get through this weekend, and then we can regroup.

#THE GRAM

Chapter 45

CasaNova87: Hawks are gonna win! *football emoji* *trophy emoji* #WeWillShowYouWhoTheRealKingOfTheJungleIs #GoHawks #PennStateIsGoingDown #BeatPennState
picture of Mason, Trav, Kev, Alex, and Noah in their football jerseys

QB1McQueen7: Golden arm! *football emoji* #WelcomeToTheGunShow #GoHawks #PennStateIsGoingDown #BeatPennState
picture of Trav, Mason, Kev, Alex, and Noah pulling up the sleeves of their jerseys and flexing

CantCatchAnderson22: I suggest you eat an extra serving of turkey tomorrow if you plan on catching me before I make it to the end zone this weekend *football emoji* #RunForrestRun #PeepTheUsername #GoHawks #PennStateIsGoingDown #BeatPennState

picture of Noah holding out a football and Alex pretending to eat it

LacesOutMitchell5: They cheer for us. How can we lose? #TheLadiesLoveUs #GoHawks #PennStateIsGoingDown #BeatPennState
picture of Noah with his arms around Em, Quinn, and Bailey

SackMasterSanders91: Don't worry. The turkey will only stretch my stomach tomorrow. I'll have plenty of room to collect those sacks this weekend *football emoji* *turkey emoji* #GoHawks #PennStateIsGoingDown #BeatPennState
picture of Kev smoldering for the camera

Chapter 46

GROWING UP IN A FOOTBALL FAMILY, Thanksgiving has never been a fancy affair. For years, the holiday was spent at one of E's games, followed by a feast at the firehouse. The standard dress code for the day would typically be a pair of jeans or leggings and a jersey. Easy peasy, pass the potatoes.

In the years since Dad died, there have been some changes.

E no longer wears a jersey since it's now a part of his work uniform. Instead, I hook him up with funny shirts, like today's: *Official Turkey Taster*.

The location now depends on if the Crabs have to play or not. E's first season with the team had myself and the Taylors hopping a flight to Dallas. B—Ben Turner, the Crabs' quarterback and E's best friend—has been a staple at our table since then, but luckily they don't play until Sunday this year, so we get to enjoy Turkey Day at home in Baltimore.

Another shift is our ever-changing guest list: I only get one Taylor at the dinner table now. Pops is still at the firehouse since it's their busiest day of the year, and JT doesn't have the time to fly home due to all the responsibilities of the Blue Squad.

But what I lack in Taylors, I make up for in Graysons.

Now that D is down in Kentucky, Mama and Papa G decided they would join us this year. To say G is stoked would be a *massive* understatement.

Shuffling down the hall in my turkey print leggings and *Turkey and pumpkin pie and football—oh my!* t-shirt, I stop to breathe in the delicious aroma wafting up from the kitchen. Wanna know what I'm thankful for this year? Mama G. That woman is a godsend. She insisted that she and Papa G come down last night to help Bette with the cooking, which earned her a *Gobble till you wobble* shirt and me the chance to sleep in.

"Coffee," Em moans when we run into each other in the hall. Yes, we got to sleep in, but we were up late and it's still the morning.

I nod and link my arm with hers. "Nice." I pluck at her *This is my food coma shirt* tee in approval. Sounds like a solid plan for later.

"Thanks. Q and I ordered one for CK too." Of course they did.

Herkie is curled at T's feet on the couch, keeping her company while she does homework on her laptop. Em snaps the band of her leggings at T's *Get your fat pants ready* shirt, stating again how happy she is that she was able to skip the trip home for this holiday. I don't blame her. Dressing up in a prim-and-proper dress to help "press the flesh" is not how today should be spent. No. Thanksgiving is supposed to be all about stuffing your face, watching football, and passing out on the couch.

"Morning, sugah." Mama G greets us, the end of sugar softening into the sound of an H with her southern twang.

"Morning, Mama." Em and I return the salutation, each going in for one of her famous hugs before continuing on our hunt for coffee.

"Have you heard anything from my boy?" Em snorts at the reference to G being called a boy; it's too funny not to.

"No..." I peer at the clock on the stove. "But Mase texted and said their ETA was around one o'clock."

Oh? Did I leave that part out? Sorry about that...but, yes...Mase—and the guys—are also on the list of attendees for this year and are driving down with G and CK. This is the first holiday I've ever spent with a boyfriend, and I can't stop the flutter of excitement that sparks to life in my belly thinking about what it means. Even when I dated the douchewaffle, we didn't do the holiday thing—guess that should have been a sign.

Inviting them all this weekend was a risk, but with the way they came to support me at the cheer competition, donning comical shirts inspired by my own wardrobe, the last of the defensive line I had around my heart crumbled.

The memory of how they cheered and hollered, making such complete fools of themselves I heard about the boisterous group in the stands before I knew it was my friends... my family—it hits me in the feels.

"Is it wrong that I'm hoping they're delayed?" Bette asks as she dances around a stuffing mix while Quinn bastes the turkey.

"No," Mama G answers, laying a comforting hand on Bette's shoulder. "I already had to banish my husband, and it's only going to get worse when the menfolk show up."

Now I understand why Papa G is sitting opposite T watching the parade.

Herkie ambles on over, nails clicking on the floor, tongue hanging out the side of his mouth, brown eyes begging for scraps from the food prep. "Not gonna work, Herk," I say with a scratch behind his ears.

"What did I say?" There's a snort from over by the couch, and if the deep baritone of it wasn't enough of a clue, the twitch to Mama G's lips confirms it came from her husband, already anticipating another dig at his expense. "These men have no patience today."

#Chapter47

BORROWING the Navigator from Brantley's fleet for our trip to Baltimore was both the smartest and the dumbest decision I have ever made—smart because it allows all seven of us to fit in one vehicle, dumb because it has given the guys four hours to razz on me. I should have gone snowboarding with my family. Who cares that technically I'm not supposed to participate in any activity that might result in an injury that could make me ineligible to play?

"Okay…" Trav claps his hands, bringing the attention of the car onto him. "I think it's time we ask what's *really* important about today."

I groan. We're ten minutes away from E's place; haven't they given me enough shit for one day? It's a holiday, dammit.

Reluctantly, I ask, "What's that, Trav?"

"How's Bette's cooking?" He rubs a hand over his belly.

Fucking Travis, forever driven by his stomach.

"Bette's a killer cook." Grayson is the one to answer. "But the turkey will *not* be the highlight of your day."

Leather creaks as Trav spins to see him in the captain's chairs. "Don't hold out on me now, Grayson."

"Just save room for pie."

My stomach grumbles as my passengers start to list off their favorite types of pie and Thanksgiving dishes. The recovery shake I had after our morning workout with the team has long since been digested, and I blow out a sigh of relief when I see the familiar gates and plug in the code given to me by Kay.

"I know most of you are new here," CK says, shutting the car door behind him. "But try not to fanboy too much."

"Yo-ho-ho." Alex slings an arm around CK's shoulders as we make our way up the walk as a group. "Look who's finally getting comfortable enough to give us shit."

"Well…if Kay is cool with you fools being here, it must mean I should be too." CK shrugs under the weight of Alex's arm. He's the most reserved of the group, so it's nice to see him coming out of his shell.

When Kay made the offer for all of us to join her family for Thanksgiving, I knew it was another way for her to prove —not that she has to—how serious she is about making us work and not running. There's still a lot to contend with, but each way we can blend our worlds together will help that much more.

If only Liam Parker could learn to mind his own fucking business. The asshat has infested the comment section of our Instagram feeds like bedbugs.

Grayson opens the front door without knocking, all seven of us pausing at the mouth-watering scents greeting us as we step inside.

A cold nose brushes against the back of my hand, and I bend down to give Herkie a few hello scratches behind his ears, getting a face full of dog slobber in the process.

Grayson doesn't bother to wait, rushing through the house on the hunt for his mama. It still amuses me how this almost-seven-foot giant is such a mama's boy. By the time we follow behind, he has her lifted in one of his deep bear hugs while she squeals, "My baby!"

The open-concept layout of the downstairs makes it easy for me to search out my girl and find her laughing at something with Em and Quinn in the kitchen. I love seeing her happy and carefree like this. With her having been so busy last week with NJA, neither of us wanted to ruin the limited amount of alone time we had by discussing how things have been around campus.

When her gray eyes finally rise to mine, I can't stop the automatic smile that blooms across my face. I only end up grinning harder when she steps out from behind the island and I take in her turkey print leggings and funny shirt.

"Hey, Skittles." I loop my arms around her as soon as she's within reach, pulling her in until there's not an inch of space between us.

"Hey, Caveman." Her arms wind around my neck and she presses her lips to mine in a kiss not suitable for mixed company.

We're both breathing a little heavier when we pull apart, and I'm pleased to see only a thin ring of gray left around her pupils. Looks like I'm not the only one who missed their cuddle buddy last night.

Hooking my finger in the collar of her tee, I say, "Nice shirt, babe."

"I was hoping you'd say that." She bounces out of my hold and into the living room, not stopping until she comes to a collection of gift bags on the ottoman.

"Gifts, Short Stack?" Trav asks, moving in closer. "Isn't that a tradition of a different holiday?"

Kay rolls her eyes, not bothered in the least by my smartass best friend. "Shut up and open your present, QB1."

"Then what?" He gives her his panty-dropper smile and I punch him—not too hard, we have a game in a few days—in his throwing arm.

"How many times do I have to tell you to stop flirting

with my girl?" I growl, not missing the way Kay's lips twitch when I do.

"Poor Nova…" Noah moves to accept the bag held out in his direction. "Afraid of a little competition."

"Sorry, boys." Kay pats both we'll-need-to-bring-in-some-one-from-the-second-string-because-they-will-be-dead   idiots flanking her. "Mase is in a league of his own."

I give a playful nudge—okay, more like a shove—to make room as I reach Kay. "Have I told you how much I love you?" I ask, cupping her face and running a thumb across her lower lip. My dick stirs in my pants when her tongue peeks out and brushes the pad of my finger.

The rustling of tissue paper sounds around us, each person lost in his own private bubble until Noah's shout of "Fuck yeah!" interrupts. Keeping Kay tucked against my side, I turn to see each of the guys holding out their very own funny Thanksgiving-themed t-shirt.

A whiff of peppermint hits my nostrils when one of Kay's curls gets caught in my stubble as she shifts so her head falls over my biceps. "You know what this *really* means, right?" She pushes onto her toes, her soft curves pressing into me, her lips brushing along my jaw as she whispers the words.

I grin, one of her hands coming up to poke a finger into one of my dimples, her eyes telling me to *put them away*. "Does it mean you *finally* accepted my membership application?"

There was a reason I chose to use t-shirts in my campaign to win Kay back. When she gifts you with comical clothing, it means you are one of her people, a member of her mashed-up family.

"I can't have you guys cheating your way in—no matter how sweet the gesture." She jerks a chin at the disrobing men around the room, each excited to exchange their U of J football tees for their new ones. "It's not *official* until *I'm* the one who picks them."

Her eyes flit to the guys again before coming back to me, my grip tightening at the flash of vulnerability that washes over her beautiful features. She brushes away my concern with a shake of her head.

Needing to see the smile instead of her sadness, I place a kiss on the top of her head and push away to join the *Magic Mike* show.

Slowly, I inch the fabric of my shirt up my stomach, and there it is—that familiar flash of heat sparking in my girl's eyes as they take in each pack of my abdominals being revealed.

"Oh, CK," Quinn coos, dangling the plastic handles of an orange gift bag from her fingers.

"We got you one too," Em adds when Quinn doesn't say anything else.

"You know what that means…" Quinn singsongs, running her gaze up and down CK's body, undressing him with her eyes. "Strip, Superman."

I bring attention back to the woman who's currently looking at me like she wants to pour gravy on me and lick it off. If she's not careful, I'll have her stripped naked and under me without a care for who else is in the house. Before I can give in to those urges, I pull on the *Talk turkey to me* shirt, smirking at the innuendo behind it.

"Eric James Dennings, you touch that pie and you won't be getting sex until Christmas!" Bette yells from the kitchen.

"Damn, babe. Why you always got to threaten our sex life?" There's a small whine in E's voice.

"Because it works."

Kay snickers at her brother's arrival, calling out, "I'll never get a niece or nephew if that's what you use for punishment."

"Didn't we agree to not talk about our sex lives, Squirt?" E may not have gotten pie, but he's munching on something when he levels Kay with a *What did I say?* look.

Kay never gets a chance to answer because Bette is shouting at the other new arrival. "Benjamin Turner, if you ever want to be allowed into this house again, you will get your head out of my fridge."

"How the hell do you do that? You can't even see me," B complains.

"She's got mom eyes, B." Kay taps at the corner of her eye as jaws drop when B steps up beside E.

"But this guy"—B pulls E into a noogie—"hasn't knocked her up yet."

"She's spent the past four years raising me." Kay taps under her eye again. "Mom eyes."

"Can we not refer to me potentially impregnating my wife as 'knocking her up'?" E breaks himself free from his friend.

All around, jaws are dropped at the—*normalcy?*—of Kay's family.

Wait…is Kay taking pictures of their bewildered expressions? Oh man, I love the shit out of this girl.

#Chapter48

MAMA G CALLS for everyone to take their places for dinner shortly after the guys all arrive. It's a good thing, because I seriously think Bette would have stabbed B if he tried to pick at the food any longer.

In keeping with our informal theme—and due to the sheer number of people here—we set up everything buffet style along the kitchen counters. Creamy mashed potatoes next to marshmallow-topped sweet potatoes. Sweet corn. Bacon crumble Brussels sprouts. Breaded and fried celery sticks and artichoke hearts. My plate is balanced on my forearm as I start to load it up with sides.

"Short Stack…" Trav stretches an arm over my shoulder to reach for the ceramic dish holding the wet stuffing while I scoop out some of the dry. "I know my boy is lovey-dovey with you, but have *I* told you I love you today?"

SMACK!

"Fuck, bro." Trav rubs the back of his head, soothing away what I'm sure is a sting from Mase's slap.

"Do I need to tattoo it on your forehead? *Don't hit on my girl.*"

I bite down on my lower lip to stifle my laughter at how

overwhelmingly possessive Mase has been. Hence the constant snapping at his best friend.

"I'm just saying..." Trav does a little twirl as he waves a hand over the food, only stopping to blow a kiss at the twenty-five-pounds of golden perfection that is the roasted turkey and its fifteen-pound fried counterpart. "This spread is a wet dream."

"Could you maybe *not* sexualize my mama's food?" G mumbles around the buttermilk biscuit hanging out of his mouth.

Plates loaded—mine with a respectable amount, Mase's with his body weight's worth—Mason guides us to the folding tables and chairs that now separate the kitchen from the living room with a hand on my lower back.

"Before everyone digs in, we have to say grace," E instructs, stopping more than one fork in midair while Bette clicks the television over from the Detroit game to the video chat system we had installed.

The screen splits in half as we wait for the calls to connect to our family members who can't be here with us.

"Dad! You're filthy." Tessa's warm chuckle fills the room when Pops' soot-covered face comes into view.

"Sorry, Teacup." Pops tries to wipe his face but only manages to smear the blackness. "Just got back from a call."

"Deep fryer?" T asks knowingly.

"Deep fryer," Pops says with a shake of his messy-haired head. "When will people learn the turkey has to be fresh and to *not* do it in the garage?"

"Is Pops giving his turkey fryer lesson again?" JT asks when he and D join the call.

"Wouldn't be Thanksgiving without it." I rest my head against Mase's shoulder as he plays with the ends of my hair.

Greetings are exchanged and JT talks shit about how I invited half the football team—cue eye roll over that exaggeration—I can't help but notice the knowing looks Bette casts in our direction.

E, our host and defacto leader for the day, leads us through a short grace and the usual spiel on the importance of family—both blood and chosen—welcoming each new addition sitting around the table. As if on cue, the siren inside the firehouse sounds and we end the call, switching back to the football game.

Dinner passes in a cacophony of conversation, but no one seems to be bothered by it. It's pure chaos and reminiscent of my childhood.

The guys may refrain from bringing up the topic of my brother's identity, but witnessing them giving in to moments of fanboying makes my entire year.

Like when Trav and Alex pinch each other over B complimenting how Trav avoided a sack to complete a touchdown pass to Alex that gave the Hawks the lead over Michigan State last weekend. That particular one is my favorite.

At some point during the meal, Herkie worms his way under the table, and he periodically rests his head in my lap, looking for food. He doesn't get any from me, but he still manages to be more successful than G attempting to eat off Tessa's plate.

"I don't think I've *ever* eaten that much." Q rubs her belly. "Don't tell my *abuela*."

A mixture of pained groans and laughter sounds from around the room, each of us finding a place to get comfortable after we were shooed away from cleanup by Bette and Mama G.

"That was only round one," I tell her, rubbing my own food baby.

"Round one? How many rounds are there?" Mase asks in my ear, shifting us so we're snuggled closer together.

"Um…" I catalog what we eat. We do dinner during the first game, dessert during halftime of the second, and then turkey sandwiches before calling it a night. "Three."

"I knew I loved this house." Trav stretches out with his feet on the ottoman.

"Of course you do. You are ruled by your stomach," G says on a laugh.

"Like you're one to talk." Em playfully slaps G on the thigh her head is resting on.

A chorus of "Preach!" comes from his fellow frat brothers.

"I don't think I could eat another bite," CK chimes in.

"Don't worry, you have time to digest. The next course isn't until halftime." I point to where the Dallas game has just kicked off.

"Heaven…this is what heaven has to be like, right?" Trav's eyes take on a look of wonder.

Conversation starts to putter off as people either focus on the game or fall into a food coma.

I feel myself start to drift toward the abyss of sleep myself when Mase's nose and stubble trail along the side of my neck, shooting tingles down my spine. I wiggle against him, my ass brushing against his growing erection.

"Keep squirming like that and I'll be eating you for dessert." His voice is gravel rough against the shell of my ear.

I feel myself go slick, and if I wasn't going commando, my panties would need changing.

"Promise?" My voice comes out breathy I'm so turned on.

"Say the word and I'll make it a reality."

My eyes close as his teeth scrape down the shell of my ear before pulling the lobe and attached diamond stud into his mouth.

"Right here?" I squeak. Damn it's embarrassing how much he affects me.

His deep chuckle rumbles through my body.

"Well maybe not *right* here." He drags his tongue down my throat in a swirling pattern. "E would kill me *before* I could get you off."

Lust causes my eyelids to grow heavy and shut, but I force them open and cast a look around the room. Across the couch, Em is now asleep on G, and he doesn't look too far away from joining her. T is passed out with Herkie on his luxurious memory foam dog bed—no surprise there.

Trav, Noah, Alex, and Kev are living every little boy's dream in deep conversation with both B and my brother, while Bette is cuddled in E's lap. CK looks to be splitting his attention between the football talk and the Dallas game. What surprises me most is Q is asleep with her head in his lap. Maybe, finally, he'll give the girl a chance—she's crushing on him hard. And Mama and Papa G are FaceTiming with D at the dining room table.

*No one will miss you two if you leave. *twirls hair around a finger and cants head to the side* And that's if they even notice you left.*

With a rare piece of helpful advice from my inner cheerleader, I take one of Mase's bear paws into my hand, his callouses brushing across the smooth skin of my palm, making me think of what they are going to feel like on the skin of my more sensitive areas, and I pull him from the couch.

Being the smart guy he is, he doesn't question, following me silently.

Nobody stops us, but I hesitate after crossing the threshold of my bedroom. If I close the door, it'll not only be obvious where we went but also *what* we're doing. I know I'm nineteen years old and there's nothing wrong with having consensual sex with my boyfriend, but E isn't the most rational person when it comes to me and sometimes he forgets these facts.

What to do? What to do?

My gaze falls to the door of my walk-in closet, and inspiration strikes. Never in my life have I been more grateful to have the kind of closet most girls dream about. The large space has bars and shelving on both sides and the back wall is the perfect display of shoe porn, but its most important feature? The lock on the door.

"I didn't think we had a closeted relationship," Mase jokes as I click the lock home.

God that devilish smirk can get a girl in trouble.

I sure as hell hope so. My inner cheerleader gives a hair flip.

"Funny." I slip my fingers under the hem of his t-shirt and pull it from his body. "We're less likely to be interrupted this way."

"Have I told you I like the way you think?" He matches my actions and has my shirt and bra on the floor before I can blink. Equally efficient, he's on his knees in front of me, pulling my leggings from my body and lifting me into his arms, spinning around.

My back hits the cold marble surface of the island chest of drawers, and I'm pretty sure he's found *his* favorite feature of my closet. With one hand spanning the width of my chest, he presses me flat while using the other to unwrap my legs from his waist. His green eyes scorch me as he stares down at me spread out like *I'm* the Thanksgiving feast.

"*God*...you're so fucking beautiful." His reverent tone slays me. "And you're mine. All *fucking* mine." He kisses up my thigh.

I gasp.

"Mine."

His mouth latches onto my clit, attacking my pussy. A cry rips from my throat at his sudden assault, the hand on my chest rising to cover my mouth, muffling the moans tripping over themselves to break free.

I'm blindsided by an orgasm, sinking my teeth into the heel of his palm.

There's no mercy.

Tongue.

Teeth.

Fingers.

Everything working together to wrest a second climax from me.

Limp, unable to move, I think my body might have dissolved into this marble. The turkey might not have knocked me out, but my boyfriend may have managed to put me into a pleasure coma.

He rises to stand, all cocky grin and lickable abs. His hair is a disheveled mess from where my fingers yanked on the strands.

Eyes locked on mine, he pushes on the band of his sweats until his cock springs free, the length straining toward me. The head is an angry purple, and the wetness of his precum glistens under the lights.

Hands slip under my thighs, holding my legs where they're hooked around his hips, and he plunges inside me in one thrust.

It's my turn to reach for him, my nails scoring his back.

His mouth covers mine and I can taste myself on his tongue.

"Mase."

"This is gonna be hard and fast, baby." His words are as much a threat as they are a promise.

My back slides across the tabletop as he drills into me, his arms flexing in an effort to hold me in place.

We continue to kiss, swallowing down each other's moans.

Without warning, his orgasm hits, his release dragging out another from me.

He collapses on top of me, still managing to hold most of

his weight off me and balancing on his elbows to keep from crushing me.

"Now that is something to be grateful for," he whispers against my throat.

I may not be able to manage the function of speech right now, but I agree one hundred percent.

#Chapter49

I'M PRETTY sure if I eat one more bite of food, my stomach will literally explode. If Coach Knight ever found out how far off the rails from the nutritionist-approved meal plan we went today, he would kill us—or worse, bench us.

It all started with *the* most amazing Thanksgiving Day feast I have ever seen—cooked by real people and not caterers—and ended with the most delicious dessert spread known to man. Holy shit Bette and Mama G can cook, and bake.

I think I may have taken Papa G's *I'm just here for the pie* shirt to heart, as I had a piece of every type offered. And oh the pie; pumpkin, apple crumble, sweet potato, pecan, and—Kay's favorite—pumpkin cheesecake. Sugar coma central right here.

Boisterous laughter sounds from the kitchen, and the leather of the couch creaks as my head lolls to the side to check it out. Kay sits on the counter surrounded by my team-mates. A chorus of *slap-slap-slap-slap* sounds as she rock-paper-scissors Kev and Alex over who gets the last slice of pie.

Kay holds up her fist in victory as her rock trumps Alex's scissor, her hips shimmying in place, bringing back memories from the closet. Her celebration cuts off when Kev takes his turn and covers her rock with his paper, her head dropping back, blonde and colored curls brushing the countertop behind her.

Grayson tries to swoop in and steal the plate right out of Kev's arms, but the defensive end dances away, doing his best to keep his prize out of reach.

The uninhibited smile on Kay's face and her eyes dancing in laughter make it easy to see her happiness clear across the room.

"It's nice"—the couch dips as Tessa plops down beside me, arm reaching across my body to point at Kay now taking on Noah and Trav in RPS—"to see her be PF with new people."

I shift my gaze, following the length of Tessa's arm, meeting her blue eyes with an arched brow. "Haven't you guys harped that Kay and PF are the same person?"

"In identity, yes, but in personality..." She pauses, glancing at Kay and back again. "No." She sighs. "Not for the last few years anyway."

Why is it whenever Tessa Taylor talks to me in private, I feel like she's my confidential informant?

"She's always been like that"—I circle a finger at my victory-dancing girlfriend—"with us." I swear Kay talks more shit to me than my teammates.

Slowly, a smile curls Tessa's lips. "Why do you think my brother pushed her to give you a chance?" *He did?*

I catch a whiff of peppermint seconds before Kay climbs over the back of the couch and into my lap, fitting herself between my spread legs. It doesn't do my already stuffed stomach any favors when she leans against my chest.

"Whatever happened to sisters before misters, T?" Kay asks Tessa, making me laugh with her mind-reading of our conversation.

"Eh." Tessa waves off the question. "Whatevs."

Kay eyes her sister for a few seconds before rolling her

eyes and shifting her attention to the Atlanta game on the television.

My arms wrap around her middle, pulling her tighter to me despite the protest from all the pie swimming in my gut. I rest my face against the side of hers, placing a kiss to her temple and breathing in the intoxicating scent of Kay mixed with me—my favorite.

"Oh, come *on*, Dennings," Kay shouts at JJ Dennings, a wide receiver for Atlanta, when he bobbles the ball for an incomplete pass.

"What I do?" E asks as he and Bette walk out of the side hallway that leads to the gym, both their clothes slightly rumpled and askew. Looks like Kay wasn't the only member of the Dennings family sampling from a side menu today.

"Not you. JJ." Kay thrusts an aggravated hand at Atlanta lining up for a third down. "He was late off the line and dropped a pass a preschooler could have caught."

"Yeah, baby!" Noah does his best Austin Powers impression. "We love it when you talk football."

Kay giggles, ignoring him to trace my tattoo instead. As the soft pads of her fingers dance along my skin while the game is on, I can't imagine anything better than this.

#THE GRAM

#Chapter50

TightestEndParker85: I wonder who she REALLY will be rooting for this weekend @UofJ411? Worried it's not you @CasaNova87? #AskingForAFriend #IHadHerFirst #HawkHunting
side-by-side picture of Kay in a Penn State jersey and a shot of Kay and Liam from high school

UofJ411: Peep my stories for our poll on this. #WhoWillSheChoose #FirstLoveOrNewLove #CasanovaWatch #CasanovasGirl
REPOSTED — side-by-side picture of Kay in a Penn State jersey and a shot of Kay and Liam from high school — TightestEndParker85: I wonder who she REALLY will be rooting for this weekend @UofJ411? Worried it's not you @CasaNova87? #AskingForAFriend #IHadHerFirst #HawkHunting
@Notnow.imreading: NOVA all the way! #GoHawks
@Oamberwhereartthou: The real question is will she be at the game? #EmptySeat

@Ofbooksandportkeys: Is it too early to tailgate?
#BestSeatInTheHouse

#Chapter51

I THROW AN ARM OUT, slapping it around until I feel my phone. Cracking one eye open, I tap the button that will silence the blaring alarm, the screen shifting from the clock to the notification banners that accumulated over night. I've gotten really good at ignoring them but can't help noticing a tag from a particular account.

TightestEndParker85.

Motherfucker.

Liam Parker.

Kay once jokingly likened me to herpes, but Liam Parker is the real genital wart.

Against my better judgment, I thumb it open, the case protecting my phone groaning as I do my best to choke the life out of it like it's Parker's neck.

It's one thing to taunt me, to come after me through social media in an effort to drum up media attention. Even Brantley has been drinking the *no such thing as bad publicity* Kool-Aid.

So...no. Starting beef with *me* isn't Liam Parker's mistake. Involving Kay, trying to get to me *through* her is. *There better not be any fucking text messages on her phone from him.*

Pain. Dismemberment. Murder. All these cycle through

my thoughts until the soft curves of Kay's body brush mine as she stretches beside me.

"Too early," she mumbles into her pillow.

I can't help but smirk, tossing my phone to the side and hooking an arm around her middle to anchor her to me. I nose aside her curls and place a kiss on her neck, breathing her in. "Go back to sleep, babe."

She mumbles something I can't quite make out but snuggles deeper into the bed.

I pull back, the bold lettering of my last name stretched between her shoulder blades calling to me like a siren. There's another incoherent mumble from my girl as I sketch the black type before extracting myself from the bed.

Herkie lifts his head as I slip into a pair of gray sweatpants, the white band of my Calvins visible above the elastic waist, not bothering with a shirt.

With a soft whistle, I motion for the dog to follow as I set off in my search for coffee.

The rich aroma of java already hangs in the air as I descend the stairs into the living room. I'm not surprised to find my boys awake; we need to leave in a couple of hours to get back to campus in time for the team's final walkthrough practice before tomorrow's big game.

Mr. Grayson slides a mug across the island to me as I approach, and Mrs. Grayson asks what I would like for breakfast. I glance around, looking for Grant, surprised he isn't in the kitchen. He hasn't been far from his parents since we arrived yesterday.

Sipping the rich French roast, I lean against the counter, content to shoot the shit, then I spot Grayson loitering at the edge of the living room, arms crossed, attention firmly on where E and Bette sit on the couch. He's way too intense for such an early hour.

"Well at least he's hot." The sound of the unfamiliar voice snaps me out of my half-awake, half-asleep state, bringing my attention to the blonde eyeing me from the television screen. "Muscles go a long way in helping us forget the bullshit that follows you fools."

Is this chick talking about me? And why does she look so familiar?

E and Bette spin to see who the woman is talking about, the former's hair a disheveled mess. It looks more like he was running his hands through it in frustration than messy from sleep.

E jerks a chin for me to join them before saying to the blonde, "And what would your husband have to say about you ogling men a few years your junior, Jordan?"

The blonde, or I guess Jordan as E called her, laughs —like throws her head back, hand smacking her chest type laughter. When she finally composes herself, she resettles on her own couch, curling one of her legs underneath her butt and letting the other dangle while wiping the last tear from her eye before focusing back on E.

"Well seeing as said husband is currently sleeping off the effects of me running my tongue down the grooves of his own six-pack, I *think* Jake will be fine."

Bette tries to cover her snort, and a handful of "Oh, shit" and "*Good* morning" come in response to that particular comment.

E rubs at the ridge of his brow, Bette cupping his knee to ease his agitation. "It's moments like this I feel sorry for your brothers, Donovan."

Oh, shit! Now I know why I recognize her. This is Jordan Donovan. She and her PR firm All Things Sports are the crème de la crème when it comes to managing an athlete's publicity. If Brantley were to hear I had face time with her, he would cream his pants.

"Please." Jordan waves a hand, brushing off the comment. "Don't make me regret leaving my bed with my very naked, very *sexy* husband to talk strategy with you by going all *we are brothers we stick together* on me, Dennings."

I'm not quite sure what's going on. I want to let myself be entertained by it all, allow it to distract me from this morning's drama, but I get the feeling that is the reason for this virtual pow-wow.

"This"—I bounce a finger between E and the television—"have anything to do with the bullshit I woke up to?"

The rage I'm starting to associate with one Liam Parker starts to bubble in my gut, spreading through my veins and causing the tips of my fingers to tingle.

"Listen, Eric." Jordan's expression changes from playful to serious as she shifts to rest her elbows on her knees. "I know technically *you're* my client, but as a sister of overprotective brothers, I will *not* have this conversation without Kay."

My lips twitch. I can't help it—I'm amused. Kay told me about how E foisted Jordan upon her after the UofJ411 account confirmed Kay's identity and her connection to E. She also told me how Jordan allowed her to call the shots on how they handled the fallout.

"Well I'm not waking her up." E flattens a hand to his chest for emphasis.

When Bette leans forward to see past her husband, the twinkle in her eye spells trouble for me. "That means you're up, lover boy."

My inner coach's voice cackles between my ears.

#Chapter52

BEFORE I HAVE to risk life and limb by waking up a sleeping Kay, our call with Jordan comes to an end when two miniature versions of her bombard her with hugs and squeals of "Mommy!"

Mrs. Grayson calls out that the omelet she made me is ready, and I thank her as I settle in on a stool at the island to eat. I moan as the savory flavors of the fluffy eggs and the spicy sausage roll over my tongue.

Some of the intensity of the morning dissipates as Bette corrals my teammates to a chair she set up by the back door, claiming the glass allows for the perfect lighting for hair shavings. She decreed there was no way we would be playing a rivalry game without representing our team pride properly.

Flying hawks, footballs, and numbers all get etched, along with her doling out fresh cuts. From over Alex's head, she meets my gaze, and I nod, telling her I'm down for my own refresh. For one, it looks sick as hell, and two, Kay loves to trace the designs as much as my tattoo. It's a win-win.

Herkie *woofs* and I spin to see a sleepy Kay coming down the stairs, curls a wild mess around her head, fist rubbing the sleep from an eye.

She wiggles her fingers in response to the collective "Good morning", yawning wide as she does so.

"Why am I not surprised?" Kay points at Bette hard at work on shading out a goalpost on Noah's skull.

"Don't worry," Bette says, not even looking up from what she's doing. "I already have the red and black pulled to add to your school spirit."

Kay accepts a mug from Mr. Grayson before walking the last few steps in my direction, settling herself between my spread knees, leaning against me with a sigh.

Around us, the guys make kissy faces and noises when I kiss the crown of her head, but Kay ignores them, sipping her coffee while I not so subtly flip them the bird. The assholes are just jealous.

"I don't know if going to the game is the best idea." E's comment causes a frown to pull on Kay's lips and a crease to form between her brows.

My muscles tense. Selfishly, I want Kay there cheering me on. It's been a few weeks since I've been able to look up into the stands and see her there, and I miss it. But, not gonna lie, a small part of me wonders if E has the right idea. Kay has only *just* started to take steps forward in broadcasting our relationship to the general public. Could this game have us starting over from square one?

So far, things have all been contained to social media, but this weekend is a big deal. Rivalry weekend is a massive ratings boost throughout college football. With only three teams in all of D1 football—U of J, Penn State, and Alabama—having one loss, the outcome of our game against the Nittany Lions could very well determine who will get a chance to play for a spot in the National Championship.

Who's to say the press wouldn't eat up this extra drama with a spoon?

"Why not?" Kay asks.

E gives me a *Show her* look. I nod, retrieve my phone from the counter, and pull up the fucknut's post.

The silence in the room grows until it feels heavy, nobody saying a word while we wait to see how Kay will react. It could go a multitude of ways. She could get pissed, sad, or what I fear most—scared.

I slip my hand under hers where it rests on my thigh, rubbing across the peridot band on her finger. Each bump of the ring's gems helps slow the erratic beat of my heart, the birthstone band an anchor that ties us—not just her to me, but me to her—together.

I never expected one person could mean so much to me. Then I met Kay. She was a game changer for me, taking everything I thought I knew before and turning it on its head.

Kay's jaw pops as she grinds her teeth, the sound of scraping enamel an audible representation of her frustration. She flicks her gaze from the screen to her brother and back again. Her chest expands with a deep inhalation and she tips her head back, the crown of it pressing between my pectorals as she looks back and up at me, storm clouds raging in her gray eyes. "Do you have a jersey with you?"

My own jaw drops; I was not expecting the question in the slightest. "No." And fuck me if I'm not overwhelmingly disappointed by that fact.

Kay continues to hold my gaze as she thinks, mouth shifting left to right, a little V appearing between her brows as she does. "Okay." She nods almost subconsciously. "Remind me we have a picture to take before you leave."

#THE GRAM

#Chapter53

CasaNova87: Me, @TightestEndParker85. That's who she'll be rooting for—ME! #StopPostingOldPhotos *side note* Is this enough proof we're official @UofJ411? #Kaysonova #MyNumber1Cheerleader #GameChanger #HawksFanForLife
picture of Kay wearing an *I like the game but I LOVE the player* shirt, Mason standing behind her with his arms wrapped around her middle, both smiling at the camera

UofJ411: Hell yeah it is @CasaNova87 #CoupleGoals #Kaysonova
REPOSTED—picture of Kay wearing an *I like the game but I LOVE the player* shirt, Mason standing behind her with his arms wrapped around her middle, both smiling at the camera—CasaNova87: Me, @TightestEndParker85. That's who she'll be rooting for—ME! #StopPostingOldPhotos *side note* Is this enough proof we're official @UofJ411? #Kaysonova #MyNumber1Cheerleader #GameChanger #HawksFanForLife
@Cr8zysockbookblock: Oh shit! #ItsAboutToGoDown #RivalryWeekend #CasanovaWatch #Kaysonova

@Dainer81: About damn time! #FinallySomeAnswers #CasanovaWatch #CasanovasGirl #Kaysonova

@Doterragirl2020: Check out that ship name! #TooCute #CasanovaWatch #Kaysonova

@Filthylittlereader: Football royalty? #ILikeIt #Kaysonova #KingAndQueenOfFootball

@Fununderthecovers: Can't wait for Saturday. It's like a modern-day duel #ThemBeFightingWords #BattleOnTheGridiron #CasanovaDontPlay #Kaysonova

#Chapter54

UNLIKE THE FOOTBALL TEAM, the cheerleaders don't stay in a hotel the night before a game, so the girls and I got to spend a few extra hours in Baltimore after the guys left before we had to return to campus.

Em and Q do have a short practice with the Red Squad, but then the rest of the night is ours.

After dropping them off at the practice gym, I drive to our dorm and open a bottle of Moscato as soon as I put my bags in my room. I'm not typically the type of person to drink by myself, but I am still mildly ticked off from earlier, and it's best for all parties involved if I take the edge off.

Glass filled close to the top—no restaurant pour for this girl—I take it and my laptop into the living area, set both on the coffee table, and take a seat right on the floor. I click the television on for background noise and open up a video chat to JT.

Instead of saying hello once our call connects, he asks, "Why do I get the feeling I should gird my loins?"

"Because you're too smart not to know I'm annoyed with you at the moment." I rest an elbow on the table and prop my chin in my hand.

We sit in silence, the face time through the screen enough

to clear the air between us. Yes I'm annoyed, but it's more from my independent nature than anything else stirring up those feelings.

A full minute goes by before JT asks, "You ready to admit this is a good plan?"

No.

"I don't like feeling like I need a babysitter." It's one of the reasons I chose to lie low and keep mostly to myself after everything went down four years ago.

"Can you *please*"—he makes prayer hands—"have me on the phone when you call him that?"

I roll my eyes.

"In all seriousness, Kay—"

"I hate when you call me Kay," I grumble.

"—Carter is a good guy. He agreed to go with you tomorrow as a favor for me, so at least try to keep those two things in mind and not give him *too* hard of a time."

Where I went with the *put my head down and hope the world will eventually get bored with me* strategy, JT took on a more proactive approach. He sought out, not necessarily the most popular, but definitely the most powerful person in our school to put an end to the in-person bullying.

"Doesn't he have a race to run?" I try again to brush it away, to minimize. Maybe if I downplay the circumstances enough, they'll go away on their own.

Do I need to drug test you or something? Because that logic has me convinced you are smoking the hippie lettuce.

"He does." JT nods, lifting a beer bottle and chugging some down.

Looks like I'm not the only one who needs a drink.

"Carter will go with you so you can mack down on your football player..." He makes highly exaggerated kissy faces, his mouth opening and closing as if in slow motion, a noise almost like dripping water sounding every time his lips form an O.

"I hate you." The pull I feel in my cheeks tells me there's no way he's going to take me seriously. "I also feel sorry for any girls you kiss if *that's*"—I circle a finger around his face—"your technique."

"Don't you worry about my technique, PF." He gives me two shakes of a backhand. "Anyway…once you're done in the tunnels and safely in your seat, Carter will head out."

I run a hand through my hair, leaving the ends pinched between my fingers and focusing on how the brightened red and pink look in contrast with the added black streaks. Bette really did go above and beyond with the school spirit.

I'm two glasses of wine deep by the time my roommates arrive home happy, loud, and full of an energy only this weekend tends to breed.

Quinn dances into the room, twirling around and picking my goblet up off the table to gulp down the last ounce left inside. "You started without us," she says with a pout.

"What can I say?" I pop a shoulder. "My brothers drive me to drink."

"I take it you talked to JT?" Em takes the open cushion next to Q.

"Yeah." I reach for the glasses Bailey sets before me and start to fill them while she works to open another bottle of wine. "I promised to play nice with King tomorrow," I say to Em before changing the subject by asking Bailey, "How was your break?"

She spent the holiday with one of their other teammates on Red Squad, and I was relieved when I learned of her Thanksgiving Eve plans because it gave me a legitimate reason not to extend an invitation to E's. My brother's identity may be out there for all the world to see, but knowing about my connection to him and being invited to meet him are two very different things.

I'm doing my best to come out of hiding, to embrace the "PF" full-time. Don't let how I invited Mase's teammates to dinner fool you; I am *very* selective on who gets to enter the inner sanctum of my life.

"It was good. The bars were packed, the food was yummy, and I got a *killer* dress for the AK party tomorrow night." Bailey retrieves a gold shopping bag from her room and pulls out a cold-shoulder red bodycon dress that will certainly have heads turning her way at the Alpha house. "Are you wearing the shirt from the picture Casanova posted earlier?" she asks after hanging her dress on her bedroom door.

I do my best not to frown at hearing his old nickname.

Guess Mason's Instagram post is making the rounds. Sure, I can admit the thought of my face—unhidden—out there for all the world to see on an account with thousands of followers makes me nauseous, makes me feel like I'll be mainlining Pepto Bismol for the foreseeable future.

But…

I was pushed too far. I tried to walk away to protect Mase, but he loves me enough to not let me. I'm not sure if I deserve a love like that, but if I'm ever going to feel worthy of it, I need to not be scared of it.

You seriously need to tell him about that bitch showing up and her lies. Yes, I do, but that can wait until *after* the game. He's going to go postal.

"No." I jump up and skip to my room to get my own show and tell. "I had this"—I spin to show the custom shirt—"made special for the Black Out." It's not one of the new ones from Mase, but I have a feeling he'll approve.

"Black to go with your new hoodie?" Em teases with an eyebrow waggle.

One home game a season, the U of J does a Black Out game. With Penn State's tradition of having a White Out game, the Hawks love to save their version for when we play the Nittany Lions.

The Black Out is my favorite game to attend. The football team, cheerleaders, dance team, band, and even the mascot get a refresh to a black uniform. Fans are instructed to wear head-to-toe black—hence my new team hoodie—and it all combines to make the atmosphere inside the stadium almost eerie to experience.

Wine flows, chick flicks are watched, and laughter to the point of bellyaches is had. Internet trolls and psycho exes aside, this weekend has been one hell of a good time, and there are still two days to go. Gotta love a holiday weekend.

#THE GRAM

#Chapter55

TheQueenB: Everyone thinks the @AlphaKappaUofJ house is the place to be. Yes that's true for our @UofJFootball victory party after we beat those Nittany Lions...but this right here is where it really begins @UofJ411. This is where our @CasaNova87 gets his pregame kiss from his queen. #PuckerUp #CasanovaWatch #CasanovasGirl #FootballRoyalty #Kaysonova
picture of the tunnel outside the U of J's locker room

#Chapter56

THERE'S an energy inside the locker room, different from any other game this season. It's like a buzz that sounds at a frequency only the team can hear.

Rivalry.

Do or die.

The spot in the Big Ten conference game up for grabs.

The culmination of our season at stake.

That's the situation for the team.

But this game? It's personal.

I want to be able to look into Liam Parker's eyes after it's over and make sure he knows *I* beat him. I want him to know no amount of shit-talking, taunting, or threats was enough to get under my skin.

My only regret? That I'm not on defense—that *I* can't be the one tackling his ass to the ground.

Good thing the captain of the defense loves our girl too, huh?

Most of the time I want to tell my inner coach to stick it where the sun don't shine, but look at him coming up with something good on fourth down.

We have a few hours to kill until kickoff, most of the team is spread around the clubhouse relaxing and trying to get in the right head space for the game. One of the perks of being such a successful football program is our boosters are super generous, as evidenced by our state-of-the-art facilities. Sure, we have your typical gym and physio rooms, but we also have two pool tables and a media room filled with leather couches and recliners, large flat-screens, and multiple gaming systems.

I make my way over to the media room, choosing an open seat as close to Kevin as I can get.

"You ready for this?" he asks, gaze flitting to mine before returning to his game of Madden.

"You know it. These fuckers don't stand a chance against us."

All around, hawk cries echo my words, bringing a smile to my face. This, this right here is one of my favorite parts of the game; the camaraderie, knowing these are my people. We win and lose together—though none us of plan on losing today.

"Kev." I shift forward in my seat, resting my elbows on my knees. "There's something I need you to do for me." The others in the room, sensing my shift from playful to serious, stop what they're doing and give me their undivided attention.

Kev's dark gaze bores into me. He sets the controller off to the side and clasps his hands to hang between his knees. "Name it."

"I need Parker to still be feeling today's game a week from now." I lift my hat from my head, fidgeting against the tantrum begging to be set free.

"Because of Kay?" He narrows his eyes, trying to read me the same way he does a quarterback on the field.

I nod. They knew some of the drama surrounding Kay and her ex—hard to avoid when it's splashed all over social media—but they didn't fully *understand* it until they got to witness firsthand E's reaction to Liam's taunt yesterday. For E to ask Kay—a lover of all things football and a genuine fan—

to skip attending today to avoid any additional Liam drama spoke volumes.

Kev pushes himself up from his chair, steps smooth and confident as he strolls through the open doors to the media room and into the main locker area. His feet land on one of the benches as he jumps onto it and draws the eyes of those closest to him. "Yo, defense!" The hard boom of his voice resonates with a captain's authority. "Bring it in."

His tone brooks no room for argument, though it's the aura of *pissed off* radiating from a player known for being one of the most level-headed that has the rest of the team closing in.

"I'm sure this request won't come as too much of a hardship for you..." He pauses to make eye contact with each of his guys. "You can think of it"—his mouth twists to the side, his head tilting left then right in thought—"as extra *motivation*."

Over the crowd gathered in front of him, Kev meets my eye, and the dangerous smirk on his lips has me grateful we play for the same team. I jerk my chin in brotherhood.

"Tonight we bring the pain to number eighty-five." Kev folds his arms over his refrigerator-sized chest. "He's messed with one of our own and needs to be taught a lesson." This time when he flicks his gaze to me, a few heads turn in my direction. "Tonight...if he's tackled under you, make sure you toss out a nice 'That's for Kay.'"

"Nova's girl?" one of our D-backs asks.

"Yes," I answer.

"It's time we remind this motherfucker," Kev declares, "*no one* fucks with a Hawk without facing the rest of the flock."

At some point after Kev's little inspirational speech, Coach Knight emerged from his office to tell us to "calm the fuck down" and to "save that energy for the field".

Shortly after that, Trav showed me the most recent repost on UofJ411, this one a shot of where I collect my pregame kiss from my girl.

My annoyance over the invasion of privacy is overridden by my worry that maybe E's concerns weren't an overreaction. I need more information.

ME: I need to know how much of a risk Liam Parker really is.

My fingers drum on the back of my phone as I wait for JT to respond to my text.

CHEER BOY: Oooo, you said his name.

Not the response I was hoping for.

ME: So???

CHEER BOY: *GIF of Lord Voldemort*

ME: You two and your whole He-Who-Shall-Not-Be-Named stuff.

CHEER BOY: Don't you dare judge us *waggles finger* You, sir, are a Potterhead as well.

Smartasses. I'm surrounded by smartasses.

ME: Fine. I concede. Now can we talk about the asshat?

CHEER BOY: Sure. The douche-canoe is a pussy.

I bark out a laugh, which draws Trav's attention, and Mr. Nosey Nelson leans to the side to read over my shoulder.

ME: I know you asked your boy to escort Kay to the tunnels.

CHEER BOY: You're talking about King playing chaperone for when PF meets you to shove her tongue down your throat for "luck"?

CHEER BOY *GIF of Bugs Bunny kissing Michael Jordan*

"I'm coming with you next time you go to Kentucky—this guy seems like my kind of people," Trav says, pointing at my phone.

Just what I need, these two teaming up.

ME: James Taylor!

The use of his full name has my phone buzzing with a FaceTime call instead of a text. I swipe to answer but hold up a finger to tell him I need a minute to find somewhere quieter, more private.

I slip into one of the unused physio rooms and wait until I hear the door click behind me before saying, "Okay, talk to me."

JT eyes me from the six-inch screen. He's in his UK cheerleading uniform, and behind him I recognize the practice gym. "I would have been more impressed if you dropped my middle name in there, but I'm not quite sure I'm grasping what you're asking?"

Honestly...I'm not either. Maybe I'm letting my feelings breed paranoia.

"Why did you ask *King* specifically? Why not Grayson? He'll be at the game." This is the part I can't make sense of.

"Ugh." JT groans and runs a hand through his dark red

hair. "Look…" He blows out a breath. "Neither one of us has enough time to get into the nitty-gritty of it, but the Cliffs-Notes version is King has a lot of…shall we say…power in our town."

"Why?" I jump in to ask.

"That's not important." He waves off my concern. "What is, is that I believe if for some reason you guys *do* run into Liam, the sight of Carter might be a strong enough message to keep him in line."

I don't know what bothers me more, the thought of having a run-in with Liam or that he might be more of a threat than I realize. Why else would someone "powerful" be needed?

#Chapter57

U OF J vs Penn State.

Rivalry game.

Black Out.

Winner takes the East Division of the Big Ten.

All week, the sportscasters have speculated, deeming it *the* game of the season.

If only they knew how this is *so* much more than a simple rivalry game.

From the things Mase has told me, there was bad blood between him and Liam before I entered his life. Now though? Learning about my own history with the twatwaffle combined with the recent taunts to drum up drama—using me—it makes this *personal* for Mase.

"I feel like I'm attending a funeral with all this black," King comments over the brim of his Espresso Patronum to-go cup.

I side-eye him as we weave our way through the under-belly of the football stadium, not appreciating the parallels he's drawing at the moment.

"Listen, Your *Majesty*"—his lips twitch at the nickname—"I love this game, so don't hate."

We flash our badges at the last security guard before the locker rooms and I shoot off a text to let Mase know.

"I would have thought *you* of all people would like it, King." Matte black is the signature color of the Royals.

He chuckles then I think he gestures that he's going to hang back, but I can't be too sure because the doors to the locker room swing open and out walks my hot-as-fuck boyfriend. *Holy shit!* Seeing him in his football uniform never fails to turn me on, but the Black Out gear ups the wetness factor in my panties to uncomfortable levels.

The jersey is black with thin red stripes down the shoulders and red and gray lettering. His ColdGear Under Armour shirt is also black and has a delicate gray weave to it, giving it the illusion of chain mail armor.

Then there's the greatest fashion invention ever: football pants. This particular pair is black with a single skinny red stripe down the sides.

Do you think it's inappropriate to request that he turn around so we can ogle his butt? Asking for a friend.

I let my inner cheerleader's question marinate—it has hella merit—as I continue my downward inspection to the black socks and cleats. The only thing he's missing is the revamped black helmet that has a badass outline of a hawk in gray.

"Eyes up here, babe."

My head snaps up, a blush heating my cheeks as I meet sparking seafoam green eyes. The matching set of dimples on display tells me Mase is enjoying my lustful attention.

"Careful..." Hands curl around my hips and he continues to step forward until my back comes in contact with the wall. "I do have a game to play." The husky timbre of his voice tells me how disappointed he is with this fact.

I run my hands over his shoulder pads, traveling across his chest then down his stomach, fanning my fingers along the muscles flexing under my touch. "After?" My question is full of promise as I peer at him from beneath my lashes.

"Without a doubt, I'll be tasting your rainbow later, Skittles."

The flush of heat spreading throughout my body has nothing to do with the multiple layers I have on and everything to do with his corny, dirty words.

"Promises, promises." I walk my fingers back up his body, hooking one in the V of his jersey's collar and pushing onto my toes. Before I can close the gap between us, Mase pulls back, stepping away until a foot of space separates us.

"Show me." He wiggles a finger in front of my chest.

I could play dumb, could feign having no idea what he wants, but I'm not that mean. Well…maybe a little bit. I did refuse to text him a picture of my shirt earlier like I typically do, but is it really so wrong to want to witness his reaction in person?

Doesn't mean I'm not going to draw this out as much as I can.

I turn to give him my back, gathering my hair in one hand and pulling it over a shoulder so the NOVA #87 on the back of my Black Out hoodie is displayed in all its claimed-by-the-caveman glory.

"Kay," Mase warns.

Ooo, someone is all extra growly today. I like it.

I bite down on my lip to hold in my smirk as I spin back around.

His intense stare is like a physical caress. He starts at the top of my black waffle pom beanie, stopping briefly at the flesh pinched between my teeth, the widening at the corners of his eyes giving away how much he wants to be the one doing the biting. He continues his downward inspection, tongue peeking out to stroke across his lower lip as he takes in the way my black fleece-lined leggings hug my legs and down to the tips of my insulated tall black Hunter boots.

It's an effort to swallow as his burning gaze locks onto where my fingers worry the hem of my—his—hoodie.

Layer by layer, I lift the sweatshirt then the thick wool sweater beneath it until...*finally*...I reveal the *My heart is out on that field* shirt I had made. There's also a football with a heart and an 87 in the middle.

I don't blink, my eyes stinging as they dry out, unable to look away. How can I when he brings a thumb up to stroke across his lower lip? I mean come on! He already looks like a wet football god dream; does he really have to pull out a move straight from the hot guy handbook?

"And mine's in the fucking stands." His voice comes out all gravelly as he lunges toward me. Hands cup my ass as he scoops me into his arms, the impact of my back slamming into the wall as he presses me against it dissolving away as his mouth claims mine.

He sucks my bottom lip into his mouth, his tongue licking across the spot my teeth abused. I sigh, running my fingers over the short hairs on the back of his head.

My legs squeeze for leverage while his hands tunnel under my layers, a sound of frustration rumbling deep in his throat when he meets the resistance of my skintight Under Amour shirt. "Why do you have on so many *damn* layers?"

I smirk against his mouth before dropping my head back to rest against the painted cinderblock behind me. "Well, you see..." I trace along the base of his skull. "I have this boyfriend."

"Tell me more."

I poke at the dimple daring to come out and play.

"Well...he plays football, and he likes to see me sitting in the stands behind his team's bench. So, when it's butt-ass cold outside, layers are a requirement if I'm going to fend off frost-bite to cheer him on."

"Smartass." I yelp when he pinches one of my butt cheeks. "It's not *that* cold out."

"It's cold enough." I wave a gloved hand in his face.

"I'm sure he appreciates the sacrifice."

"So he tells me." I smirk, playing along, sobering when his forehead comes down to rest against mine.

"Sounds like a lucky guy to have you cheering him on from the stands through such *treacherous* conditions."

"He is." My eyes cross in an effort to maintain eye contact as our foreheads press together.

"You two are giving me a toothache." Carter's voice echoes down the tunnel.

"Shut it, King," I volley back. "You're supposed to be a *silent* chaperone."

Calloused hands come up to cradle my face, bringing me back to the moment. "I love you, baby," Mase says, dropping all pretense of the game we've been playing and causing my heart to turn over, showing its soft under belly.

I reach up to wrap my hands around his wrists as they hold us in place. "I love you too."

Our eyes lock, transmitting all the love and lust we feel for each other.

"Isn't this sweet?"

This time, the voice we hear is a sneer, not a tease, and it comes from my right, not my left—not King. It is familiar, though, and unwelcome...a voice that spells trouble.

Instinctively, I tighten both my arms and legs around Mase in an attempt to keep him in place.

"Parker." Mason's voice is venomous.

Nothing good can come from this—*nothing*.

I know how Liam thinks. This isn't some chance encounter. He wasn't getting the reaction he wanted on social media or from sending Chrissy/Tina to my dorm, so he purposely came looking for us to start something. Maybe he thinks he can draw Mase into a fight and get him benched for the game; I don't know.

Behind me, footsteps rush in our direction, but I don't

dare take my eyes off Liam to check if it's King. The former is coiled tight like a snake, waiting to strike.

"You know, Parker..." King tuts, cool as a cucumber, ready to face down a challenge like this is your typical Saturday night. Who knows, with his reputation, it might be. Out of the corner of my eye, I see him round Mase and move so he's positioned between us and Liam. "I would have thought you'd know better than to mess with one of my people." King shakes his head like a disappointed parent. "Guess you took one too many hits to the head on the football field."

Liam scoffs, his face twisting, thrusting an arm out to point at me aggressively. *That's a mistake.* "She's not Royalty." *That's another mistake.*

A sense of foreboding like someone walking across my grave washes over me as Liam's head tilts to the left in consideration.

"TRAVIS!" I shout as loud as I possibly can, my lungs screaming with the effort, my vocal cords vibrating like razor wire. I pray he can hear me over the noise inside the locker room.

Mase's grip on my butt turns punishing as my yell brings Liam's attention onto me.

The red doors to the locker room push open with a, "What's with the full na—" Trav's words cut off as the clack of his cleats comes to a stop.

Using every ounce of strength in my thighs, I rise to see over the curve of Mase's shoulder pads and meet Trav's worried gaze as he stands with the door propped open with a foot. "Get. The. Guys."

A hawk cry rips through the air, bringing what looks like most of the Hawks' roster to the door. Why do I feel like it's not going to be enough?

Liam clicks his tongue, too stupid or too cocky to heed the precarious situation he's found himself in. "Unless..." His gaze bounces between where I'm clinging to Mase like a koala and King. "Is Nova not the only one sampling my leftovers? Is the football princess bending the knee for your Royals and doing more than kissing the ring?"

A hush falls over the tunnel while every muscle of Mase's body that I'm in contact with seizes.

With a calm reminiscent of the eye of a hurricane, he slides his hands down the backs of my thighs, hooking them under my knees to unwrap my legs and lower me to the ground. He tries to move me behind him, to safety.

I clutch at the front of his jersey. While I can appreciate the instinct to protect me, what he fails to realize is I feel the same toward him.

Unfortunately, Mason is literally twice my size, and I'm dragged with each stomp he takes toward Liam.

King plants himself in front of us, and Trav's arms lock around Mase's neck while Kev and Alex flank our sides.

"Don't," Trav says through gritted teeth as we struggle to restrain Mason.

"The fuck you say about my girl?" I've never heard him sound so feral.

"Mase"—I flatten my palms, dig my heels into the floor for traction, and push—"he's not worth it," I plead.

He struggles against the arms binding him. "He. Doesn't. Get. To. Talk. About. You. Like. That."

"Please." Push. Step. "Mase." Push. Step. "This is what he wants."

I'm sweating by the time we manage to back him into the locker room, my beanie falling to the ground in the process.

"That *fucker* needs to be taught a lesson."

His teammates maintain their hold on him while I reach up to cup his face in my hands.

"He's not worth it," I insist, but he won't look at me. "Please." I try tugging on his ears—no dice. "Please." Finally he drops his gaze to me, his pupils dilated in banked fury.

With a jerk of his chin, he's released, and the next second I'm crushed to his chest, my forehead knocking against the hard plastic of his chest protector.

"Anyone want to tell me what all the commotion is about?" Coach Knight bellows as he pushes through a cluster of players.

"Nothing," Trav answers for the group. "It's handled, Coach."

"Kayla." Coach Knight comes to a stop when he spots me in the mix. "You can't be in here."

"I know. I'm sorry." I wiggle out of Mase's hold. "I was just leaving." I turn for the door.

"The fuck you are." Mase tugs me by the hand, preventing my exit. He's beyond pissed. He's dropping F-bombs left and right, a vein pulses in his temple, and his chest is heaving like he just ran a ninety-yard touchdown.

"It's fine." I show him the text that came through from King. "He's gone."

One, *one* stride is all it takes for Mase to be in front of me, no thought to our audience made up of his teammates, a hand curling around the back of my neck. This is my possessive caveman, and I have to push onto my toes under the strength of his hold.

"Kay." His lashes fan across his cheeks as he closes his eyes, breathing me in.

"I know, Caveman." I don't need to hear the words to know what he's thinking, what he's struggling to articulate. "Now use it and go kick some Nittany Lion ass."

Hawk cries answer my words and are the soundtrack behind the gentle kiss I place on the underside of Mase's scruffy jaw.

I hurry out of the room to meet King, and something tells me this is far from over.

#Chapter58

THE ENTRANCE TUNNEL echoes with the final strains of the school's fight song, my body vibrating with each beat of the drumline's bass drums. The adrenaline I typically get before a game has nothing on the murderous rage rolling through me from my encounter with Liam Parker.

I already wanted to kick his ass, but clearly this motherfucker has a death wish coming at my girl like that. My hands fist at my sides, the knuckles cracking at the memory of his vile bullshit.

"You straight, man?" Trav asks, clapping a hand on my shoulder.

I nod even though I'm not. "This isn't over." My voice is eerily calm compared to the riot of emotions coursing through my body.

"Fuck no." He holds out a fist and I bump it twice. "But after." He points toward the field with his helmet, a reminder to keep my head in the game.

"After," I promise.

The palpable energy only the Black Out game can bring bleeds into the tunnel as the intro video flips over to the live feed, AC/DC's "Thunderstruck" blaring through the speakers. With a collective hawk cry, the team rushes out to take the field.

The scent of sulfur hangs in the air from the fireworks set off prior to our entrance, a fog of white smoke falling over the crowd as we run through the path created by the band.

The stadium is a sea of black, the creepy dancing shadows almost making it seem empty except for the uproarious cheers of tens of thousands of Hawks fans.

Jogging over to our bench with the rest of my teammates, I round it and take a moment to find Kay in the stands. Typically I wait until after the coin toss to search her out, but I need eyes on her, as if seeing her in her seat is all I need to reassure me she's safe.

Some of my tension eases, my shoulders loosening when I catch sight of her bright smile and shy wave. With a quick thump of my hand over my heart and a point at her, I run to join the other captains for the coin toss.

Hand in hand, Trav, Alex, Kev, and I make our way out to the fifty where the referee and camera wait. My lip curls when I see Liam amongst the white jerseys walking out with those chosen to represent Penn State.

At my left, Kev hums the funeral march, and on my right, Trav gives the hand he's holding a *Keep your head* squeeze.

"Tell me, Nova"—Liam's teeth flash in a smile behind the faceguard of his helmet—"how bad did my sloppy seconds fall apart after I was gone? She may be a football princess, but she sure as shit is a drama queen."

I lunge forward only to be jerked backward by my friends. I'm seething, heart racing, breathing heavy.

The referee steps between us, commemorative coin in hand, gaze bouncing from white jerseys to black, waiting for the sportsman handshake.

Yeah, that's so not happening, buddy.

As if able to hear my inner coach, the ref shakes his head

before going over the spiel about the football embossed on the silver being heads and the hawk representing tails.

The Nittany Lions win the toss, electing to receive first. Fine by me. Let my boys on D get their first shot at teaching this scumbag a lesson about respect. The way Kev's dark eyes twinkle in the shadow from his helmet tells me he's having similar thoughts.

"Blow a kiss to Kay for me." Liam pulls off his helmet and puckers his lips at me.

Black-jersey-clad bodies step into my field of vision in an instant, my friends circling around me. "You keep her name out of your *fucking* mouth," I snarl like a rabid beast, my size making it possible to see how Liam's smile widens over Alex's shoulder.

Liam is purposely baiting me. I know it. My guys know it. Doesn't reduce the itch to lay his ass out right here, right now, leaving his body sprawled on top of the hawk printed on the turf.

The shrill of a whistle cuts through my haze of fury and I allow myself to be guided back to the Hawks' bench.

Ripping my helmet off, I hold it down by my side, shoving all thoughts of Liam away and focusing on the person who is important here—the blonde with the colorful streaks grinning down at me.

I lift my arm to point at her with my helmet, give a wink, and return her blown kiss. Before I turn away, Kay makes a Y with her hand, waving the same *hang loose* gesture she gave Pops during NJA's competition. I do the same with my free hand, and I need to remember to ask her about the significance behind it.

There's a skip to my step as I make my way back to the sidelines, ready for my front-row seat to the pain about to rain all over the douche-monkey.

The whistle blows.

The quarterback calls the play.

The ball snaps and the lines go into motion.

The clash of pads against pads is like music to my ears, especially when one of our safeties flattens Parker on his back.

After no gain on the play for the Nittany Lions, the lines reset for the second down, holding them to only two yards.

Third and eight, the quarterback hands off the ball to Parker, and he barely makes it a yard before Kev drives a shoulder into his middle, lifting him off the ground and driving him into the turf. Kev stays in his face until the refs force them apart.

The smile on my friend's face as he jogs off the field, helmet in hand, indicates how gratifying the hit was.

Game on.

#Chapter59

THERE'S a pit in my stomach unlike any other I've ever had for a football game before—and I've sat in the stands while E played in the Super Bowl.

I haven't been able to sit still since I made it to my seat, keyed up and unable to shake off the confrontation with the asshole.

G and CK both had more than a few choice words when I told them about everything that went down, and I'm grateful JT was the brother to which King decided to relay what happened. JT's texts had a protective edge to them, but E would have sped up the I-95 to kick Liam's ass if he heard.

What has me the most nervous is I know my boyfriend. There's no way he's going to let an insult against me go unanswered. The way he stalks around the sidelines is downright lethal, and I didn't miss the white-knuckled grip he had on his helmet when he blew me my pregame kiss.

I jolt as I swear I feel the vibration from Kev's latest tackle. For this entire set of downs, the Hawks' defense hasn't taken any prisoners, pummeling and punishing the Penn State offensive line.

The play is called dead with the blast of a whistle, but Kev remains on top of Liam. Kev's knee is braced on the turf, the toe of his cleat digging in, his foot arching with the effort. His hands are fisted in Liam's jersey, the faceguards of their helmets bumping against each other as Kev gets all up in Liam's face. Granted, they're too far away for us to actually hear anything, but the subtle flex and pop of Kev's wrists gives away that it's not a friendly little chat.

I don't even realize I'm holding my breath until my body sags from my rushed exhalation when the refs step in to separate them.

"Welp." G claps his hands together as we watch a now smiling Kev jog to the sideline and share a complicated fist-bump, hand-slap bro handshake with Mase. "So much for dick weasel being safe from your boy since he's on offense."

"Truth." There's a glimmer of approval behind the black frames of CK's glasses. "Looks like the whole team's got your back."

Those familiar warm and squishies I've come to associate with our crew, our family growing, bubble inside. I link my arms with CK and G, the first of my brothers after JT, and rest my head on the curve of G's biceps—because, let's be real, there's no possible way for me to reach his shoulder.

The polite thing to do would be to retake our seats, but no one around us complains as we remain standing, watching Mase and the offense take the field.

Trav's first completion is a fifteen-yard pass to Alex, who runs it for another twenty before finally getting tackled at the Penn State thirty-five.

Holy shit! What did they put in the Gatorade?

I snicker at my inner cheerleader's colorful commentary on the *full steam ahead* approach to the game.

The next play is a handoff to Mase. He jukes, finding a hole in the line, and punches through to run the ball in for the Hawks' first touchdown.

Cannons blast, the band plays the fight song, and the tens

of thousands of Hawks fans inside a sea of one hundred thousand cheer ourselves hoarse.

My boyfriend stands in the end zone, arm raised perpendicular to the ground and pointing at the Penn State bench with the football before spiking it in a declaration of war.

7-0 Hawks.

It isn't until the second quarter that the scoreboard changes again thanks to a broken tackle from a Penn State running back.

7-7. Tie game.

Every *single* down Liam plays, there's a Hawks' player on him, each tackle more punishing than the last. I ain't mad about it.

The two-minute warning comes and goes with Penn State forced into another punt. With good field position thanks to a solid effort from our special teams unit, Trav gets to work putting more points on the board before the end of the first half.

His voice rings out loud and strong as he calls the play. The center snaps the ball, Trav spinning it in his large hands as he drops back, looking for a receiver. It's a good thing I'm wearing gloves; otherwise G's forearm would be sporting a line of crescent-shaped nail marks from the death grip I have on it.

I see the play a split second before Trav, Alex shaking off his defender to free himself for a lateral pass. Bending his elbow, upper arm flush to his side, ball parallel on his forearm, Alex tucks it in tight to his body. He looks downfield for a clear route, but there are none.

Alex pepper-steps, narrowly avoiding a tackle until Mase frees himself, stopping a defensive tackle, creating a hole big enough for Alex to spin through and score.

14-7 Hawks.

The second half is more of the same. Each hit on Liam by the defense—especially from Kev—is more and more bone-crushing. The intensity inside the stadium only increases with each second ticking off the game clock.

A quarterback sneak ties the game in the third.

I wring my hands together, thankful for the gloves keeping them warm. Without them, my manicure would be shot to shit from this nail-biter.

A set of field goals keeps the game tied, one of them a fifty-six-yard bomb from Noah.

17-17.

Fourth quarter.

Two-minute warning.

Penn State has the ball in the U of J red zone.

The quarterback calls an audible.

Our defense blitzes the quarterback. He dumps the ball off to eighty-five.

Kev, reading the play beautifully, goes in low on the tight end, taking Liam down to the turf at an angle, causing the ball to fumble from the douchebag's arms.

I swear the stadium shakes as the crowd of over a hundred thousand jumps to their feet, screaming in reaction to the loose ball.

The players scramble on the field.

Dogpile on top of the ball.

Whistles blow.

Referees break up the play.

And one of our cornerbacks comes up with the ball.

Red—or in today's case, black—ball.

The sound is deafening.

A minute and a half to play with two timeouts.

Ball on our own fifteen.

Time for Trav to lead our boys to victory.

Not one person retakes their seat.

Yard by yard, they march downfield.

Ten seconds left on the clock. Trav pump-fakes and hands the ball off to Mase, who runs it in for a nineteen-yard touchdown.

The extra point is good.

The game clock ticks down to zero, and the U of J Hawks are now the Big Ten East Division champions.

The goalposts come down as thousands of U of J fans rush the field, the green turf becoming a sea of black.

G and CK help me over the railing so we can join the melee, and I run for the Hawks' bench, needing the extra height advantage it will lend me if I'm to have any hope of finding my man in the crush of people now on the field.

Of course he sees me first, his long legs already eating up the distance between us. He looks so fucking sexy, helmet in hand, mouthguard pinched between his teeth, hair in sweaty disarray from playing.

"Congra—" Arms band around me, lifting me from the bench so he can kiss me breathless.

Even through the fleece lining of my leggings, I feel the coolness of the helmet as it presses under the curve of my ass when my legs wrap around Mase's waist. I cling to him like a monkey, not giving a damn about his sweat-soaked jersey, the cheering fans, his celebrating teammates, or the constant strobe of camera flashes. Nothing matters except for this kiss.

His tongue licks across the seam of my mouth and I open, the hint of orange left over from the Gatorade lingering as I stroke it with mine.

"NOVA!" Trav shouts. "We just finished a football game—stop playing tonsil hockey and get your ass over here."

I unhook my ankles, expecting him to lower me to the ground, only to shriek when I'm hoisted over his shoulder. "*Mase.*" I smack his delicious-looking ass. Yes, I said delicious. Do I need to remind you? Football pants. "Put me down."

"Hell no, Skittles." It's his turn to slap my ass, only he

follows it up with a *honka-honka* of the cheek he abused. "You're my trophy."

From my upside-down vantage point, I make out four sets of cleats and the familiar pairs of Jordans and Chuck Taylors as Mase steps inside the circle of our friends.

I go from one set of arms to another, being passed between the guys like I really am their trophy. I'm too damn proud of them to mind.

Eventually the reporters find their way to our small cluster, each vying for the first postgame interviews with the stars. Mase wraps an arm around my shoulders, tucking me against his side, his helmet coming up to obscure my face as he starts to back away.

I fall for him a little bit more at how he instinctually shifts to keep me out of the public eye. Yes it's true I'm doing my best to ignore the attention on us on the school's Instagram, but being with him during a national television interview is next level.

"Mase." I place a hand to the flat of his stomach. "Stop." I jerk a chin toward Trav. "Go. This is *your* moment."

His eyes narrow, displaying his displeasure. "No. I want to be with you. They can interview me in the locker room."

As swoony as I think the statement is, I won't allow it. He's earned this moment in the spotlight—he needs to bask in it. Plus, this is exactly the type of press coverage that will help him come draft time in the spring.

*The draft. *readjusts bow* Talk about something you* don't *want to discuss.*

"No." I reach up to cup his scruffy jaw, my thumb running along the stubble. "You've *earned* this. Let your star shine bright."

His hand covers mine on his face, palm warm and dirty. "Fine." He strokes along the back of my knuckles. "I don't like it, but *fine.*"

He swoops in for one last kiss before letting me go then

whistles to grab G's attention. It's only once I'm safely flanked by him and CK that Mason allows himself to be pulled into the closest reporter's interview.

I chance a peek as we walk away, and the smile on his face is as bright as the stadium lights above. There is no doubt in my mind that this is the first of many interviews he will be doing throughout his career.

"Come on, Smalls." G plucks at the pom on the top of my hat, bringing my attention his way. "Let's get you a coffee the size of your head to get you in the party mood."

Right, victory party at the AK house. *Oh, the joy—not!*

#THE GRAM

#Chapter60

UofJ411: Someone's fired up #LetMeAtEm #CasanovaWatch
boomerang of Mason being held back during the coin toss
@lt.sgottabethebooks: Better look out @TightestEndParker85.
Our @CasaNova87 will kick your ass today in more ways than
one #PassThePopcorn
@JJennifermarie119: I put my money on @CasaNova87 any
day of the week over @TightestEndParker85. #PlacingBets

UofJ411: That HAD to have hurt #Ouch
boomerang of Kev tackling Liam
@Hbietsch: I know @TightestEndParker85 isn't the quarterback,
but this right here is why we call #91 @SackMasterSanders91
#BaggedLunch #HowsTheTurfTaste?
@Heymom05: @TightestEndParker85 #DoYouNeedSomeIce?
@Hippychick782000: Awww…do you have a boo-boo
@TightestEndParker85 #WhatABaby

UofJ411: Now THAT'S a kiss #InstaWorthy #Kaysonova

picture of Mason kissing Kay on the field

@JJUllom: All the heart eyes *heart eyes emoji* #KingAndQueen #Kaysonova

@Juliedreamsofbooks: Talk about a Kodak moment #PicturePerfect #FootballRoyalty #Kaysonova

UofJ411: Not your typical trophy #HoistMeUp #Kaysonova

picture of Mason carrying Kay over his shoulder after the game

@Kmford2317: @CasaNova87 could carry me away ANY day of the week #CasanovaWatch #ClaimingHisTrophy #Kaysonova

#Chapter61

THE VICTORY PARTY is already well underway by the time we arrive to a hero's welcome at the Alpha house. With showers and post-game interviews, the whole thing took much longer than I would have liked, and I'm itching to get to my girl.

The house is packed wall to wall with people, hawk cries ringing out from them and various teammates scattered throughout the rooms. I'm jostled, high-fived, and pulled in for selfies all before I even make it to the staircase across from the front door.

Inside my pocket, my phone vibrates for the billionth time, the steady stream of congratulatory text messages and phone calls as well as comments from Brantley about my on-field interview doing its best to drain the life out of my battery. My notifications are also blowing up thanks to the highlight reel UofJ411 has been posting, and even I can admit I've watched the boomerang of Kev tackling Liam at least a dozen times.

I push through the crush of partygoers, the first order of business to drop my bag in my room then find Kay. While I appreciate—both on a personal and career level—Kay forcing me to participate in the on-field interview, all it really meant was more time spent away from her.

Unlocking the door to my room, I grin at the pile of discarded clothes in the center of my bed. Sure, I would have rather found my girlfriend lying there naked instead, but at least this way I won't have to fight through miles of fabric to get my hands on her silky skin.

For as much as I want to dive right in and spend the night buried between Kay's thighs, it's probably a good thing we need to put in some face time at this party before that can happen. With the amount of adrenaline pumping through my bloodstream from both the game itself and from dealing with Peckerhead Parker, I'm not sure I'd be able to hold back, which can be dangerous given how much larger I am than Kay. The last thing I would ever want to do is hurt her by being too rough.

The sounds of the party are muffled two floors up, so I can make out the faint strains of laughter spilling from the open door to Grayson's room.

Leaning a shoulder against the doorjamb, I cross my feet at the ankles and take in the scene before me. Kay, Em, and Quinn are a mass of limbs on the bed, bent over each other, laughing while Grayson regales them with some story about God knows what. Even CK, although shaking his head, looks amused from his perch against the dresser.

I don't need to know the details of the story. All I care about is how Kay seems to have shed most of the tension from what happened before the game.

Her hair is a riot of blonde and U of J pride curls, her cheeks are flushed, and my name and number are stamped across her back. *Fuck me!* She's so beautiful like this—happy.

"Caveman!" she cheers when she sees me, disentangling herself from her friends to jump from the bed and rush into my arms.

"Skittles." I fit her body against mine and drop a kiss on top of her peppermint-scented head. "You might want to slow down on the partying if you want to last all night." I tap the top of the to-go coffee cup in her hand.

"You're lucky you're cute." She pinches my chin between her fingertips, her nails painted school-spirit black. "Because your jokes need work."

The day this girl stops giving me shit is the day I have to worry. I give her a squeeze and avail myself of a sip of her pumpkin-flavored coffee.

"Yo, lovebirds." Trav pushes his face between us. "You can do each other later. I need a beer."

"Jelly," Kay teases, booping him on the nose.

"Damn straight," Trav admits without any shame. "Now come on, Short Stack…" He hooks an arm around her shoulders and pulls her to his side instead of mine. "You can help me find the lucky lady who'll get the privilege of sharing my bed for the night."

"Ew." Kay pops him on the chest. "I want *no* part in helping you play jersey chaser roulette."

"I thought we were besties? Your taste in football players may be questionable…" Trav looks over Kay's head at me, winking. He lives for getting under my skin. "But you have good taste in girlfriends. So, who better to help find QB2 a playmate?"

"*Gross.*" She shoves his arm off her as we enter the den. "Do you *really* call your dick QB2?" A mixture of disgust, humor, and genuine curiosity crosses her face.

"What?" Trav fills a cup with beer, handing it off to me before filling another for himself. "You have a better name? What do you call Casanova's?"

Pink climbs up Kay's neck, staining her cheeks with a pretty blush as she turns her back on my best friend, leaving him to come to me. She scrunches her nose and digs a finger into one of my dimples as I grin down at her. I know what she calls my dick, and now she knows I'm thinking about it.

As per usual, the den is sparsely populated, and it's easy

to claim one of the leather armchairs. I stretch the arm holding my beer along an armrest and hook the other around Kay's waist to pull her onto my lap.

Home. That's the thought I have every time she settles with me. She's my home.

"Just remember, Travis…" Kay says, resting her head back on my chest. "No glove, no love."

Howling laughter meets her advice, and she receives a knuckle bump any time one of my teammates passes where we're seated.

Conversation cycles as different people filter in and out of the room. At some point, someone changes the channel to *College GameDay* on ESPN for the weekend's highlights, but it mostly serves as background noise.

"I think this is my favorite out of any of the times you two have trended." Noah, never understanding the concept of personal space, crowds Kay and me to show us a picture on his phone.

On the screen is a shot of the kiss Kay and I shared when I first found her on the field. I'm not sure who took the picture, but they captured every ounce of the animalistic passion I was feeling for my girl perfectly.

It's taken from the side, so you're able to clearly see how her legs are wrapped around me, feet hooked together, one hand cupping my face, the other clutching the hair at the back of my head. It also shows my hand gripping under her thigh and my helmet resting against her ass while the other is hooked around her back. We look like something out of a movie. Oh look—there's a hashtag that says just that.

"Oh my god!" Kay buries her face in my chest. She's slowly been making an effort with her media presence, but I know it's still not her favorite.

Me? I have no qualms. "I'm making this my new background."

Kay's head pops up, eyes wide. "Really?"

She's adorable. "Fuck yeah, babe." I place a kiss to the tip of her nose. "Look at us—we're hot."

The most breathtaking smile I have ever seen transforms her face. "Would it be corny if we had matching backgrounds?"

"Who the fuck cares? Give me your phone." I switch my beer to the arm behind her and hold out my now free hand.

She smirks but does as I ask. Entering her passcode—now the date I asked her out—I take care of sending her the picture and setting it as her background. We're so cute, kinda makes you sick, huh?

Alex and Grayson are over in the corner doing their best to create a reenactment of the picture with Em and Quinn acting as photographers.

Suddenly, like a record scratching, all conversation cuts off and it feels like all the air gets sucked out of the room.

Every muscle in my body locks up, causing Kay to peer up at me. Out of the corner of my eye, I see the questioning look she's giving me, but my attention stays solely focused on the swinging door leading into the room from the hallway.

In my lap, she goes rigid, all the earlier ease evaporating in an instant, replaced by an under-five-foot ball of anxiety as she follows my line of sight...

To where Liam Parker stands in the doorway.

Chapter62

ONE MINUTE I'm luxuriating in the feel of Mase's fingers tracing shapes on my skin, no longer restricted by my Cold-Gear top. The next I'm wondering if I fell asleep from those drugging touches because I'm staring at a literal nightmare—Liam Parker.

What the hell is he *doing here?*

My mind whirls. This is bad.

This is so, so bad.

The...*incident* in the tunnels was one thing, but showing up at what is essentially the U of J's sport teams' home base is a whole new level of stupidity. How did he even get in here?

If the way the team was during the game is any indication, there's no way this showdown ends without bloodshed.

There's a tremble in Mason's hands as he lifts me with him as he stands. Jaw clenched, vein pulsing at the side of his neck, eyes never straying from the threat before us, he slowly lowers me until the rubber soles of my boots touch the hard-wood floor.

A slimy feeling travels down my spine when Liam cackles at how Mase shifts so he's in front of me, using his large frame as a barrier between myself and the threat.

"Wow, Kay." Liam looks around at all the Hawks players

shifting into the danger zone in support of us. I hope he's regretting only bringing two of his teammates with him. "Guess you really are a full-service type of girl, huh? First the Royals and now a whole football team?"

"I told you…" Mase hooks a hand around my ribs and shifts me behind him more. "Keep her name *out*. Of. Your. *Mouth*."

I grip the back of Mase's polo, peering around him in time to see a smarmy smile overtake Liam's face. *This isn't going to be good.*

"Poor, poor Nova," Liam coos in false sympathy, setting my teeth on edge. "How's it feel to know it was *my* name she moaned first?"

There's a collective hiss at Liam's question, and my knuckles turn white around the fabric clutched in my hands.

"Stay the fuck away from *my* girl." Mase takes a step toward Liam and I move from behind him, wrapping my arms around his middle like a snake to keep him in place. He's a powder keg waiting to explode.

With the increased press coverage the rivalry game brings, the last thing Mason needs is to allow himself to be manipulated into a fight. Off-field antics and drama can have as much of an impact on a player's chance at a pro career as those on it.

Liam tries again. "Tell me, Nova, does she still do that thing with her hips when she's on top?" He gyrates in a way that looks more like a drunken monkey than anything sexual.

"Fuck. You," Mase bites out, boiling in fury.

"Though I will say, having her flat on her back was fun too." Liam taps his chin with the tip of his finger.

I shift my gaze to G, sending him a pleading look. I'm no match for Mason's size, and I'm going to need backup if I have any hope of restraining him.

"You talk a big game, Parker." Mase's voice is an eerie monotone as he speaks, and goose flesh covers my arms. "But from my recollection, the only one having the experience of being flat on their back tonight was *you*." The side of his mouth lifts then he says, "So why don't *you* tell *me*...how'd the turf taste?"

Snickers sound from around the room, including some from both of Liam's teammates.

Mase tips his chin down to check that I'm alright. In his concern for me, he doesn't see Liam lunge for him.

I don't think. I only react.

The drive to protect the man I love has instinct taking over and I jump in front of him, my only thought to push him out of harm's way.

Pain explodes on the side of my face.

My feet leave the ground.

My head hits something sharp.

Then...

Nothing.

Everything goes black.

Okay, okay I totally hear your shouty capitals before you even type them. I'm sure you're like WTF ALLEY!!! I need to know what happens.

Good news! Book 3 is available now And there's no cliffhanger!!! *Playing For Keeps (#UofJ3)* Read FREE in KU HERE!

Jordan Donovan (E's mentioned PR person) is the matriarch of the BTU Alumni world and you can meet her in *Power Play* if you were curious about her story.

Need emotional support? Need a place where you can WTH did I just read and HOLY SHIT Alley really took her Evil Queen status to a whole new level?

Maybe you just have some crazy theories to run other like-minded people? Want to help plan Liam's death? Flip off that gossipy UofJ411? There is a spoiler room, but it's for the whole series so read PFK and join the #UofJ Spoiler Group HERE.

Are you one of the cool people who writes reviews? Game Changer can be found on Goodreads, BookBub, and Amazon.

Dying to know more about the Royals? Well good news. Savvy King has forcefully shoved BTU6 out of the way is out now. This Royalty Crew U of J Spin-Off Novel *Savage Queen* is available to Read FREE in KU HERE! Keep scrolling for a peek at chapter 1.

Randomness For My Readers

Whoop!

Oh my goodness I can HEAR you all saying "What in the damn hell, Alley! Again?!" To be fair…any of you who have Died me or yelled in the LTS spoiler group my response *because I'm evil like that* was wait until book 2's cliff.

Oopsie!

Have no fear book 3 *Playing For Keeps* is out now and you can read it here. And it **DOES NOT** end in a cliff!!! *Yay! Spirit Fingers!*

For those of you who have read my words before you may have noticed a few cameos from my BTU Alumni Squad. If you are new to my crazy and haven't run screaming from the room you can be sure to check out the BTU Alumni while you wait for #UofJ3. Don't worry these are stand-alones.

So I like to give you my fun facts in bullet style but I'll leave this one out on it's own because it's **special.**

I actually wrote the U of J books before I ever published my first book *Power Play*. I had been invited—no idea how, so don't ask me—to join a NaNo writing group on Facebook with so many of my favorite authors and thus this brain child was born.

So now for a little bullet style fun facts:

- The U of J books went through some major rewrites and I made Jenny live the angst like 8365830 times while I changed things around, but what never changed was how this book ended. #SorryNotSorry
- Jordan Donovan (E's mentioned PR person) is the matriarch of the BTU Alumni world and you can meet her in *Power Play* if you were curious about her story.
- I LIVED for the theories you all came up with in the LTS spoiler room, and I'm sure you noticed while reading, I was ALL ABOUT the misdirection in my teasers *evil laugh*
- Most of the IG handles you see in the comments are from my reader Covenettes. So many are great bookstagrammers I would check them out.

If you don't want to miss out on anything new coming or when my crazy characters pop in with extra goodies make sure to sign up for my newsletter! If my rambling hasn't turned you off and you are like "This chick is my kind of crazy," feel free to reach out!

Lots of Love,

Alley

Acknowledgments

This is where I get to say thank you, hopefully I don't miss anyone. If I do I'm sorry and I still love you and blame mommy brain.

I'll start with the Hubs—who I can already hear giving me crap **again** that *this* book also isn't dedicated to him he's still the real MVP—he has to deal with my lack of sleep, putting off laundry *because... laundry* and helping to hold the fort down with our three crazy mini royals. You truly are my best friend. Also, I'm sure he would want me to make sure I say thanks for all the hero inspiration, but it is true (even if he has no ink *winking emoji*)

To Jenny my PA, the other half of my brain, the bestest best friend a girl could ask for. Why the hell do you live across the pond? Mase is yours and **yes** he is the *ONE* hero I will confirm you can claim. I live for every shouty capital message you send me while you read my words 97398479 times.

To Meg for being my first ever beta reader who wasn't related to me. I'm so grateful this series brought you into my life.

To my group chats that give me life and help keep me

sane: The OG Coven, The MINS, The Tacos, The Book Coven, and Procrastinors & Butt Stuff (hehe—still laugh at this name like a 13 year old boy).

To all my author besties that were okay with me forcing my friendship on them and now are some of my favorite people to talk to on the inter webs. Laura, Maria, Kelsey, Lindsey, Kristy, Stefanie, Becca, Samantha (both of you), Renee, Dana, Lianne, and Anna.

To Sarah and Julie the most amazing graphics people ever in existence. Yeah I said it lol.

To Jules my cover designer, for going above and beyond, then once more with designing these covers. I can't even handle the epicness of them.

To Jess my editor, who is always pushing me to make the story better, stronger…giving such evil inspiration that leads to shouty capitals from readers that even led to a complete overhaul of these first 3 U of J books.

To Caitlin my other editor who helps clean up the mess I send her while at the same time totally getting my crazy.

To Gemma for going from my proofreader to fangirl and being so invested in my characters' stories to threaten my life *lovingly of course*.

To Dawn for giving my books their final spit shine.

To my street team for being the best pimps ever. Seriously, you guys rock my socks.

To my ARC team for giving my books some early love and getting the word out there.

To Christine and Wildfire PR for taking on my crazy and helping me spread the word of my books and helping to take me to the next level.

To Wander and his team for being beyond amazing to work with and this custom shoot for all of the Mase and Kay books. And Wayne and Megan for being the perfect models! Seriously I think the world can hear my fangirl squee whenever I get to message with you both on IG.

To every blogger and bookstagrammer that takes a chance and reads my words and writes about them.

To my fellow Covenettes for making my reader group one of my happy places. Whenever you guys post things that you know belong there I squeal a little. And for letting me use your IG handles.

And, of course, to you my fabulous reader, for picking up my book and giving me a chance. Without you I wouldn't be able to live my dream of bringing to life the stories the voices in my head tell me.

Lots of Love,

Alley

For A Good Time Call

Do you want to stay up-to-date on releases, be the first to see cover reveals, excerpts from upcoming books, deleted scenes, sales, freebies, and all sorts of insider information you can't get anywhere else?

If you're like "Duh! Come on Alley." Make sure you sign up for my newsletter.

Ask yourself this:

 * Are you a Romance Junkie?

 * Do you like book boyfriends and book besties? (yes this is a thing)

 * Is your GIF game strong?

 * Want to get inside the crazy world of Alley Ciz?

If any of your answers are yes, maybe you should join my Facebook reader group, Romance Junkie's Coven

Join The Coven

Stalk Alley

Join The Coven

Get the Newsletter

Like Alley on Facebook

Follow Alley on Instagram
Hang with Alley on Goodreads
Follow Alley on Amazon
Follow Alley on BookBub
Subscribe on YouTube for Book Trailers
Follow Alley's inspiration boards on Pinterest
All the Swag
Book Playlists
All Things Alley

Also by Alley Ciz

#UofJ Series

Cut Above The Rest (Prequel) <—Freebie for newsletter subscribers. Download here.

Looking To Score

Game Changer

Playing For Keeps

Off The Bench- #UofJ4 Preorder, Releasing December 2021

The Royalty Crew (A #UofJ Spin-Off)

Savage Queen

Ruthless Noble

BTU Alumni Series

Power Play (Jake and Jordan)

Musical Mayhem (Sammy and Jamie) BTU Novella

Tap Out (Gage and Rocky)

Sweet Victory (Vince and Holly)

Puck Performance (Jase and Melody)

Writing Dirty (Maddey and Dex)

Scoring Beauty- BTU6 Preorder, Releasing September 2021

About the Author

Alley Ciz is an internationally bestselling indie author of sassy heroines and the alpha men that fall on their knees for them. She is a romance junkie whose love for books turned into her telling the stories of the crazies who live in her head…even if they don't know how to stay in their lane.

This Potterhead can typically be found in the wild wearing a funny T-shirt, connected to an IV drip of coffee, stuffing her face with pizza and tacos, chasing behind her 3 minis, all while her 95lb yellow lab—the best behaved child—watches on in amusement.

facebook.com/AlleyCizAuthor
instagram.com/alley.ciz
pinterest.com/alleyciz
goodreads.com/alleyciz
bookbub.com/profile/alley-ciz
amazon.com/author/alleyciz

Printed in Great Britain
by Amazon